Dedicated
…to the Street
Thank you

D1556879

In Memory of
Bebe Moore Campbell
Rest in Peace, Sister

For more imformation of Dutch, contact:

Myspace.com/kwame_teague

or

Myspace.com/kwamefreedom

1

Prologue

It was the Fourth of July, bombs bursting in the air, but the real independence being celebrated was Dutch's victory over Kazami and the virtual annihilation of his organization in Northern New Jersey and Atlantic City in the south. It was a one-sided war. With Kazami dead, all the crews his organization umbrella'd fell into smaller factions, making them an easy target for Dutch's united assault.

Some came over to Dutch's camp; the rest required mournings and murals. Blood ran in the streets and the murder rate skyrocketed. But the members of Kazami's criminal organization weren't the only victims.

Dutch knew the Nigerians were dangerous; therefore, he left them no base on which to rebuild. Nigerian store owners, club owners, everyday workers and any Nigerian that was remotely connected to Kazami in any way were killed or forced to relocate. Once Dutch had established his dominance – uncontested – the violence stopped just as quickly as it had started.

And so it was, that Dutch threw a huge block party to celebrate and allow the pent up tension of the streets to be released in laughter, love and dance. The block party was held on Bergen Street, between Lyons and Lehigh Avenue, a major thoroughfare lined with stores, shops and delis. The bars, like The Four Leaf, kept their doors opened and Dutch paid in advance to make sure the beer and liquor flowed freely into the crowd. Roberto's Pizza parlor, where Dutch had once worked, and where it had all started, stood on the opposite corner and supplied the pizza.

The block was packed with ghetto legends and soon to be stars. Roxanne Shanté, the original Queen B of The Juice Crew was there with her son and her cousin Mook, looking all brown sugary with her chinky eyes smiling. Haitian Shakim, Queen Latifah's partner was there with Clinton Avenue's own Lakim Shabazz, who

2

already had a record out. And a young and gorgeous Faith Evans, that everyone called Faye, was there with his little sister Gaye, Candi and her partner Maureen that catz knew from the Salt N' Pepa video, *Tramp*.

Mischievous little children ran around shooting Roman Candles off into the sky and exploding firecrackers, whole packs at a time, which sounded like a shootout with .22's.

POP! POP! POP! POP! POP! POP! POP!

Nigguhs on that dog food, deep in dope fiend nods or pilled up on 550's and 529's, bottom lip protruding, glanced up long enough to curse the kids out.

"Little ass bastards! Yo mama shoulda' swallowed ya!" they barked hoarsely, voices as gravelly as Uncle Qwilly's.

But the kids were like flies: once shooed off, they scatter, then form Voltron and swarm again.

The DJ's were two catz from the Hooterville section of Newark, Reggie Nobles, a.k.a. Redman, and his man, Rocafella. Redman had his sound system set up in the parking lot of Butter's store and kept the crowd jumping and shoutin' out the ghetto celebs.

"We got Black Fam, a.k.a. Danny Dynamite out here! Tanya Mincey...I see you sweetness, Maine Ills, Lil' Mike, Dom, Ali Smalls and to my main man, Dutch! Nigguh, I see you!"

Reggie kept the fever going, playing a little reggae and a little hip hop, but the main staple was club music. Like go-go from D.C. or booty music in Miami, a party wasn't a party in Newark without classics like Love is the Message, Love Thang, One Night Love Affair, Dr. Love and Love Sensations (but sang as "club sensations" after the famous spot on Bradford Place). Every record was about love in some form or fashion – good love, bad love, real love – but, love is love and Newark gave it up.

Record: "Is it all over my face?!"
Crowd: "Heeellll Yeeeaaah!!"

3

Record: "'Cause I'm in love dancing'..."

The females cabbage patched and whopped while the nigguhs two stepped and bopped, and Craze was in the midst of it all. He was the ladies man of the crew and the chicks loved his Big Daddy Kane hi-top fade, the dookie rope around his neck, as thick as an industrial strength chain.

"Oohh, Chris...come 'ere...dance wit me."

"That's fucked up, Chris, I beeped you. Why you ain't call me back?"

"The batteries yo, them shits dyin' on me," he lied, because that was before chicks got up on thatexcuse.

"Yo, Roc...you blind mothafucka...who gave you the grill?" Craze joked, yelling from across the street.

One eyed Roc shot him the finger.

"Nigguh, fuck you. Come say it to my face," Roc hollered back.

"Oh, that's your face? I thought I was talkin' to yo ass, you ugly bastard!"

All in earshot that heard it fell out laughing, even Roc. He promised to fuck Craze up when he caught him, then turned his attention back to the grill. Truth be told, Roc was doing his thing, grilling up burgers, chicken, steaks, hot dogs, fish and shish-ka-bobs on a six-foot long industrial grill. "But, no swine! So don't even ask!"

He looked like an official chef with his chef hat cocked to the side and leaning, chef's apron and the butt of his nine sticking out at the small of his back. But, that was for another type of beef, because he was a chef at murder, too.

Roc bopped to the music while serving the hungry crowd, but when Reggie played his song, *It's Not Over*, he all but abandoned the grill and pulled Ayesha out of the lawn chair she was kicked back in.

"Rahman! Ain't you 'posed to be cookin'?" she grinned, standing on her tiptoes to put her arms around his neck.

"Can't you hear, woman? They playin' our song," he flirted, doing his little two step.

Now I'm an Aquariu.s
You know what that means?
That means that no man in the world can let go
Of this Aquarius.
I got something that you don't ever want to turn down.
I got something for your mind, your body and soul
Every day of my life...every day of hi-life
Woo Woo Babbyyy...it's...not...over...

"Hey! I'ma beat -" Roc growled, trying to grab at the four little boys from the firecracker crew as they ran through, grabbing all they could grab and then sprinting off, dropping chicken and burger.

Ayesha laughed as Roc yelled after them.

They ran by Zoom, Mustafa and the Zoo Crew, who were shooting dice with Smiley and a few other catz.

Zoom jumped in their path, making them dip and dodge like four miniature Barry Saunders. He laughed as they scampered off.

"Man, you gonna play or what?" one cat huffed, mad because Zoom was breaking him.

"Ah! Get 'em girls!" Zoom sang, releasing the transparent blue cubes from his hand. They looked like tiny ice cubes, bouncing across the pavement until they tumbled over and melted on his point.

"Four! That's what you get for rushin' this ass whoopin'. Smack yourself," Zoom bragged, raking up the piles of money at his feet like fallen leaves.

"Ay, yo, Zoom...what up wit' yo peoples," one gold toothed, Chancellor Avenue cat asked, referring to Angel, down the block.

5

Zoom saw Angel and smiled. He knew how she got down, but apparently the dude didn't. "Oh, she cool, Money," Zoom gamed him. "Go 'head…you could bag that."

"Word? Ai-ight, bet," he replied, then strutted off to do just that.

"You foul, Zoom," Mustafa chuckled, giving him a pound.

"Chancellor nigguhs is just like them Harlem nigguhs, think they pretty," Zoom smirked. There was no love lost between Bergen and Chancellor.

Angel sat, distanced from the crowd, on a milk crate with her back propped against a light pole. She was watching everyone and saw the smiling dude approaching, one gold tooth gleaming.

"Excuse me, Miss, but ahh, I can't help but to notice you all alone over here," he tried to croon, voice light like he sang for Blue Magic or something. Even though she had on a baggy MCM velour short set, the fabric couldn't hide her curves, nor could the cap-styled Kangol, over her eyes, conceal her beauty.

"I'm wit' somebody," she replied without looking at him, her hand propped under her chin.

"I can't tell. He must be crazy to leave you all alone out here lookin' so lovely."

"Naw, you don't understand," she answered, giving him an evil smirk and pulling up her shirt so he could see the chrome .38 Bulldog stuck in her waist. "I said, I'm wit' somebody."

My man wasted no time in heading back from whence he came.

Dutch stood, hands clasped behind his back, surveying the whole scene. He had mingled early on, speaking with the Abdullah family out of Atlantic City – Bilal, who was really from Newark, but made his name in Elizabeth Pioneer Homes – the Wright brothers and the sons of the infamous Akbar.

Many of these men were already legends, and much richer than himself, but he was just beginning. Soon, he too would be a legend.

He watched Fat Tony pull up to the wooden police horses that served as barricades. Fat Tony's driver opened the door of the navy blue Lincoln Continental, and then Fat Tony climbed his sumo-like body out of the back seat. He was a grumpy man, but when he saw Dutch, his face lit up.

"Hey, kid, come 'ere! I came all the way here to see ya and you ain't even got the decency to open my fuckin' door?" Tony scowled.

"My days of openin' doors are over, Tony," Dutch replied.

They shook hands and Tony patted him on the back.

"I know, just bustin' your balls a little bit," Fat Tony chuckled, because power respected force. He looked around at the block party. "You do this?"

"Yeah."

Fat Tony nodded, then said, "Funs good, you know, it's a fuckin' holiday. But ahh...don't do this too much, capece? It's not good...brings too much attention to your name. That fuckin' Gotti over there is fuckin' killin' me with his flashy shit," he shook his head. "You mark my words, it'll be his downfall.

Don't let it be yours. Remember, the real power is *behind* the throne," Fat Tony scolded him.

"They can't stop what they can't see," Dutch agreed.

"Yeah...I like that. They can't stop what they can't see. Let's go inside, I'm sweatin' like a fuckin' hog over here."

Dutch and Fat Tony went inside Roberto's Pizza parlor. Dutch saw a young cat sweeping the floor and smiled, remembering when he used to sweep these same floors.

"Hey, Tony, look!" Roberto exclaimed, "the kid used to work for me, now I'm makin' pizza for him. Whadda world, ah?" he chuckled.

Fat Tony gave Mrs. Piazza a kiss, and then Dutch did, too. Fat Tony asked her to make him some linguine with red pepper tomato sauce "to go", and then he and Dutch went into the back room and sat at the small table in the center of all the restaurant supplies.

"Okay, here's the deal," Fat Tony began, wiping the sweat from his face with a handkerchief.

"The guy I told you about is on his way to meet us. He's called, Ceylon, and I gotta tell ya, he's like the fuckin' Pope of the drug world. France, Germany, Australia, South America, North America…he nods, and it's done. His people practically own the Panama Canal from a smuggling sense. He could travel around the world wit' a dollar, which means he's connected like you wouldn't believe."

"What you say his name was?"

"Ceylon. He's a Turk. The Turks and the Sicilians have a long history in heroin, so, he's well respected in the old country. Now, I gotta tell ya', I know the guy, but I was surprised when he called on me. He says he's aware of the situation and he wants to meet with the man responsible. I'm thinking', *for what*, you know, because the streets are peasant food to him. No offense."

"None taken."

"But, if Ceylon wants to meet, that means he wants to do business. And, Dutch, I'm telling' ya', you do business with a guy like that, you play fair, and believe me, he can make you untouchable."

"I always play fair," Dutch said as he smiled his infamous smile.

A few moments later, Roberto knocked, and then opened the door.

"The guy's here."

"Graci," Fat Tony thanked him in Italian.

When Ceylon walked in, Fat Tony stood up, so out of respect, Dutch did the same. His first impression of Ceylon didn't match the stature of his reputation. *The Pope*, as Fat Tony referred to him, was an impishly small man with a large head. His receding hairline and wire framed glasses made Dutch think of a college professor who bored you with monotone lectures. But, his voice, was light and nasal, with a hint of a foreign accent.

"Good to see ya', Ceylon. It's been a long time," Fat Tony shook his hand.

"Yes, my old friend, it has," Ceylon replied evenly with a warm smile, then turned to Dutch.

"Ah, Ceylon, this is the guy you asked about. Dutch, meet Ceylon."

Dutch and Ceylon nodded to one another, neither man extending his hand.

"Dutch?" Ceylon quipped, "Like Dutch Schultz?"

"Naw, like Dutch, I pay my own way in this world," he replied calmly.

Fat Tony excused himself, as he had done his part, the rest was up to Dutch.

Once Fat Tony closed the door behind him, Ceylon said, "I will get down to business, because the nature of success is rooted in simplicity. You have done me a service and I will offer you a service in return."

"What service did I do you?"

"Do you play chess, Dutch?"

"Only when I wanna make a point," Dutch smirked, letting Ceylon know that he knew why he'd asked.

Ceylon smiled at his witticism. He could see that the young man in front of him had a natural charm of personal magnetism and the animal instinct so important for leaders.

"You are a pawn...and I say that without contempt. It is merely a fact in the world we both inhabit. But, you have removed a troublesome castle, the Southern Nigerians. The money they were making in New Jersey was a large percentage of the funds being used to fund the war with the Nigerians in the North. We do not want that. The Nigerians in the North are Muslims, but believe me, our interest is not religious, it is oil. Nigeria is a part of OPEC and their vote is important to our interests. It's that simple. To stop a tank, you cut the gas supply, rendering the tank useless. This is the service you have done by removing the Nigerian castle."

Dutch had been listening intently to this geopolitical explanation of Ceylon's. "And the service you want to do with me?"

"I will supply you in whatever quantity you need, of the highest quality. Your business is your own; my price will be inconsequential to the amount you will be making. The only stipulation, the one that cannot be broken, is that you not allow the Nigerians to re-enter the drug trade in New Jersey."

Both men had the same interests, but for different reasons. Ceylon needed Dutch's type of strength in the streets to keep out the Nigerians and Dutch needed the drug connect of a lifetime. The two men, upon agreement, shook hands for the first time and initiated the beginning of a dynasty.

** ** ** ** **

Angel lay back on her bed with her hands behind her head. It sounded like a sex party going on throughout the house. Zoom across the hall, Craze in the living room and Dutch down at the other end of the hall. Headboards banged, bedsprings squeaking like a chorus of gleeful mice and there was a chorus of feminine squeals and moans, mixed with manly grunts and groans.

"I wish they'd shut the fuck up," she huffed, and then raised her voice, "It ain't like they killin' you!"

It was hard being the only female in the crew, even if she *did* sexually prefer the same thing they did. At that point in her life, she didn't go hard over sex. When she had been with Diamond, that was pleasure, but the things she did to establish *Angel's Charlies* and her network of gold diggers was strictly business. She didn't develop her lust for sex until after she went to prison.

Back then, they all lived on Renner Avenue, in the same two-story house. Rahman and Ayesha lived upstairs, while the three of them lived downstairs. It was one house, but basically two separate dwellings, both equipped with kitchens and bathrooms.

She rolled over on her side, facing the wall. She couldn't sleep and it wasn't because of the noise. She was used to it. Angel couldn't sleep because she was thinking about the murder she had committed.

It was her first, the first of many, but at that time, the only one, so she had been thinking about it since it went down a few days prior.

Angel's primary position had been to set up the after hours joints and to set up her team of chicks. She hadn't been involved in the murder side of the game until Dutch had picked her up like,

"Take a ride wit' me."

He was pushin' the same BM Angel gave him after he got out. B.D.P.'s *The Bridge is Over*, was the street anthem of Newark at the time. Originally, Supercat's dubs, the spine tingling piano riffs, deep pulsating bass line and K.R.S One's lyrical energy sounded like music to midnight marauding nigguhs with murderous intent.

The car smelled like frankincense and Dutch's wood tipped Philly cherry cheroot cigar. It was a smell that was forever burned in her mind because she could still remember it, it was so vivid. She remembered Dutch handing her the gun.

"You scared?"

"Of what?"

But she *had* been scared. Not scared to do it, but scared because she *wasn't* scared. She was about to take a life for the first time and she felt nothing. There was no hate or anger, she had never seen the dude before in her life, yet she knew instinctively – even before she did it – that it wouldn't bother her at all.

Holding the gun to the soft flesh of his temple, how the shot sounded at point blank range, the soft sigh he gave right before the lights went out in his soul – like a woman swooning away – and the smell of shit, as his body relieved of the burden of life, released it's waste. Angel remembered it all. But, even *that* didn't keep her awake. Now that she had taken a life so easily, she thought about taking another…her father's.

Just thinking of what he did to her for so long, the way he had violated her trust and her body, all the confusion, hate and rage welled up in her like an inferno – exploding in her chest. But, he was still her father, and a small part of her still held on to that. So, she did what she usually did when she couldn't sleep – she went to talk to Dutch.

Angel climbed out of bed and walked out of her room wearing only an oversized Giants football jersey. She walked through the living room and saw Craze with a girl bent over the couch, banging her back out. Angel had to hold her breath because the room smelled like rotten fish.

"ILLLLLLL! What the fuck? Is you fuckin' her on her period?! DAMN!" she cursed in disgust, but kept it moving.

She got to Dutch's door and didn't bother to knock because she could hear what he was doing down the hall. She opened the door to find a dark-skinned chick with big titties riding Dutch – reverse cowgirl style – eyes rolled up in the back of her head and mumbling and shivering like she was in a cold trance.

"Angel! Close the fuckin' door!" Dutch barked, gripping shortie by her hips.

"No! I gotta talk to you," Angel replied.

"Later."

"Now," she retorted, because she always got her way.

The girl wanted to protest Angel's presence, but it felt too good to really give a fuck. Besides, having someone watching her, turned her on and she began to really go buck.

"Hurry up!" Angel huffed; glancing at them out of the corner of her eye, then rolled them and sighed hard.

The girl who was with Zoom came out of his room with a sheet wrapped around her, about to go into Angel's room.

"Ay, Ay…that ain't the bathroom!" Angel piped up. "*That's* the bathroom," she barked, pointing to the bathroom door before mumbling, "stupid bitch."

By then, Dutch had busted his nut and was shoving shortie off of him. "Ai-ight, go head…get off me," he mumbled dismissively.

The girl sucked her teeth, but did as he said. She grabbed her clothes, holding them to her chest and moved past Angel. Usually, Angel would say something slick like, "Can I get next?" but, she wasn't in a joking mood. She went inside the room and was about to get on the bed, but stopped, pulled the sheet up and lay on the bare mattress. Dutch slipped on some cut off jogging pants, and then turned to her.

"I can't sleep," she said simply, arms folded across her breasts.

"Ay, yo, you gonna have to start takin' medicine or something for that shit, yo. You can't keep bustin' up in here like this," Dutch scolded her mildly, even though he had been ready to put shortie out anyway. He started to say something else, but when he looked at Angel, he saw that something was really on her mind.

Angel looked at him, hesitant to tell him her terrible secret, but she had to tell someone, and there wasn't anyone she trusted more than Dutch.

"I…I gotta tell you something…something you can't tell *nobody*. Not even Craze…you hear me?" Angel told him.

"Ai-ight, what is it?"

13

"Dutch...I'm serious."

"Am I smilin'? I am too. What up?"

Angel took a deep breath and answered, "It's about my father."

Dutch listened while Angel explained how her father used to molest her. The more she talked, the more she opened up – telling him detail after detail and how she felt confused and scared and mad and crazy all at the same time. It was the first time he would ever see her cry, but not the last.

He held her in his arms while she fought through tears to the conclusion. "So, what you wanna do?" he asked, already knowing the answer.

She looked up into his face and answered, "I wanna kill 'em."

Dutch nodded.

"Then, he'll die...tonight," Dutch stated, because he believed in not waiting once a decision was made.

"But...am I wrong? He's my father."

"Naw, Dada...he stopped being your father the minute he put his hands on you."

Angel wiped her face on the collar of her shirt, and then nodded.

"Now, go get dressed."

** ** ** ** **

They left the house without telling Craze, Zoom or Roc. No one would ever know, except Dutch and Angel, what was about to happen. They drove to Dayton Street – no radio, no words. It wasn't that late, so Dayton Street was still alive with activity. They entered Angel's old building from the back and walked the eleven flights to her mother's apartment. Dutch told Angel not to let her mother see her, so she waited on the stairwell, listening. If her father was there, then she'd show her face.

Dutch knocked, and within a few seconds, Angel's mother said, through the door, "Yeah!"

"Is DeJesus home?"

14

"Who wants to know?"

Dutch looked up and down the hallway before responding, "I really ain't tryin' to shout in through the door. Can I speak to DeJesus, please?"

"Well, you're gonna have to, 'cause he ain't here"

"It's kinda' important I get up with him. He played a number with my boss and I'm here to pay off."

There was a short silence, and then Dutch heard the bolt locks and chains being removed from the inside of the door. Angel's mother opened the door just enough to put her head and hand out. "Just give it to me."

Until, that moment, Dutch had never seen Angel's mother before, but he instantly recognized where Angel had gotten her features from. The only difference was the years, and DeJesus' beating of the beauty out of her. Her stringy black hair was matted and tangled, her strong Latina features sallowed and fresh, red bruises covering her cheek.

"Yo, no offense, but ahh...I'd rather give it to him myself, you know? I mean, DeJesus would be pissed at me, and I don't want any problems. You know how he is," Dutch explained, using the evidence of her bruises against her. He could see, from her change in expression that she knew *exactly* how DeJesus was.

She studied Dutch's face for a moment, weighing out the situation. "He's probably at the fuckin' bar up on Frelinghuysen. You know the one?" she asked.

"No...but I'll find it," he said, then pulled out a few hundred dollar bills and handed them to her.

"What's this?" she asked, quickly crumpling the bills in her hand and slipping it back inside the door.

"I changed my mind...you hold it," Dutch told her, knowing that she'd need it, because she was about to be a widow.

He and Angel walked around to Frelinghuysen Avenue. As they advanced, Dutch stopped in a small alley, looking on the ground as if he'd lost something. Angel watched him curiously. Locating what he had been searching for, Dutch bent down and picked up a pipe about the length of a bat, and handed it to Angel.

"Don't use no gun…get it all out," he told her.

Angel took the pipe and they continued their walk. On Frelinghuysen, they found a bar close to the corner and peered inside. He didn't have to ask if she saw him, because she went around him and opened the door. Dutch pulled his gun and followed her inside.

The bar was dimly lit, except for the beer signs hung unsparing throughout, most of them glowing red. The interior was half full with factory workers, alcoholics and over-the-hill prostitutes. Her father sat with his back to the door, laughing and drinking with two other men.

The chatter was lively, but when Dutch and Angel entered, and people saw the look in Angel's eyes and the pipe in her hand, things began to quiet down and patrons parted like the Red Sea.

DeJesus noticed how quiet it had become, so he turned around, just in time to see Angel approaching him. He squinted through his intoxicated state and the dim lighting, finally recognizing her face.

"Angel?"

"Yeah, of death, you sick son of a –" she began, bringing the pipe up and over her shoulder, as if she was swinging an ax, before spitting out the last word of her sentence and striking the crown of his head, "bitch!"

The two men he had been talking with leaned back so far that they fell out of their chairs trying to get out of the way. DeJesus screamed like a man gone mad from the pain as blood sprayed from his cracked cranium. Several patrons jetted for the door, but encountered Dutch, who was standing in front of it – gun aimed.

"Everybody sit the fuck down! You ain't goin' *no*where…and you ain't *seen* shit!" he ordered.

The people rushed to comply, but the bartender tried to inch his way to the phone before Dutch foiled his plan by reaching across the counter and grabbing his black ass by the collar.

"Mothafucka, you deaf? Put your head on the bar!"

While Dutch ran crowd control, Angel mercilessly beat her father into a bloody pulp. Blood spattered with every heavy iron swing, splashing tables, walls, bystanders and Angel herself. She was releasing every ounce of pent up emotion - her frustration, her pain, her shame – and replacing it with a bloody rage.

Dutch had wanted her to do just that, but he also had an ulterior motive. As Pitbulls are trained with the taste of blood, so was he training Angel – because the most vicious of any species is the female.

DeJesus had died several blows ago, but Angel continued to pound his skull into red, jelly tapioca. She did as Dutch had told her – she got it all out. When she had finished, she turned calmly, dragging the bloodied pipe behind her. Looking into her eyes, Dutch saw the Angel that had been released, the only Angel the streets would ever know.

Dutch put his gun to the bartender's head. "Now, gimme' your wallet," he demanded calmly.

The bartender hurried up and did as he was told. Dutch took out his I.D. and read it aloud, "Melvin Tindell…okay Melvin, I'ma hold on to this, you hear me?"

Melvin nodded his head vigorously. "I – I – I seen nothing."

"That's good, but if *any*body saw somethin', I'm holdin' *you* responsible. Do you understand?"

"Man…come on…I –"

"Do…you…understand?" Dutch repeated, lowering his face and bringing it to eye level with Melvin's.

"I understand," he sobbed.

Dutch smacked his cheek, and then let him go before turning to the crowd. "And…if I gotta come back for any of ya'll, blame Melvin here for rattin' you out," Dutch quipped, using a psychological ploy that would have everyone watching everybody else and keeping each other's mouths closed.

Dutch and Angel walked out.

Their bond up to that point had been tight, and this only cemented it. It would stay that way until…

DUTCH
RETURNS

Chapter One
Alexandria, Virginia

Joseph Odouwo was a hard man. Even though he was of average height and build, at 61 years old, he was still every bit his nickname – the Nigerian Butcher – ruthless, even merciless to a point. The only things that had aged were his graying temples and the wrinkles creasing his dark, leathery skin.

The fire still burned inside of him intensely and kept him amongst the most powerful Nigerians of the underworld.

Odouwo had been raised with a strict Christian upbringing – his mother made sure of that. She had been raised during the British colonization and had admired the White man's ways and education.

A member of the Igbo tribe by birth, they had adopted the Western ways more quickly than other Nigerian tribes – such as the Fulani, Ife, Youraba and Hausa. She had named her son, Joseph, after the husband of the virgin mother, Mary, but he preferred to think he had been named after Joseph, the Hebrew slave that had risen to power in Egypt and ushered in a new era for the biblical Hebrew people. From a young age, Odouwo idolized the powerful. What he learned from the British weren't the affectations of etiquette and education; rather he learned how to obtain power by manipulation, deceit and force. He learned and mastered the White man's greatest contribution to civilization – Organized Crime.

He and a young band of assassins, called the Ekwensu – a Nigerian word meaning "messengers of death" – who were hired guns for the British against anyone in Nigeria who aligned themselves against the British crown.

By the time Nigeria gained her independence in 1960, Ekwensu had become experienced gun runners in Nigeria and neighboring Chad. In 1966, Odouwo provided the weapons for a group of Igbo army officers who overthrew the central and regional governments, killing the Prime Minister, Balewa, as well as the political leaders of the North and West regions.

But politics were only a side bet for Joseph. His bread and butter were the gun and drug trades.

Through his British connects, his Nigerian tenacles spread to North America, where many Nigerians had relocated, seeking asylum from the civil war. Aligning themselves with various gangs on the East Coast and Mid-West, the Nigerians muscled their way into the billion dollar heroin trade. The Ekwensu flourished in America, taking the drug profits back to Nigeria to ensure Igbo political power.

Joseph remained in Nigeria, but his chief general in America was a young upstart named Ojiugo Kazami, the son of his dead brother. Kazami was the Butcher Incarnate and would have taken over for Odouwo had it not been for one thing… "Dutch."

The name lingered on Odouwo's tongue like curdled milk. Since Odouwo had no sons of his own, his nephew had become the closest to an heir for him. To have him butchered and beheaded – the ultimate disrespect – was something that Odouwo could never forget. So, he turned to the ********** mafia family, who at the time was headed by Frankie Bonno. He struck a deal, but…Dutch had other plans.

Once Dutch had literally blown trial and escaped into France, Odouwo had been hot on his tracks, only to find that the man whom he was now backed by was a man stronger than the mafia itself.

But, his vengeance would not be thwarted, and once realized, would be even sweeter.

For assistance, Odouwo turned to an old Igbo associate – a man whom he didn't trust, but had used many times - a man that had become the White man's puppet, even to the point of copulating with a German wife. *Disgusting*, Odouwo thought, but, the man had a daughter who had been raised in America – of their ways and established in one of their most powerful institutions – the Federal Bureau of Investigation.

In the international game of politics, it was always advantageous to have an American ally, and Odouwo sought his in the form of a woman. She was a beautiful young woman - a hybrid, comprised of the best of both worlds – the White man's and Odouwo's. Her father was the White man's puppet, and now Odouwo would make her his Nigerian whore.

Looking into her piercing gray eyes, Odouwo knew she was not to be trusted...but she *was* to be desired. Her butter smooth complexion against his dark hue and the way his swollen blackness slid effortlessly in and out of her creamy center invigorated his senses.

Joseph slid a small pillow under the small of her back, then sat up and lifted her legs, spreading them wide. The penetration from this angle made her gasp and claw at the mangled, sweat stained sheets. She tried to wiggle away, but her struggles only excited Joseph more, making him pound her harder with the entire length of his shaft.

"Jo-Jo – ohhh please...right there..." she moaned as her head flailed from side to side. Joseph grunted, then sunk into her as deeply as he could, releasing himself in spasms and spurts.

He lay on top of her, exhausted, while looking down into her face and pushing aside her sun-kissed colored locks. "After this is all over," he smiled, the afterglow of sex in his face, "I want you back in Nigeria. I have a position for you."

Yeah...on my back, she thought to herself. *Thanks, but no thanks.* She rolled over and went to the bathroom, ass swaying and giving Joseph thoughts of going another round. Once in the shower, she quickly scrubbed the scent of sex off of her, vigorously cleansing between her legs and letting the water cascade through her hair.

"After this, a position?" she quipped, remembering Joseph's words. She laughed it off because she truly had other plans. She had come too far now to become some type of concubine to an old man – even if he *did* know how to make her cum. *No, not in this lifetime.*

She stepped out of the shower and looked at herself in the mirror. She loved the way her dreads had a reddish, auburn glow and none of that natty black shit that most dreads looked like. It gave her European features that exotic touch – almost mysterious – which is why she'd dreaded her hair in the first place.

Growing up, being a mixed child had been confusing for her, to say the least. Her parents had sent her to the best schools – mostly White, private schools. She had a few friends, but she just didn't fit in. The White girls looked at her like an oddity, an almost-but-not-quite. And the White boys viewed her as an object to conquer out of curiosity. She tried to escape that by going to a historically Black college, much to her parent's chagrin.

Despite their objections, she enrolled in Howard University and tried to immerse herself in Black life. But even there, she was viewed with suspicion and jealousy. The guys latched on to her light skin and gray eyes, which made the Black girls despise her. Then, the issue of apartheid gripped Black colleges nationwide and the *Proud to be Black* theme made her mixed heritage something to be scorned. She dreaded her hair in a show of solidarity. Still, she was only almost-but-not-quite. And, instead of being flaunted by guys on campus, she became strictly an after hours booty call.

She dropped out of college and decided to join the Army. It was there that she was introduced to lesbianism. Lesbians don't discriminate, lesbians don't judge, they just want to taste your pussy. The experience was not only sexually liberating, but culturally as well.

At the same time, the Army gave her strength she didn't have as a civilian, so she thrived, signing up for Army intelligence. She passed the aptitude tests with flying colors and excelled in the field. Not even two years later, she had become a federal agent. It was mostly desk work and boring field work, until Joseph Odouwo approached her about Bernard James. It wasn't just the half of a million dollars he offered, it was an opportunity to be accepted, to be enlisted for a cause…a Nigerian cause.

He had appealed to her Nigerian heritage and she threw herself into the case, looking at Dutch from every angle before she approached her superiors and inquired about being assigned to the case. They were skeptical at first, but when they saw how much she knew about it, had studied it and that she offered an insight that they hadn't previously thought of, they were all ears.

"Send you to prison with Alvarez?" her commanding agent responded with surprise.

The plan was perfect. When she saw the structure of Dutch's organization, and saw that Angel was a dyke, she knew that she could get to her. She just hadn't counted on Angel getting to her, too. That was one angle she hadn't figured into the equation.

She emerged from the bathroom with a large towel wrapped around her waist. Joseph stood in the middle of the bedroom in his burgundy silk pajama bottoms and sipping a glass of cognac. He smiled as she approached him.

"Goldilocks," he sang, running his fingers through her hair, "the name fits you…in more ways than one. The perfect thief in a world full of bears."

Goldilocks smiled, "The federal element is of no consequence to us any longer. They have served their purpose."

"What orders did they give you?"

24

"The chief trusts my integrity. Communications are on my initiation because they have no official jurisdiction in France, and we both know that France could care less about American intelligence," she giggled. "I must give it to Dutch...he picked the one spot in the world where the mutual hatred of the authorities will protect him. Either way, I am on my own until such time as Dutch returns to American soil."

"But, he won't."

"Not if I can help it," she vowed intently.

"We have come a long way, you and I. And you have proven yourself worthy of the Ekwensu. But now that we have reached our goal, take caution. James is not a man to be underestimated."

"Neither am I," Goldilocks smiled mischievously.

"Death is too good for him. I want him to live as I do...in pain. Take everything from him...everything he loves...and only in the end, take his life...slowly," Odouwo instructed her, relishing the thought of Dutch, finally broken, his pride reduced to nothing. "Then, bring me his head."

Goldilocks rose up on her tiptoes and kissed Odouwo. "I have to go now, but, I'll keep you informed." She took up her clothes and dressed.

On her way out, he called to her one more time, "Kim...be careful," he said, knowing that for what she was about to undertake, she would need to be.

** ** ** ** **

Newark, New Jersey

"What the *fuck* was on ya'll minds, huh?! Digamé! Leavin' me behind like that, not knowing if ya'll fuckin' dead!" Angel screamed on Craze as he drove along the Garden State Parkway in a rented Lincoln. "I should smack the shit outta you...can I smack the shit outta you? Come here," she barked, pulling his shirt with her free arm and turning his face to hers, then kissing him dead on the mouth.

"You tryin' to make me wreck, crazy mothafucka?" Craze replied, putting his eyes back on the road.

Angel was too happy to be upset, but she still had three years of frustration to get off her chest.

"And what? Ya'll all in fuckin' France la-la'n and wee-wee'n while I'm cooped up in a fuckin' cell for three years! Oh what, it was just *fuck Angel,* huh? Qué sera, sera. Ya'll ain't shit," she screamed, then winced in pain because she had leaned her slinged arm too heavily on the armrest.

"Ain't nobody forget you, ai-ight? But –"

"I ain't tryin' to hear that shit," Angel sucked her teeth, turning up the radio.

Craze turned the radio back down. "Look…what the fuck you expect? For us to kill a whole fuckin' court room, then come see you on visitin' day? Stupid ass…fuck you wanted, a forwardin' address? Nobody forgot you. Dutch talked about you every fuckin' day…but we had to let shit cool

down, ai-ight? And then, here you and Roc is heatin' it right back up!" he glanced over at her. "What the fuck is goin' on? I come back and hear ya'll fuckin' warrin' in the mall, and I find you wit' a gun in his face."

Angel sucked her teeth.

"Well?" Craze pushed, ridding his blunt of its accumulated ashes as he switched lanes.

"He shot me!"

"For what? What the fuck happened?"

"So, Dutch talked about me, for real? What he say?" Angel questioned eagerly, trying to change the subject.

"Angel, I'm serious."

"I'm serious too! The mothafucka shot me and it ain't ova'...fuck that. Sangré por sangré" – blood for blood in Spanish.

"Damn. There you go with that Spanish shit. What you say?"

"Nothin' yo'...nothin'," she answered, looking out the window, thoughts filled with Dutch. She had known that he wasn't dead. She knew it in her heart, and now to know for sure, nothing else mattered. "So...how is he? What up wit' this move to France?"

Craze looked at her, smirked, then blew out a stream of purple haze. "Trust me, baby, the game...will never be the same."

** ** ** ** **

Willingboro, New Jersey

Rahman sat in his driveway looking at the home he thought he'd never see again. He'd gone to the children's school prepared to die. His only hope was that he hadn't lived in vain. Remembering the look in Angel's eyes, there was no doubt in his mind that she would've killed him...

Then Craze had walked in and his presence opened up a whole 'nother chapter. Deep down, Rahman had known that Dutch was alive. Even deeper, he'd *hoped* that he was alive – although he wanted no parts of that life anymore...or did he?

He looked at the brick and stucco house his family lived in. It had been bought with drug money.

The Cadillac Escalade he was sitting in had been bought with drug money. The cause he had taken lives for – was prepared to die for – was largely financed by drug money. True, all of it came to him before he got locked up, but the fact remained that he was still enjoying the fruits of his gangster past.

And what of France? He remembered when Dutch had frequently taken trips there back in the day, but he never knew why. Never really gave it any thought...and now, he was being invited as well. *What was Dutch up to...and how could it really*

27

help him in ridding the streets of the poison that made them all wealthy?

One thing was for sure, Craze was right. With Angel out of the way, he could really clean up the streets of Newark. *But, then what?* Like Craze said, the police, the courts, even the mafia and other powerful factions wouldn't just stand by and let him dry up such a potent source of illegal funds without a fight. *So, could he really take them all on and win?*

Rahman shook his head, rubbing his hands over his face. No. He wouldn't go to France. He owed it to his family. They needed him as well. What good was saving the world if you couldn't even save your own family? He had cleaned up several large areas of the city and helped alot of people. That would have to do for now.

He opened the car door and eased his large frame from the seat. Stretching and taking in the fresh air, he truly felt blessed to be home.

"All praises are due to Allah," he whispered, chirping the alarm on the SUV and heading for the front door.

Once inside, he saw his three children huddled around their Mommy. They were so engrossed in their grief that it took a second to realize that he was there. His son, Ali, looked up and his eyes became as big as plates.

"Mommy, look! Abu's home! Abu came back!" he cried, then scampered over as fast as he could, his sisters, Aminah and Anisha, hot on his heels.

"My daddy's home! My daddy's home!"

"We love you, Abu!"

"I knew you was comin' back!"

They all exclaimed, covering his face with kisses and embracing his neck when he got down on his knees to be on their level.

"That's right…Abu's home, and I'm home to stay!" Rahman shouted, eyes brimming with tears.

When he looked up at Ayesha, he expected to see her coming to greet him as well. But, she sat on the couch, hugging herself like she was cold, rocking back and forth. Her Kohl eyeliner ran in black streaks down the length of her face where tears had previously run, but, in her eyes was nary a tear...just a cold, hard gaze.

"As Salaam Alaykum, Ummi," Rahman smiled, standing up. "I can't get no hug?"

Ayesha remained expressionless, finally breaking the silence with, "Ali, Anisha, Aminah...go in the back. Abu and Ummi have to talk."

The children whined in protest, but they could tell by her tone not to dally too long. They were just happy that their father was home and scampered off into the T.V. room.

Rahman had expected her to be upset. He knew she had a right to be. But, he felt that coming back made everything alright.

"Now, about that hug," he smirked, trying to break the ice that hung in the air, almost as invisible as the frost. Ayesha rose slowly, regarded him a moment, then slowly approached.

"Listen! I know you're upset, but it's all o – "

The swift smack Ayesha delivered to his jaw silenced him instantly.

"How...dare...you...How dare you just walk into this house after what you said to me. After what you've put me through for the past 24 hours," Ayesha hissed, the sound of her own voice making her madder, so mad that she trembled. "Not knowing...if you were alive or dead, not knowing...waiting for that phone to ring and they tell me...," her voice was swallowed in sobs.

Rahman moved to hug her, but she tensed rigid and held up her arms. *"Don't* touch me."

"Ayesha, listen...what could I do? Let those babies just *die*? Huh? Is that what you wanted?" Rahman questioned.

"I don't know what to expect from you anymore, Rahman...I really don't."

"From now on, I promise, things will be different. I'ma be —"

"I want a divorce," Ayesha stated simply, meeting his shocked gaze with a firm one of her own."

"Ayesha..." Rahman sighed, "let's not —"

"A divorce, Rahman. You can initiate it, or I can through Khul. Either way...it's...it's...over," she stated, stumbling over the *it's over* part.

Rahman couldn't believe what he was hearing. *A divorce?* "After all we've been through...you just wanna let it go *like this*?"

"*We* been through?" Ayesha chuckled. "*We*? No, *me*. What *I've* been through. When you wanted to run the streets, doing God knows what, who was the good little wife at home? And when your life finally caught up with you and you went to prison, who was there by your side? And when you came home, ready to change the world, who had to grin and bear your absence? Then, you have the nerve to tell me you're *leaving* to *die?...Leaving?* What a joke, because, nigguh, you was never *here*," Ayesha broke it down to him, then turned, went back to the couch and sat down.

"So, just like that?" Rahman asked, trying to calm the raging pain he felt building inside. "Don't I have no say in this shit?"

"You had your say when you walked out that door 24 hours ago," Ayesha replied calmly.

Rahman searched his heart and soul for the words...to somehow dispel this nightmare become reality. But, none came. There was nothing he could say, so he turned and headed back out the door.

** ** ** ** **

Irvington, New Jersey

Delores Murphy entered her apartment and dropped her purse on the couch. She had just come home from church and she was ready to eat. She had been going to service regularly for the last few years, but it was more out of upbringing than faith. Her mother had been a devoted Christian, and Delores had rejected that lifestyle. But, she was soon to turn fifty and, after all the years of doing it her way, the sheer burden of life incited her to seek spiritual solace.

She had always believed in God, but, like most people, that's where it ended – verbal affirmation, but no active strivings. To her, religion seemed to be so confusing – especially now, with books like The DaVinci Code, Gospel of Judas, Gospel of Barabas and many others, all giving different versions of the man they called Christ. But she was no fool; she knew spirituality without boundaries – which is what religion represented – usually degenerated into sensualism, and finally, base materialism. While she didn't feel like she could find the answers on her own, she just didn't know who could help in the process. And, above all, Delores needed answers. Her life was one big question mark, a waiting period, each day diminishing her hopes of ever being truly happy.

She started to check her phone messages, but her rumbling stomach took priority. She popped a Lean Cuisine microwaveable meal of shrimp scampi in the microwave, started it and then went into her bedroom to take off her Ann Taylor suit. Looking at herself as she undressed, she felt like there was nothing to be ashamed of.

She was forty-nine and still looked incredibly attractive. She continued to be propositioned by the mature gentlemen's class of bachelors and had the build and resemblance of Allen Iverson's mother, only a shade lighter. She didn't work out regularly, but she did like to take brisk walks on nice days and she watched what she ate. Delores Murphy took care of herself, but she wanted more than health, she yearned for happiness.

The timer on the microwave went off just as she slipped into her house robe and slippers.

Returning to the kitchen, she removed the dish from the microwave and emptied its contents onto a clear, glass plate. The ringing of the phone stopped her from taking a first bite of the shrimp dinner.

Delores answered, "Hello," only to listen to a request from a strange voice, then replied, "Wrong number," and hung up.

She decided to let the messages play while she ate. The machine said that she had three new messages.

BEEP: Mrs. Murphy…this is Doctor Eckstein. Just got your lab reports. No need to come in, just wanted to congratulate you on a clean bill of health. Just watch the salt intake and you should be fine.

Delores celebrated the news by adding a liberal amount of salt to the bland, store bought scampi.

BEEP: Mrs. Murphy…umm…this is Nina again and… well…I'm … I've decided to relocate.

Where, I don't know…but…I know what you said…but, Mrs. Murphy, *please*…I need to know before I go if…

The message went on too long and Nina's pleas were cut off.

"If…" that was the last word she got in, and for Delores, it summed up her whole life…*if*. She prayed the girl would go on with her life before she became like Delores, waiting for the answer to that very word…*if*.

Delores put down her fork and walked over to the answering machine, ready to delete the third message, because she thought it would be Nina calling again. But, it wasn't…

BEEP: Mrs. Murphy, this is Shirley Green at the VA Hospital. Please, call me as soon as you can at 5 -5 - 5…9…3…2…6. I'm calling about one of my patients here who believes you're his wife. His name is Bernard James. It really is urgent.

Silence...total and complete silence...

The blare of the city, the babbling television, even the hum of the appliances were swallowed by the all encompassing silence. The first thing Delores became aware of was the beating and skipping, beating and skipping of her own heart. She was too scared to move - like a person dreaming, afraid to lose the vision - but her knees became too weak to stand, so she knelt on the floor. She knelt before the answering machine like a worshipper before an altar, awaiting a revelation from a higher power.

Her trembling fingers reached out too replay the message, and she did...three times. By then, all of her frozen emotions had thawed and she cried the cry of release - like the slaves on Juneteenth, like a prisoner fresh off of death row and like a woman who was finally free to love.

"Thank you, Je-...*God*. Thank you God...thank you!" she murmured fervently, the prayers giving her the strength to rise to her feet. She started to call Nurse Green back, but, for what? She knew where the VA Hospital was and it was there that held the answer to her prayers. She grabbed her coat and threw it on over her house robe and slip. Delores giggled feverishly to herself because she was never a woman to leave her house less than immaculate. But, then again, she never had a reason like this to leave the house.

Snatching up her keys and purse, she headed for the door, and when she opened it, her eyes widened in amazement. Craze stood there before her, just about to knock.

On impulse, Delores wrapped him up in a big hug, exclaiming, "He's alive! Thank God! He's alive! He's alive!"

Craze was shocked that she already knew. "I know, Ma. That's what I came to tell you."

"Tell me? You knew?" she asked, and then reality sunk in. The *he* they were referring to, weren't one and the same. The *he* Craze was speaking of…was *Dutch*.

** ** ** ** **

Seth Borden Housing Projects (Elizabeth, New Jersey)

"Where you been?"

"Out."

"Fuck you mean, *out*? I asked you a fuckin' question!"

"Just like I said…out! I didn't know I had to report to you."

Angel snatched Goldilocks by her arm, yanking her over to her. "You damn right, you gotta report to me, huh, tu comprende?" Angel sneered.

"Yeah, whatever," Goldilocks flippantly replied.

Angel back slapped her so hard, Goldilocks spun around and fell on her ass in the middle of the living room.

With the training Goldilocks had, she could've smashed Angel with ease, but she was the submissive partner, that was her role, and she knew how to play it well.

"Why'd you hit me?" she questioned, tears welling in her eyes.

"Get up," Angel commanded her coldly. When she moved too slowly, Angel kicked her leg with the side of her foot. "Get…*up!*'

Goldilocks got to her feet, tears flowing freely.

"I'm sorry, okay? I just…needed to get away…to think."

"Get away from what? Think about what?" Angel asked, suspiciously. She was vexed because Goldilocks wasn't home when she got there. She had just been tellin' Craze about her and that she wanted Goldilocks to go to France with them.

Craze was skeptical. He didn't know her, but, Angel was adamant. Explaining how they did time together, and how Goldilocks had stuck by her through the whole Rock – Roll ordeal. Craze had checked with Dutch on bringing her.

"If Angel say she solid…then cool," Dutch had said.

Angel assured him that she was solid, only to get home and find her gone, and then unwilling to account for her absence.

"Remember you told me that...if Dutch was alive, that it wouldn't matter? That you'd always be with me?" Goldilocks reminded her.

Angel didn't answer, but her gaze confirmed the memory.

"But, that's not what I heard on the phone. When you called to tell me about Dutch and about France, I didn't hear that it wouldn't matter. I've *never* heard your voice so alive. So...so...full. Not even when you told me you love me..."Goldilocks sobbed and explained.

Angel sighed, letting the steel out of her taut shoulders and lowering the wall on her emotions.

"Do you love him, Angel?" Goldilocks questioned, eyes like glass pools of innocence.

"He means a lot to me, Goldi. Nothin' can change that. But, you mean a lot to me, too," Angel confessed.

"Then...I'd rather not go to France with you," Goldilocks announced, wiping her eyes and feigning conviction. "I'd rather just...just say good-bye now...before I get over there and you hurt me."

Angel pulled Goldilocks to her, body to body.

"Ma, believe me, I would never hurt you," Angel vowed, caressing Goldilocks' cheek.

"You say that now," she replied, the tears welling back up. She wanted Angel to feel like she had convinced her to go so that it would remove any lurking suspicions anyone may have about her wanting to go. And, Angel was falling right into her trap, or so she thought.

Angel did indeed have feelings for Goldilocks, but her reasons for making sure that she came with her, weren't purely based on emotions. Angel wouldn't leave her in the states with the knowledge of where Dutch was. For Angel, Goldilocks would go or die. Both women had hidden agendas.

"Have I ever lied to you, huh?" Angel smirked, running her thumb over Goldilocks' peach colored lips.

Goldilocks shook her head, looking into Angel's eyes.

"And I never will. I can't leave you, Goldi. You have to come with me, okay? You have to. Them French bitches can't eat pussy, you know?"

Goldilocks smiled, parting her lips and taking Angel's thumb into her mouth, then pulling it out and kissing it. "I love you, Angel."

"Siempre."

** ** ** ** **

Once it hit her who Craze was talking about, she broke their embrace. "What did you say?"

"Your son," Craze said, then lowered his voice, "your son wants to see you right away."

Delores heard him, but didn't want to hear him. Her mind was on getting to the VA Hospital.

Still, the mother inside her breathed a sigh of relief, knowing that her only child was still alive, confirming what she already knew. "Where is he?"

"I have to take you to him."

"Not...not now, Chris. I can't explain, but...I can't do this now," she informed.

Chris watched her fidgety demeanor and noticed that she was dressed in a robe under her coat and couldn't figure it out. He thought she'd be happy to hear about Dutch, but, if she was, she wasn't showing it.

"But, Ma...it's like...a long way...so we have to do this now."

"I can't. I have to go," she replied, backing towards the elevator.

"Aren't you happy that he's alive?" Craze questioned, not sure that she was.

Delores stopped and pondered a proper response. "I'm glad...that he's not dead," she answered.

Craze walked up to her as she frantically pressed the elevator button. "Is everything okay, Ma?"

"Yes...yes...I just can't explain now. How can I reach you?"

"You can't. But, I'll reach you. Soon...Tuesday...is that good?"

The elevator doors slid open and Delores stepped inside.

"Yes...Tuesday...I'll explain everything. And, Craze? Tell Bernard that I may have a surprise for him as well."

The doors closed with a ding, leaving Craze scratching his head.

** ** ** ** **

Angel opened the door for Craze with a kiss and a hug. "What's up, Papi? What she say?"

Craze was about to answer until he saw Goldilocks sitting on the couch in a pair of cut off shorts and a wife beater. She eyed him right back with a smirk that acknowledged his appraisal. He looked at Angel in her yellow LRG velour suit. It was baggy, but her ravenous beauty couldn't be hidden. *What a waste*, he thought to himself, looking at the two gorgeous females.

"So, you must be Goldilocks, huh?" he finally said, extending his hand.

Goldilocks didn't shake his hand, she stood up and gave him a full body hug, "And, I know, you're Craze. Angel told me you was a cutie," she flirted.

Angel sucked her teeth and chuckled. "Naw, I said he had a fat booty!" she joked, grabbing him on his ass. "Should be on a bitch."

Craze slapped her hand away. "Ai-ight, don't get fucked up in here, Dada."

"Who's Dada?" Goldilocks inquired.

"That's what family call her," Craze explained, "You know, like Jaws? Dada...dada...dada.

'Cause she like a fuckin' shark."

Angel's cell phone rang with the sounds of a Don Cauldron medley. "Yeah..." she answered, then rolled her eyes to the ceiling and thrust the phone at Craze, "It's for you," she said blandly.

Craze took the phone. "Hello?"

"When do we leave?" Rahman asked on the other end of the line from a phone booth.

"Leave? I ain't think you wanted to go."

"Yeah, well," Rahman replied, looking around at the downtown traffic, "I feel like I need to go away for a while. Hard to see the picture when you're in the frame."

Rahman had decided not to go. He had decided to step back and just concentrate on family. Ayesha had changed that and left him only with himself. Rahman knew One Eye Roc was still very much a part of him, and he needed the time to really figure out who exactly he would be. Besides, Dutch was still his man.

"Ai-ight...cool. I need to holler at my man and get ya'll passports done up. We all leavin' by different routes, feel me? Call me tomorrow and I'll have that for you."

"One."

"One."

Rahman hung up the phone and took a deep breath. He had once told Ayesha that he couldn't be a Muslim and a gangster at the same time. He thought he had chosen, when in fact, he had only compromised. He was a gangsta' Muslim, but now...it was time to get off the fence.

Chapter Two

The concorde taxied onto the runway smoothly . That was when Nina opened her eyes, took a deep breath and mouthed a silent thanks to God. She hated to fly because it gave her a queasy feeling in the pit of her stomach – not to mention the butterflies flittering frantically inside, not only in her stomach, but her fingertips, the inside of her thighs, and the small of her back.

"Thank Zoo for flying Marseille Provence. Please remain seated until the plane fully stops," the voice of the French stewardess' heavy French accented English was heard over the PA system, but many people disregarded the request and prepared to deboard.

When Nina stood, her whole body felt like a limb that had fallen asleep and that prickly sensation covered her like goose bumps. But, she knew it wasn't because of the trip - it was first-class luxury all the way. No, the feeling was internal and had more to do with the *reason* she was making the trip than the trip itself.

Since boarding the plane at LaGuardia, a need to turn back, to run, continued to twist her emotions. *This is crazy*, her head continued to warn her, reminding her of the life she had built for herself.

She was at a point in her career where she could write her own ticket wherever she chose to relocate. Her finances were finally stable and flourishing, after paying off all the debts she had accumulated since college. She owned her own home and paid her own bills. Then, the capstone to her life structure had been added by Dwight – a loving, supportive brother, who wasn't intimidated by the fact that she made more than he as a mechanic, nor was he afraid to stand by her side. But, there she was, leaving all of that behind in exchange for a path of rose petals. A path that led to an unknown destiny…a path that led…to Dutch.

As she entered the terminal, her senses were overwhelmed with the sounds, sights and scents of France. So many different languages created a cacophony in her ear, but it was the French tongue that gave it rhythm. French, that language of love. Even if you didn't understand it, French was still like music to your ears...a poem you couldn't grasp, but you could feel.

"Bonjour, Mademoiselle. Venillez me moutrer votre passeport?" the young man from customs asked pleasantly for her passport.

"Bonjour," Nina replied, using the only French word she was sure of. "But...I don't..."

The customs agent sighed and mumbled sarcastically to himself, "Choutte. Une Americaine," then to her, "May I see your passport?" he stumbled clumsily over his English grammar.

Nina noticed his attitude, wondering if it was because she was Black. She didn't know about the disdain that the French have for Americans. She handed over the proper documents and he examined them.

"Nee-Na Mara-teen??" he tried to pronounce.

"*Nina* Jam- I mean...Martin. Nina *Martin*," she corrected him, while in the process, correcting herself.

Nina James. She had written it over and over on the tablet of her mind, like a schoolgirl with a crush. *Nina James*. She took a deep breath and added, "I have nothing to declare."

He took a cursory look through her small carry-on suitcase and travel bag, then smiled weakly.

"Enjoy your stay."

Before she could respond, he was on to the next person behind her. Nina gathered her luggage, looking around for Dutch. All she saw were scurrying bodies, family members greeting one another and a tall, blonde woman, apparently cursing out a short, balding, middle-aged man. Her words were French, but body language is universal.

She stepped out of the terminal and was hit by a peculiar odor – tangy, musty, almost like the stale insides of a gym - it was definitely body odor. The flowers being sold all around her brought occasional relief through breezes but, the stench, although not strong, was pervasive. Nina would soon learn that France was the country of love, but it carried the odor of human frailty.

Taxis lined the front drive of the terminal. She looked around, and still no sign of Dutch. She had no number to call and no address to go to. Her heart dropped, thinking of what could've happened.

After all, Dutch was a wanted fugitive. He was also a gangsta', playing a gansta's game. Just like the day she went to the courthouse only to arrive too late, she thought maybe something happened and Dutch wouldn't show up.

"I told you this was crazy," she mumbled to herself. It was in that moment that she saw a classic '55 silver Rolls Royce parked five spaces down. A large delivery truck had been blocking her view, but as it pulled away, she could clearly read the sign that the driver was holding up: Nina Martin.

A smile spread across her face, and the butterflies returned with a vengeance as she gathered up her luggage and hurried over to the driver. "I'm Nina Martin," she announced proudly.

The driver smiled, bowed slightly, then said in a British accented version of English, "Velcome to France, Miss Martin. May I take your bags?" he offered. Once they were all loaded up, he opened the back door, took Nina's hand and helped her into the backseat before seating himself behind the wheel on the right-hand side of the car. "I trust you are comfortable? There is wine and an assortment of cheeses, should you so desire. We'll be at the estate very soon," he advised, then pulled away from the terminal.

The French countryside made for beautiful scenery with the rolling hills and endless fields of grapes and flowers. It was just as Nina had imagined it. Thinking about all she had read about France in school by James Baldwin or from Josephine Baker, and of course, Nina Simone. But, her mind wasn't on the scenic route. She wanted to see *him*. For her, *that* was the beautiful scenery her heart yearned for.

When the driver turned off of the main road and the car began to ascend a steep hill, in the distance, she could make out a beautiful, castle-like structure up ahead. The hill was steep, below it, a rocky precipice that ended in a beautiful field of lilac and lavender. As the car climbed, she giggled to herself that this was truly the stairway to heaven the O'Jay's sang about.

The castle-like structure was truly breathtaking, a palace built for royalty. It sat on a huge plateau which had rows and rows of grapes and flowers to its immediate right. The palace was built in Gothic fashion, with spires, portals and flying buttresses. The driveway doubled back on itself, with a large fountain in the middle.

Several columns held up the stone awning, with bronze lions on either side of the entrance. To the left was the carriage house, which held several expensive cars. The driver pulled right up to the door, then graciously assisted Nina from her seat. She looked around, amazed by her new surroundings, but what amazed her most was not above her, but at her feet.

Rose petals – the same petals that led her through her own home and extended across the den, both continents and continued into this palace built for a king…and queen.

She looked at the driver, who smiled at her in a fatherly way. "Don't worry about your luggage, Miss Martin. Please," he held out his arm, "as the French say, entrez."

Nina's butterflies had moved to the soles of her feet, but instead of pushing her back, they seemed to carry her through the front door. Inside, two sets of stairs circled up to the balcony above, but the rose petals continued straight through the domed lobby. Her heels clacked across the shiny marble floor, through a beautiful dining room with a dining table which seated twelve on either side. Up ahead, she saw a blooming rose garden that filled the air with its fragrance.

Once outside, in the courtyard area, the petals continued, but she could see now, where they ended. Standing in the middle of the garden, dressed in dark blue jeans and a white tee – typical American thug gear - was Dutch. That was her moment of clarity – the moment when everything she'd let go of, or could've had, no longer mattered. All that mattered was the man in front of her, holding a bouquet of orange callalillies.

"Hello, Nina…it's been a long time," Dutch greeted her, that smile that made her want to strip right there on the spot, spreading across his face. "You still look beautiful."

She felt like a schoolgirl, bashful, yet eager to learn. "Too long, Bernard. And, you ain't lookin' too bad yourself," she replied, wanting to run to him, jump in his arms and wrap her legs around his waist – but the schoolgirl inside wouldn't let her.

"Yeah, I ain't?" Dutch remarked, playfully brushing away imaginary lint. "Well, I look even better from up close. Come 'ere," he smirked, opening his arms wide, Nina immediately rushing over and devouring his embrace.

The moment their lips met, she knew she was in trouble - tasting him after so long, waking up wet, going to bed wishing – and realized that she had never wanted anything as much as she wanted him right then.

They heard someone behind them clear their throat so loudly that they broke their kiss, but kept the embrace, looking in the direction of the noise.

"Excuse the intrusion," Ceylon smiled, bowing slightly with his head, "but, I heard Miss Martin had arrived. So, I had to see who had my young friend so…smitten."

"Nina, this is my business partner, Omar Ceylon, Dutch introduced.

Ceylon stepped over and took Nina's outstretched hand and kissed it. "Shall I compare thee to a summer's day? Thou art more lovely and more temperate."

Nina blushed, "Nice to meet you, Mr. Ceylon."

"Please, call me Omar," Ceylon said, then turned to Dutch. "I just wanted to tell you that Craze says that all is well. Everyone is en route, although traveling separately."

"I'm glad to hear that. 'Preciate it, Cey."

Ceylon nodded. "I will leave you two to get, uhh... reacquainted."

As Ceylon disappeared into the house, Dutch turned back to Nina.

"Bernard, I just wanna say – " Nina began, but Dutch silenced her by gently putting his finger to her lips.

"Hold up, baby. We only get to do this once, and I wanna make sure I do it right," Dutch said, handing her the callalillies, then sinking to one knee. He took her hand, looked in her eyes and said, "I can't front. I was buggin', wonderin' if you would use that ticket...you know...be on that flight. But, when I heard that you did...Nina, in my whole life, I've never bowed to nobody. I prided myself on that.

But I bend my knee now, because of all the women that's ever been proposed to, you're the only one worthy of a bended knee. And, I'm asking...that you'll be my wife," Dutch proposed, pulling out a ring box and flipping it open with his free hand.

Nina didn't even see the ring, she was so busy looking into his eyes through the tear clouded lenses of her own. Her words caught in her throat and all she could do was nod her absolute acceptance.

But, when she did see it, she let out a gasp. As Dutch slipped it on her finger, she couldn't believe the size of it. It was an eight carat canary yellow diamond surrounded by an intricate spiral of baguettes.

My God, it's beautiful," she gasped, wrapping her arms around his neck. "I love you, Bernard James."

"I love *you*...*Mrs*. James," he smiled.

This time, when their lips met, the kiss was more intense than the first. Their bodies pressed against one another until they could feel each other's anxiousness through the fabric of their outfits.

Dutch and Nina had been wanting each other too long not to devour each other on the spot. Like Janet Jackson sang, *any time, any place.*

Dutch slid his hand under Nina's dress, palmed her ass, and then lifted her off of her feet. Nina wrapped her legs around his waist, allowing Dutch to carry her into the stone gazebo made in the shape of a Roman love temple. He sat her on the railing, pulling his pants down while pulling her panties aside and entered her fully, with one stroke. Nina's wetness gushed, taking her breath away and causing her to moan his name.

"*Dutch.*"

"Damn, you feel so good," Dutch whispered in her ear. Then, tracing his tongue along her neck, he long-dicked her with a passionate rhythm.

"I want you so bad...I...I...I dreamed of you every night," Nina moaned.

"Tell me your dreams," Dutch urged.

Nina imagined all the times she had fantasized about making love to Dutch. Feeling him deep inside like he was at that moment, the mental images turned her on even more, making her spread her legs wider and grind into Dutch's every thrust, throwing the pussy back to him. She bit down on her trembling lip against the painful pleasure, feeling his balls banging against her ass.

"Tell me you need me," Nina gasped.

"I need you."

"Tell me you love me, Bernard...tell me you love me."

"I love you, Nina."

"Tell me I'm all the woman you'll ever want."

"No other can compare," Dutch replied with a grunt.

The satisfaction of the last statement sent Nina over the top. She arched her back, relaxing her walls and letting the orgasm shudder her entire body.

Nina's juices covered Dutch's dick, giving their sex that sweet, slurping sound that, along with Nina's cries of passion, made Dutch release himself deep inside her, leaving them both panting and exhausted.

After the couple showered, teasing and touching their way into another steamy session, the chef prepared them a lunch – of succulent steak with mushrooms, covered in a red wine sauce, steamed broccoli and seasoned mashed potatoes – and then, Dutch wanted to show Nina around the estate.

It was a sprawling estate, consisting of some 10,000 acres and sat on a plateau. One side overlooked a lush valley filled with an array of flowers. The other side, overlooked a small village and the not too distant shores of the Mediterranean Sea.

The estate itself, besides the palace-like chateau, boasted its own field of merlot, cabernet franc and sauvignon grapes as well as 100 acres of lilacs, roses and lavender. Directly behind the house, opposite a helicopter landing pad, was a stable which held Ceylon's collection of prized Arabian horses.

There were horses of all different shades, but Nina was especially attracted to a jet black one with a tuft of white in the shape of diamond on it's forehead.

"I like this one the most," Nina commented, leaning up to stroke the horse's face. "Can I ride him?"

Dutch arched an eyebrow. "What a Pioneer Houses chick know about ridin' horses?" he chuckled.

"When I was younger, they used to have these programs, you know...to take city kids to camp and stuff. Would you believe I went to one in Voorhees, New Jersey? That was the *real* Camp Crystal Lake...you know, from Friday the 13th?" she explained. "Anyway, they had some horses and they let us take turns riding them. I *loved* it, *and* the counselor said that I was a natural. Trust me, I know how to ride," she flirted, "as long as it's a stallion."

"Yeah?"

"Yeah."

Dutch smirked. "Well, you got a thoroughbred here, shortie."

"When can I ride?"

"You already did," Dutch joked.

Nina playfully hit him. "I'm talkin' about the horse. *This* horse," she said, pointing to the horse.

"Soon. First, I got something else to show you."

As they strolled hand in hand across the estate, a playful breeze spread across the plateau and Nina closed her eyes, enjoying the sensation. Everything was so beautiful, so perfect...almost too perfect.

But she prayed that this time would be the exception.

They came up on a hanger-like wood structure. Inside, a few men in overalls were hauling burlap bags full of grapes and dumping them into large bronze vats – six in a row, down the length of the hanger and the tangy aroma of the fruit tilled the air. Dutch reached into a bag, pulled out a few grapes, popped one into his mouth and fed Nina another.

"This is the winery, this is where we make these grapes into a red wine of the St. Emilion type.

See these vats?" he pointed out, "you ever see women on T.V. standing in a big tub, mashing the grapes with their feet?"

Nina nodded in affirmation.

"Well, this does it automatically. That is, unless you want to do it the old fashioned way with those pretty little feet of yours," he chuckled, making Nina giggle.

"Naw, I think I'll leave it to the machines."

"After the impurities are filtered out, and all the ingredients are added, it's stored in wooden barrels like this," he concluded, leading her over to a row of barrels stacked along a wall. He looked around, then called out to one of the attendants. "Apportez vous, s'il vous plait une bouteille," he said, asking for a bottle in flawless French.

Nina was taken aback, pursing her lip in an impressed fashion. "You speak French like a native."

Dutch shrugged. "What can I say...I'm nice wit' my tongue," he winked.

I know that's right, she thought to herself, remembering their shower escapade.

The attendant brought him an empty bottle. Dutch used the spout on the barrel and filled the empty bottle with red wine, then handed it to the attendant, who corked it. He then handed the bottle back to Dutch and then walked away.

"What they say is true...wine gets better with time," he began, giving the bottle to Nina. "And this...is for our tenth anniversary. By then, like this wine, what we share will be that much sweeter," he finished, pulling her close and kissing her passionately.

Climbing the stairway to heaven
Step by step...
** ** ** ** **

If any woman could identify with what Nina was feeling, it was Delores. But, for her, it was 30 years more intense. Three decades of going back to school and working full time until she got the job with the state, where she stayed for almost 20 years - not to

48

mention, raising a son alone. She barely had time for herself, but she etched out a niche of a social life.

On the surface, Delores looked to be a woman who had it all together, but, underneath, her heart was going through every phase Langston Hughes spoke of in his poem A *Dream Deferred*. Delores' dream had dried up the day Bernard had walked out of her life. The void he left in her heart festered, and at times, memories of him became the emotional equivalent of rotten meat. There were times when she cursed him for abandoning her. But, at other times, when she heard the music that had been the sound track of their love, thoughts of him turned sticky and syrupy sweet.

Her emotions swung like a pendulum between syrupy and stench, but as time wore on, her youthful femininity became matronly, her eyes developed crow's feet and she watched her only child grow into a murderous monster, her deferred dream began to sag like a heavy load. But, before it could explode, the phone rang with the answer to her prayers.

She had rushed to the VA Hospital, kissed his sleeping face and awakened her prince with it. The smile she received in return brought out her natural woman. Delores made all the arrangements to move him home with her, promising him the best medical care, even if it cost her last dime.

The last few days had brought her glow back - making love to the only man she had ever loved, washing his back as they bathed together, getting her hair washed in return and quiet moments when neither said a word, letting their eyes say it all.

As Linda Jones' *Hypnotized* played on the CD player, Bernard proved he still had his swagger, despite his debilitated condition.

"I bet you don't remember this song?" Delores teased, swaying in his arms.

"Do I remember? Please, baby girl," he chuckled, and then began to croon in a shaky falsetto, "Hypnotized...youuuu got me...hypnotized."

Delores giggled. "No, I don't mean the words, I mean, what comes to mind when you hear it?"

Bernard closed his eyes and hmmmed as if he was thinking, then he groaned softly. "What?" Delores asked.

"I see Linda in that sexy sequined – " he began, but Delores cut him off.

"Nigguh, don't get hurt up in here."

He chuckled. "Okay, okay...let me see...I see...a fine caramel flavored little girl tryin' to prove she was grown," he quipped.

"Little girl? I wish. Believe me, by the time we met, the little girl was long gone," Delores commented wistfully.

"Naw, baby girl, it wasn't gone. She wasn't gone. I admit you were hip to the hip talk and partial to the ways. But...you was like a young bird, just trying on her wings, you dig? Not quite sure if they could hold her up, but damn, if they wasn't pretty to look at," he chuckled, dipping her ever so slightly. "Pretty and proud, saying to the world, look at me. Look at my beautiful wings. But fear kept you on the ground until life made you take flight."

Delores laid her head on Bernard's shoulder, thinking about the picture he had just painted and how it fit her frame. She thought back to that particular time – the time in every young woman's life when she judges her worth by her physical proportions and her ability to attract. Seeing themselves through other's eyes, until they're forced to look inside and see the woman they truly are. Therefore, she knew his assessment had been correct.

"But, when you took flight," Bernard began again, savoring the memory, "Baby girl, you *soared*. I mean like, wow. You know? Watchin' you all this time...I was like...I was so proud...so proud.

Linda Jones faded out in the background and silence was the only sound. Delores slowly raised her head from Bernard's shoulder, then backed away from him. "What do you mean...*watchin' me all this time?*" she questioned.

Bernard looked at her, but couldn't keep eye contact. He turned away instead and dropped his head.

Delores put her hand on his shoulder and turned him back around. "Bernard, where have you been?" she probed, her eyes frantically searching his.

"Right here," he whispered, "I've been...here."

Delores opened her mouth, but no words came out until she finally managed, "I...I...don't understand."

"I was here, Delores...sometimes close enough to smell your perfume. Not every day, but never not for long."

Delores turned away, running her fingers through her hair. She didn't know what to say or how to react. After all this time, waiting and yearning like she had, and *Bernard was there*?

"When it snowed...it was me that shoveled the walk sometimes...days! Would see you go to school...nights when you'd get all fixed up and some cat picked you up in his Cadillac, took you out...made you smile..." his voice trailed off, choked emotions finally given air. "That was the life you needed."

Delores spun around on him, furious, "You think that's what I wanted? All the time I —"

"It ain't about what you wanted, it's about what you deserved," Bernard cut in.

"You took that choice away from me! You! What I wanted, needed, deserved didn't matter, it was what I had to do without you!" Delores screamed, but Bernard barked back.

"Well, what was you gonna do *wit'* me?! A heroin addicted ...drunk...killer?! Gave me your money so I could shoot it in my

51

veins? Gave me your life so I coulda' destroyed it right along wit' mine?"

Delores came to him. "I could've *helped* you."

"The Lord himself couldn't help me," he huffed, lighting up a Kool cigarette. "Bible say vengeance is mine say the Lord. Well, I thought I was *vengeance*, therefore I was doin' the Lord's work. I was sick, I realize that now, but, back then, I thought I was bein' a man," he confessed, blowing smoke through his nose like a bull. "When I left you and went back to 'Nam, I continued my war. The war I told you I was fightin', killin' crackers. Them redneck, back woods motherfuckers...kind spit in my daddy face, just 'cause he can...But killin'..." he shook his head slowly. "No matter the reason, do somethin' to a man soul. No man can live like that...no man. I needed somethin', anythin' to numb me to the pain I was feelin' deep down. That's when I found heroin."

Bernard sat down on the couch, coughing uncontrollably. Delores sat next to him, patting his back.

"But, when the war was over...why didn't you come back to me?"

"Because I was hooked," he answered, looking her directly in the eyes. "I was gone, tryin' to feed that monkey. I was a bum...penniless...homeless. I wasn't the man you knew, I was nothin'. All I had was who we were. I couldn't let who I had become ruin that. I couldn't...I'm sorry. I just couldn't."

Bernard hit the cigarette one more time and then put it out.

"Then...you know?" Delores probed hesitantly.

Bernard smiled softly and took her hand. "I know everything," he answered, knowing what she was referring to. "He probably don't remember, but once...he must've been four or five, I don't know. I taught him how to tie his shoe," he chuckled, thinking back to the only time he had spoken to his young son. "He was at school...preschool. You know, just runnin' around like kids do,

52

laces just a draggin'. So, I walks up and I say, *boy, can't you tie your own shoes?* He just looked at me like this," Bernard commented, showing Delores his ice grill.

She snickered at his expression.

"Like...*nigguh, who is you?* I say, *a man always tie his own two.* Like that. Then I bent down, tied it once, then untied it. He got it in two tries," Bernard stated proudly.

Delores smiled momentarily, remembering her son's short lived innocence, and knowing he had been there, gave her a strange comfort. Then, her thoughts soured. "So, you know what he became?"

"Yeah...his own man," Bernard replied. "Don't get me wrong, I don't approve of *what* he was, but I do approve of who he was. I believe if he woulda' lived, he woulda' learned the difference."

If? She thought, then took a deep breath.

"Bernard."

He looked over at her.

"He...is alive," she told him, and Bernard just looked at her.

Chapter Three

"Chief, this is Reese. I have yet to make contact with the target."

"Have you reached France yet?"

"We're en route as we speak. Alvarez and I are traveling through the British West Indies into Britain and then out to France."

"We have agents awaiting your go ahead stationed in Paris."

"Good, but because of the sensitive nature of the operation, I'll be severely limiting our contact."

"Are you sure?"

"Yes, sir."

"Okay...keep your eyes open and remember...you report directly to me."

"Yes, sir."

"And Reese...be careful."

** ** ** ** **

The Bell helicopter created a mini hurricane of swirling wind as it touched down on the estate's landing pad. Dutch stood, watching the copter through the tinted lenses of his Versace sunglasses. The wind made his silk pants flap and wave, giving them the rippling effect of water. He smiled to himself, seeing the faces of his family, finally reunited.

He thought of Zoom and Shock, wishing they had lived to see this day. They had risen from petty car thieves to ghetto drug lords to the international opportunity they now had. Having the team back together, he knew it was time to put his master plan into action.

The first to get off the copter was Rahman, his hulking frame bent low to deboard. Since they had last seen each other, Rahman had been big, but not diesel. The two men approached one another, keeping solid eye contact. Dutch extended his hand, 'Peace, Rahman. I'm glad you made it, Ock." Rahman grasped his hand,

and then they each pulled one to the other for a manly embrace. "I'm glad *you* made it," Rahman smirked. "You look good...not as good as me, but ahhh," he joked, playfully throwing Dutch a jab.

"Like we always said, they can't stop what they can't see."

"There go my baaaabbbyy!!" Angel exclaimed, leaping from the copter and into Dutch's arms. He spun her around and then set her down, kissing her with a quick lip smack.

"Step back...lemme' look at you, girl," Dutch told her.

"*Damn*, it's good to see you, boy!" Angel couldn't stop grinning. "Muhfuckas *swore* you was dead, but I knew we fuckin' troopers! Walk through hell and steal the fire," Angel exclaimed.

Goldilocks had appeared next to Angel, never taking her eyes off of Dutch. Her first impression upon finally seeing him was that Angel's prized picture didn't do him justice. He was younger then, cockier and wore that cockiness like a badge of honor. Now, his cockiness wore the assuredness of power. Dutch was fine enough to make a crooked chick straight. The attraction Goldilocks felt was magnetic, almost primal. Dutch was the alpha male at its best. She shook it out of her mind. She knew she had a job to do and nothing would stop her. Still, even a black widow sexed her prey before...

Goldilocks audibly cleared her throat and Angel turned first to her, then back to Dutch.

"Oh..." Angel snickered, "Dutch, this is Goldilocks... Goldilocks, this is Dutch."

Goldilocks held out her hand, but Dutch pulled her to him and gave her a family hug. "Naw, Ma. If you fam' to Angel, then you fam', period."

Dutch looked at Goldilocks and his gaze was like an aphrodisiac to her senses. "Believe me, I've heard *a lot* about you," she smirked.

"I hope it was all good."

Angel looked at the row of flowers and quipped, "What up wit' all the fuckin' flowers? Lemme find out you been over here sellin' tulips and shit."

Dutch chuckled. In the distance, he saw two horses galloping towards them. "Just in time. I got somebody I want you to meet."

Nina and a female horse trainer came trotting towards them, Nina riding the black stallion she'd seen in the stables, the trainer on a chestnut brown mare.

"How was it?" Dutch asked, helping Nina down from the saddle and giving her a kiss.

Angel wrinkled her brow, trying to place where she'd seen Nina's face.

"You know me, I ride 'em hard and put 'em away wet," Nina quipped, wrapping her arms around Dutch's waist.

Dutch turned to the family. "'Yo, that there is my man, Rahman."

"Peace, sister."

"That's my ace boon, Craze."

"How you, Ma?"

"That's Goldilocks...and...my little sister, Angel, but we all call her Dada." The crew introduced, he then said, "Everybody...this here is Nina, my fiancé," Dutch announced.

Angel frowned up and asked, "Fiancé? Since when is you gettin' married?"

"Since I got engaged. I-"

Then it hit Angel, her eyes widened and then narrowed to a dangerous slit. "Bitch, now I know where I seen you! At the fuckin' club, suckin' up and ridin' nigguh's dicks! Dutch, I *know* this ain't that bitch from Elizabeth!" Angel huffed.

Nina was taken aback by Angels calling her a bitch, but it didn't last but an instant. "Bitch? Hol' up, who the fuck are you talkin' to?" Nina screamed back, ready to bring that ghetto shit to South France.

"Fuck, is you deaf?" Angel fired back, taking her arm out her sling, ready to set it. "*You*...bitch!!"

"Angel!!" Dutch barked, restraining Nina by her waist because he had felt her flinch to pull away. "Ay, yo, what the fuck is wrong wit' you?! Chill!!"

"What's wrong wit' *me*? I'm lookin' out for yo' dumb ass...ask *her*! Why you ain't gettin' on her?" Angel countered.

Dutch shook his head. He and Angel had bumped heads over Nina when he had first met her.

He couldn't believe she was still on that bullshit. "Dada, let it go, ai-ight? Let it go. We'll talk later, okay?" he told her firmly.

"Whatever!" Angel huffed, grabbing her travel bag. "If it ain't Roc tryin' to be the ghetto Bin Laden, here you is fuckin' fallin' for some chicken head slut. The whole fuckin' family losin' they damn mind! Just show me where I'm posed to sleep!" she bassed, pushing past Craze, Goldilocks in tow. She and Nina eye boxed as she walked off.

Dutch turned to Craze, "Same 'ole Angel, huh?"

"We shoulda' been got her spaded," Craze quipped, half jokingly. "I'ma take Roc in, too."

"You talk to my mother? What she say?" Dutch questioned Craze.

Craze shrugged, not knowing how to put it. "I mean yeah, but she was like...in a hurry."

"In a hurry? To do what?" Dutch was used to his mother's strange ways, but he was sure she'd be ready to see him.

"I don't know. I told her I'd call her on Tuesday, well, tomorrow. I'll call her tomorrow."

Dutch nodded. "Okay, you do that," he replied, then shook Rahman's hand. "Ay yo, Roc...go 'head and get settled. We'll talk later."

As Craze and Rahman walked away, Nina folded her arms over her breasts. "Some sister" she remarked sarcastically.

"Look, you just gotta get to know her."

"Oh, I'ma get to know her real well, she come out her mouth like that again," Nina vowed.

"She won't."

"And, why would you have to talk to her later about us? Who is she to you, Bernard?" she demanded to know.

Dutch gently took her by the arms and kissed her on the forehead. "Believe me, it ain't what you think. Me and Angel fam'...that's all. Besides...she's," he smiled, "a vegetarian."

"Huh?"

"She don't do the beef."

Nina rolled her eyes. Dyke or no dyke...her whole attitude was of a female in love, and Nina saw it instantly. The way Nina saw it, either Dutch was blind, or he thought that she was. Nina shook her head, because her mind was like, *if this was heaven, then who in the hell left the gate open for this devil bitch?*

** ** ** ** **

The rest of the day went smoothly. They had too much love for one another to spend their first day beefing. That would come later. They, along with the rest of the crew, celebrated the reunion with a large dinner, reminiscing and catching up.

Rahman couldn't front; he had to admit to himself that it felt good to be back with the family.

But the enjoyment gave him an uneasy feeling of guilt. Everything this scene represented went against what he now professed. He didn't drink, but the wine flowed all around him.

The conversation ran from raunchy to grimey and Rahman dismissed himself from the table.

"Where you goin', Ock?" Dutch said between laughs, Nina on his lap.

"Just need to make a phone call," Rahman replied, forcing a smile.

Craze and Dutch both laughed out loud.

"I see shit ain't change with your mother. Ayesha still got that ass on lock," Dutch joked.

Rahman chuckled. "That's ai-ight, yo. You'll be checkin' in soon enough yo damn self. Tell 'em, Nina."

Craze hooted on Dutch, then made the sound of handcuffs. "*Lock* Down!"

Dutch grinned, looking at Nina, "You wouldn't do that to me, now would you?"

Rahman didn't hear her reply as he made his way to the kitchen phone. He dialed the number, then waited for the operator to put him through.

"As Salaam Alaykum," Ayesha answered with a laugh in her throat.

He could hear the kids in the background and could just imagine the vibe at home. "Wa Alaykum As-Salaam," he replied.

"Where are you?" she questioned, the playfulness in her voice gone, leaving only a business-like tone.

"Somethin' came up."

"Like what?"

"Somethin'."

"Where are you?"

"Out of the country."

- Silence -

"Ayesha?"

"What?"

"I'm sayin'…that's all I can get? What and where? No how *you doin'*?" Rahman tried to chuckle and lighten the heavy tension between them.

Ayesha sighed audibly. "Why are you doing this, Rahman? You're not being fair to me," Ayesha expressed. "I pray you're well, but, Rahman, you already know where we stand."

"No, I know were *you* stand," Rahman replied, "what about where *I* stand? Ain't I part of this here?"

"I have a life to live too, Rahman, just like you. Let me live mine."

It was true that part of the reason he had come to France was so he wouldn't be around to give Ayesha the divorce. He thought that distance made the heart grow fonder, but he was slowly realizing that it could make a heart grow colder just the same.

Irritated by her demeanor and cool aloofness, he snapped. "Live yo' life? What…you in a rush?

You got somebody in mind?"

CLICK

"Ayesha…Ayesha…" he barked, but she had hung up. He started to call back, but he thought better of it. He knew he had been wrong. Ayesha had never given him any reason to doubt her fidelity.

But, still, if he was wrong, then what was *she* for not letting him make it right?

Glancing at his watch, he knew it was time for salat. He went up to his room, performed ablution, and then laid down his prayer rug As he prayed; he tried to concentrate on the words of the Qur'an as he recited:

> *In the name of Allah, Most Gracious, Most Merciful.*
> *All praises are due to Allah, the Lord of the worlds,*
> *Most Gracious, Most Merciful.*
> *Master of the Day of Judgment.*

You do we hold up and you we seek for help.
Show us the straight way
Show us the straight way
Show us the straight way...

He repeated the line thrice, because he sincerely felt lost. A darkness was setting over his heart which he fought desperately with the light of Qur'an.

Who was he?

He had seemingly failed as a husband, maybe even as a father as well. He had tried to fight the ills of society, but went about it the wrong way. The only thing he had ever done well was be a gangsta'.

It came natural to him – the swagger, the dog eat dog mentality, the cold viciousness behind the cool demeanor.

Who...was he?

Tears traced his cheeks, then fell to the floor as he finished his prayer. He sat on the bed, head in hands, only to have his thoughts interrupted by a knock at the door.

"Yeah," he called out.

"Yo...Dutch wanna see us all in the study," Craze informed.

"Right."

"Roc...you heard –"

"I said Ai-ight!" Rahman repeated more aggressively. He wiped the tears from his face, folded his prayer rug and followed Craze's fading footsteps to the study.

Once Rahman reached the study, he realized that it was much more than an average study. It was the size of a small public library. The walls held shelves upon shelves of books and ancient artifacts that reached the ceiling, the top shelves, only reachable by wheeled ladders. Along the back walls was the entrance to a patio, doors open, letting in the crisp night air of France. In front of the patio was a large desk, behind which Ceylon sat and Dutch propped himself up on a corner.

Angel and Goldilocks sat to Dutch's left on an antique leather couch with gold railings. Craze had settled in a high backed leather arm chair to Dutch's right, near a bar. Dutch motioned for Roc to take a seat in the other arm chair, but he declined, opting to lean against a bookshelf, arms folded.

Dutch looked at everyone with a slight smile on his face. "First off, I want you all to meet Omar Ceylon," Dutch motioned to Ceylon, who raised his glass in acknowledgement.

"I've heard so much about all of you. Dutch speaks very highly of you," Ceylon remarked.

"Ceylon has been the man behind our connect all these years...and my reason for coming to France all the time, back in the day," Dutch explained.

"And all this time, I just thought you had a thing for French pussy," Angel joked.

Dutch laughed. "That, too...but business always came first," he replied, taking a sip of his drink.

"Family business...and believe me, its good to have us all back together." Dutch directed his last comment at Rahman, looking directly at him, but Rahman diverted his gaze. "I only wish that Shock and Zoom, God bless the dead, were here to see how far we've come, yo. Nigguhs runnin' around, stealin' cars, robbin' catz, then the Port and killin' Kazami's bitch ass."

If Angel had been any closer to Goldilocks, she would've felt her tense up and seen her eyes take on a sinister hue at the sound of Kazami's name.

"Now, this..." Dutch spread his arms to all the opulence around them to behold.

"Yeah...but what is *this*?" Angel questioned, "I mean, its fly and all, but what the fuck? Get to the point."

"He is, if you shut your dumb ass up," Craze cracked.

"Fuck you, puta. I wanna know *now*. I just hope it ain't got shit to do wit' all them flowers out there. Between Dutch gettin' married and Mother Theresa over there, I figure ya'll nigguhs goin' soft"

Angel snipped, gesturing to Rahman.

Rahman bit his tongue. He knew the situation with Angel was far from over and would have to be dealt with sooner or later. But, if she kept up with the slick mouth, it would definitely be much sooner than later.

"As a matter of fact, it *does* have to do wit' flowers, wit' your smart ass mouth," Dutch told her, "the poppi and the coco."

Dutch looked around to make sure he had everyone's attention, as he always did when he put a plan into motion. "For years, me and Ceylon have had a few scientists working wit' the two seeds. They were trying to create a hybrid between the two. One that would keep all the essential elements of cocaine, but contain the stronger addictive quality of heroin."

"Like speed ballin'," Angel suggested.

"Yes, and no. Speed ballin' is a combination of highs. What we're talkin' about is this..." Dutch said, tossing Angel a small glass vial.

She caught it and examined the contents. After tasting it, she said, "It looks and tastes like coke."

"Exactly. We ain't tryin' to create a new drug, just improve on the old one. The high of coke, but the addiction of heroin. For anybody who smokes this, sniffs it, whatever...within three days, they'll have a heroin monkey on their back – one they have to feed more and more, creating virtual heroin addicts out of crackheads, without them ever knowing why," Dutch explained, his smirk saying *checkmate* to the game.

Rahman shook his head in disgust. "Man, you'll create zombies...worst than '84 and '85 when crack first hit."

"Naw, Rahman, because it'll never hit the streets like that," Dutch replied, leaving confused faces on everyone in the room except for Ceylon and Craze.

"I don't understand."

"We're settin' up a meeting with several of the major cartels as we speak. The deal is this: for every three ounces of pure they manufacture; they have to buy one ounce of our hybrid to match it. If even one cartel bucks, or doesn't agree to our terms, then we put it out at 50% of its full strength – which means, no one in the world will be able to sell coke because once the fiends taste ours, nothin' else will satisfy their urges."

Dutch poured himself a glass of Hennessy, letting his words sink into their heads.

"Yo, Dutch," Angel spoke first, eyes glazing over with greed, "at that ratio, and knowing the production of coke a year...that's like..." Angel stopped for a moment to compute.

"Roughly 40 billion dollars the first year, Dada," Craze cut in, already knowing the plan.

"Forty fuckin' billion dollars," Angel repeated, shaking her head, "Forty fuckin' billion...that's Sosa money...we gonna be like fuckin' Sosa."

"Naw," Dutch corrected her, "Sosa is the type of muhfucka we extortin'. We extortin' the game, Dada...like Jay-Z said, *Stick up the world and split it 50/50...*"

Goldilocks couldn't believe what she was hearing. The potential in his plan was mind blowing.

Her calculating mind began to plan how to get in fully before she carried out her mission.

"Excuse me, Dutch, but...I have a question," Goldilocks began.

Dutch gave her his attention.

"What's to stop the cartels from dissecting your coke and creating a similar hybrid? Like with roses and stuff?"

"The synthetic involved," he answered. "In plant reproduction, what you're talking about is called grafting. You have the original plant, then you attach the second plant with some kind of adhesive to hold it together...glove, tape, etcetera. Genetically, that's what the synthetic does, it holds the two together until they become one. Then, the synthetic is basically discarded. Without it, the DNA of the two plants wouldn't synthesize. But once it does, it's no longer necessary; therefore, by the time it reaches the stage of maturity, no longer detectable."

Dutch could easily answer questions from every angle, because he had been working on the concept for years. Now, all that was left to do was put it down in the streets and enjoy the fruits of his labor.

Rahman stepped forward.

"Yo, Dutch...even though its been awhile, I'm sure you know what I'm about now. So, you tellin' me you brought me here to help you destroy *more* lives in the hood?"

Dutch approached Rahman and said, "No, I'm tellin' you that the ends justify the means, Roc. Yeah, you right; I know what you about. I respect that. But let's say everybody in the hood stop taking drugs and stop selling drugs...stop strippin' and everything else. Then, they turn to you and say, *'Okay Ock, what now?'*" Dutch asked, holding his arms at his sides.

"Then what? How you gonna feed 'em, Roc? How you gonna give 'em a roof over they head, huh? Before you build a nation, you gotta have an economic structure and before that, you gotta have land. Africa is dyin' despite the fact we got all these ball players, moguls and otherwise jiggy style Uncle Toms because they won't invest...won't build it up. Tanzania, Ghana, Liberia, Nigeria..." Dutch ran off, counting on his fingers.

65

When Goldilocks heard him mention Nigeria, her ears perked up again.

"You think you the only one care about Black people, Ock? You think I want forty billion so I can buy these cracker Bentleys...rock their platinum? Fuck them, I want my own! Period. I'm just like you, Ock. The only difference is, I ain't got a cause. I got a *solution*," Dutch concluded, he and Rahman keeping firm, but warm eye contact. "People get high, killin' theyselves...that's their choice. My concern is with the ones we can save. Otherwise...let the dead bury the dead," Dutch said, turning away and returning to his perch on the edge of the desk.

Rahman understood everything Dutch was saying. He didn't want to agree, but deep down, he did. On the other hand, selling drugs was selling drugs. Even if it was *their* choice to get high, it was *his* not to assist them in destruction. The way of the righteous isn't always in what they do, its in what they don't do, regardless of the outcome.

Rahman started to reply, but Angel spoke up before he got a chance. "I don't know why you even wastin' your breath on this nigguh, Dutch. Fuck 'em if he don't understand."

Rahman directed his full attention to Angel, eyes ablaze. "Ay, yo...you got one mo' fuckin' time to come out jib fly like that, ya hear me? Next time, I'ma –"

Angel jumped up and Goldilocks did too, but Angel told her, "Naw, this between me and him," then to Rahman, as Goldilocks sat down, hesitantly, "or what, Roc? *What?* You gonna *kill* me? Huh? You already tried, remember...and you *missed*!"

"Missed?" Rahman echoed. "You think if I was tryin' to kill you, I would've missed? Do you?"

"Bullshit," Angel barked back.

"How many times you known me to miss, huh? I coulda' walked up in that store and *deaded* you, believe that!" he huffed.

66

"But you *shot* me!"

"And because of that, you was gonna kill me? You got hit in the fuckin' arm, and you threaten to kill nine little girls or me?!"

"Did they look scared when you got there?? I wanted *you*, not them, and I *knew* you'd come! And I wasn't gonna kill you," Angel added, almost as an after thought.

Now, it was Rahman's turn to say, "Bullshit!"

"I *wasn't*. I just wanted my blood back," Angel shot back.

"Is that what this is all about...your blood?" Rahman questioned in a strained tone. "Fuck it...you want blood..." he looked around, first at Dutch, and then at Craze, "somebody gimme a gun!"

"Yo, Roc, chill. Angel, let that shit go. Its over," Craze suggested, waving his hand lazily and sipping from a bottle he'd gotten from Ceylon's winery.

"Naw...she wants blood...gimme a gun," Rahman insisted, trying to bring the situation to a head once and for all.

Craze looked at Dutch, who smirked, then shrugged his shoulders. Craze gave Rahman his chrome .380. Rahman cocked it and put it on the table between Angel and himself.

"There...you want blood...shoot me. That's what you want? There it is," Rahman urged, calling Angel's bluff

Angel looked at Rahman, then at the gun, then back to him. She picked up the gun and examined it.

"Well, what you –" Rahman began to say, but was cut off by the impact of the blast that pierced his shoulder. "Aaaawww fuck! This bitch shot me!" he exclaimed, holding his bleeding shoulder.

"You told me to!"

"You wasn't posed to do it for real, stupid fuck! I was just makin' a point!"

"Point taken," Angel shrugged, calmly putting the gun back down on the table.

Ceylon, always the consummate courtier, didn't even raise an eyebrow. He had watched it all unfold, curious as to where it would lead. He swished his snifter full of brandy, then remarked, "An odd form of chivalry, but chivalrous nonetheless."

Dutch turned to him, "In the streets, chivalry is called *shootin' a fair one*."

"I must remember that," Ceylon replied, standing up, "Please, Rahman…come with me. I have some experience with bullet wounds and such."

"Let me see," Angel tried to examine it, but Rahman snatched away. " It ain't nothin' but a flesh wound and you hollered like a bitch. Aaaww!" she moaned, mocking him.

"Fuck you," he growled, following Ceylon.

"Word up, Roc…you *did* sound like a bitch," Craze joked as he and Angel fell in behind Rahman and Ceylon.

"And fuck you, too," Rahman shot back.

Goldilocks was the only one to remain behind with Dutch. "I guess Ja Rule was right, Pain is love," she snickered.

Dutch shrugged and held up his drink.

Goldilocks studied him for a minute, weighing him out in her mind. She had been sent to destroy him, but was met with a strange attraction. Her fire had been kindled when she heard him curse Kazami, and then…almost in the same breath, changed the game as she knew it and even spoke on investing back in Nigeria. So, she asked, "What you said…about Africa…Tanzania… Nigeria…would you really do that? I mean, invest and stuff?"

'Dig, Ma, I never talk just to be talkin'. Its time to take the game to another level. It's only so many basketball teams and colleges you can buy. But, at the end of the day, you still pay taxes to the *real* bosses."

"I heard that."

"You know what taxes really are? State sanctioned extortion. The governments are the real gangstas," Dutch remarked.

"Then, I guess women are the gangsta's gangsta, because Angel says you taught her that pussy controls the game," Goldilocks smirked, a flirtatious spark to her tone.

Dutch scratched behind his ear, slightly amused. "Yeah…in a way, it do."

"Is Nina a gangsta?" Goldilocks asked, but she could tell by his expression, it was an inappropriate question. "Too personal? I'm sorry…I was just wondering if Nina knew how lucky she really is."

"Maybe its me whose lucky."

"Maybe…" Goldilocks smirked, backing away, "maybe… Goodnight, Dutch."

"Yeah…goodnight," he replied.

Goldilocks exited the room with a sultry strut and the last thing Dutch saw was her hand, lingering on the doorframe as she turned the corner, her red tipped nails resembling blood stained claws.

Chapter Four
St. Tropez

Craze was right in his element...this was the lifestyle he shined in – the pretty thug, international playboy type role. That's how Craze had spent the last few years. He was a regular at spots like Le Club 55, Les Caves Du Roy and The VIP Room as well as Salle Blanche in Monaco. The only French or Italian he knew was how to order drinks and how to proposition pussy, but words were unnecessary for that, because his style spoke volumes.

Craze liked to swing at the Cannes Film Festival because he wanted to get a big name in international films. He had financed a few Italian flicks that had done fairly well. He also fancied himself a designer of women's clothing, putting together risqué ensembles that the rich and licentious devoured.

For a nigguh with style like Craze, the lack of inhibition of South France had his name written all over it.

He had put together Dutch's bachelor party and had gone all out. He had a 150 foot yacht called Zanzibar, after the famous club in Newark. It was tri-decked and boasted all of the amenities of a mini club, house theatre and pool. At this bachelor party, Craze, Dutch, Rahman and Ceylon were the only males. Everyone else were long legged model types of every flavor, barely dressed and extremely open to suggestions.

Angel had come, but Goldilocks stayed behind because she had other plans. Rahman had come to celebrate his man's pending nuptials and to see for himself if this type lifestyle was still in him. He knew Craze would wild out, but he didn't know the half.

The bachelor party had a masquerade theme – partly because he didn't want Dutch to be recognized by anyone that could take it back to the states, but the other reason was because he knew women behind masks feel free to do freaky things. The whole vibe was like Mardi Gras on the open waves of the Cote D'Azure.

Women ran around in masks and barely anything else – asses boomed and silicone filled titties jiggled in every direction. Pecks on the cheek became tongues in the ear and dancing bodies became four part daisy chains in the middle of the floor. The smell of pussy and perfume filled the air and cries of passion weaved melodically with the pounding rhythms of Euro-house music.

Craze was right in the midst of it all. He had one blonde chick bent over on the steps of the pool, who had her face nose deep in the pussy of another blonde who could have been her silicone twin. The combination of Viagra and Ecstasy had him like a stallion, slaying pussy after pussy.

Dutch laid back in the corner of the mini club getting his dick sucked by two Italian chicks with deep, Mediterranean tans and even deeper Mediterranean throats. He didn't smash any of the chicks, but seeing his nut run down their European faces - as the house lights tinged it red, yellow and orange – was it's own thrill.

Surrounded by pussy, Angel tried to get her freak on, but she couldn't keep her eyes and mind off of Dutch. She could see him across the club through the dancing and fucking bodies – enjoying the oral pleasures of two women. Her mind went back to her 21st birthday, their picture together and the words she hadn't told any other man.

"You the only nigguh I wanna fuck," she had told him, meaning every word.

While Dutch was getting brains, Angel was across the room getting a pearl tongue massage, both at the point of climax and…their eyes met for an orgasmic instant.

Rahman was totally out of his element. Looking around, the whole scene reminded him of Sodom and Gomorrah. Faceless women, soulless bodies – all running around, chasing that forbidden fruit, which was all the more tempting because it was forbidden. Bodies everywhere interlocked in various positions of sixty-nine, daisy chains and human scissors, their faces contorted in that painful expression of pleasure. Nothing about it turned him on in the least – therefore, he knew that at least this part of his life didn't appeal to him anymore.

He wandered the yacht aimlessly, turning down the propositions of countless wet pussies. His thoughts soon turned to Ayesha and he had a sudden urge to call her, so he found the house phone and called home.

"As Salaam Alaykum."

"Wa Alaykum As Salaam. How are you?"

"You wanna talk to the kids?"

"Yeah, but I want to talk to you, too."

SILENCE

"Look, Ayesha, I know what I put you through is inexcusable, but yo, do it gotta be unforgivable? All I'm trying to do is bring light –"

Rahman's attempt at reconciliation was cut off by the sound of his young son's voice.

"As Salaam Alaykum, Abu!"

It was then that he realized Ayesha hadn't even been on the phone. She had gone to get the children right after she'd asked if he wanted to speak to them. He knew then just how bad it really was.

They were a continent apart, but they couldn't have been more emotionally distant had they been in the same room.

After speaking to his children, he hung up, looking for a place to be alone and hoping that the yacht would dock soon. He traveled to the upper deck, where the music only reached by vibrations, and the only bodies were the stars above. He heard light classical music coming from one of the cabins and found Ceylon inside, playing himself in chess.

Ceylon looked up from the board with a smile. "Aahhh, Rahman...please...do join me!"

Rahman came in and sat on the other side of the chessboard.

"Do you play? Of course you do, you're a thinking man – and all thinking men play chess, even if its not on a board," Ceylon shrewdly surmised.

Rahman smiled slightly. "I used to, when I was locked up," Rahman told him. "You always play yourself?"

"Why, yes. Can you think of a better opponent?" Ceylon asked. "Man...is his own worst enemy."

Ceylon slid his black bishop across the board and took the white rook, then sat back in his chair.

"How is your shoulder feeling?"

Rahman rotated his shoulder once, "A little stiff...other than that, it's cool."

Ceylon smiled at Rahman, knowingly. "Tell me something ...why are you here?"

"I've been asking myself the very same question."

"Well, here's one you may not have asked yourself...why...am *I* here?" Ceylon probed, and Rahman looked at him quizzically. "Of course, I may presume that you have surmised that maybe I'm some type of international drug peddler – being that our mutual friend introduced me as his connect.

But...connect to what?"

"I really haven't thought about it."

"But, believe me, its in direct relation to why you are here...you see, Rahman...you, Dutch and myself represent three quintessential types of men. You...are the proud warrior, the visionary. Dutch, on the other hand, is like the prince, making a bid for the throne. While I...am not a king myself, I am a king maker, which in many ways makes me more powerful than a king…yes? The three of us together, represent…dare I say…the trinity of power, and it is just this trinity of men that control this world."

Rahman sat back in his chair and replied, "You mean, like secret societies? Illuminati, Jesuit orders and people like that? Mr. Ceylon, I don't believe in conspiracy theories. Sure, there are catz in funny hats that speak in babble behind closed doors, but my thing is, if they're so secret, how do we even know they exist?"

"Excellent point," Ceylon chuckled, "it would be the opposite of what they said the Devil did.

While he convinced man he didn't exist, the societies convinced man that they *did*. Subterfuge. Their pretense to secrecy would be mass publicity…hiding right out in the open."

"Exactly."

"But, my young friend…where is a better place to hide?" Ceylon countered, checkmating Rahman's point.

Rahman nodded his concession. "Touché…I'll give you that. But to then say they control the world is a stretch. Only God can control the world."

"Which brings us to the age old question…did God create man, or did man…create God?" Ceylon proposed.

Rahman smirked. "There's only one way to see it, because if man created God…who created man?

"Darwin," Ceylon chuckled, "that is to say, natural selection."

"But, natural selection is based on no more than chance, which is only a secularized way of saying the unknown. You can't remove the X from the equation."

Ceylon nodded, returning Rahman's concession. "This is true. I'm sorry to have digressed, but you have a rather interesting mind, and I just wanted to explore a bit…my point is, you are here and I am here for one reason. A man once said that ends are often merely hopes, but means are *facts* which are in some men's control. We...are here for the means and if the *hoped* for ends are to be reached, then...carpe diem...carpe diem," Ceylon repeated.

Rahman knew exactly what carpe diem meant, because he had studied Latin in prison. It meant...seize the day. Rahman took Ceylon's point outside to ponder.

Outside, he leaned his elbows on the railing, and looked down to the water below. The light of the moon and the yacht shimmered off of the water like jewels that you pick up with your hand – a shimmering illusion for a fool to dive in after, only to find nothing in the shadowy depths.

As he stood, Dutch walked up behind him, pulling the black and white bandana from his mouth and nose that he had been wearing for a mask.

"I figured I'd find you up here, and it look like I'm just in time. You lookin' at that water like you ready to dive in and swim ashore," Dutch joked.

Rahman chuckled. "Naw, I'll wait 'til we dock. That party scene just ain't my scene no more."

"No more? It never really *was* your scene, Roc. Remember back in the day – Cancun, the bike rallies and shit? You was *never* the wild nigguh on the pussy tip. You was selective. Either that, or you brought Ayesha, like sand to a beach," Dutch cracked. "But, its all love, yo. I dug how you and wifey swung out, you know, through thick and thin."

Rahman remained silent, listening to Dutch remind him of the way things *used* to be.

"I said to myself back then, if I ever do get married – and back then, that was like impossible to even consider. But I said, if I do, that's how I want it – like Roc and Ayesha. God bless 'em... So what up, how she doin'?"

"She want a divorce."

The announcement stunned Dutch into silence.

"She told me right before I came over here, yo," Rahman painfully admitted.

"So, what you doin' here? Why you ain't back in the states wit' dirt on your knees and flowers in your hand?"

"I'm runnin'."

"Yeah, well...no matter where you go...there you are."

Rahman nodded slightly, then skeet spat into the open air. "So, what you want from me, Dutch? With this plan of yours...where I fit in?"

Dutch turned around, leaning his back, with elbows against the rail. "Craze done got soft. I love that nigguh like a brother, but he lettin' all the bitches, the cars and the movies turn him out. The nigguh getting high, fuckin' wit' these European sluts, jet settin' all over the place..." Dutch shook his head. "He more fit for gettin' that entertainment money...that paparazzi shit. He ain't gonna be directly involved in this. I already told him, and after he bitched a fit, he understood, snorted a line and went to sleep."

Dutch looked Rahman in the eyes. "I need you to be my right hand now - coordinate shit from the front line – while I deal with the cartels. Ceylon has us covered politically. I've got the heads of the major gangs in the states on their way to Paris for a meeting. I'll explain in more detail when I know if you gonna rock or not. You know me...it's on a need to know basis."

"Then, I need to know."

Dutch looked him in his eyes and knew what Rahman was saying. He was ready to rock.

"But...I need something, too."

"Yeah?"

"Everywhere we movin', in every hood...I want an area strictly clean...run by me and my team," Rahman demanded.

"Not a problem."

"Nigguhs violate, I handle it *my* way…no questions asked."

"Done."

Rahman knew he was accepting from Dutch what he had basically turned down from Angel, but the difference was simply scale. Newark was one thing, but to have a Muslim area in every hood, safe for children to play and life to flourish was too much to pass up. That, and the fact that 40 billion dollars could do a whole lot, a whole lot sooner than his monopoly of the East Coast. He knew the benefits would be along the way, but deep down, he knew he had made a deal with the Devil to get it.

** ** ** ** **

Nina loved the ambience of the flower garden. The mingled fragrances of the assorted flowers was like an ever changing potpourri, depending upon which way the wind blew. The soothing babble of the man-made stream filled with exotic fish that appeared iridescent under the lights of the estate. She was in love. She had, or could have anything that she wanted. Her life was beautiful, but she couldn't get around the tiny gnawing void within her. She knew what it was; it was everything she had left behind. *But, shouldn't everything she had gotten compensate?*

Nina had thought that it would…knew it should, but it had yet to happen When Dutch told her about the bachelor party Craze had planned, she had urged him to go, even though he offered to stay.

"We can have our own party," he had slyly suggested, tickling her neck with his kiss.

"No, I bet Craze went through a lot to put it together, so…go…really."

"You sure?"

"I'm sure. I'll be fine."

But, she wasn't fine; she was lonely. She wished Tamika could've somehow come with her. She missed her best friend terribly. Tamika was finally starting to get her life together after the scare that the torched club had brought her, and Nina wanted them to share in each other's newfound happiness. She could just hear her now.

"Grrrl...you marryin' *Dutch?*" Tamika would've squealed, doing her skank booty dance. "I knew yo', wanna be boujie, ass wanted a thug on that ass!"

Nina laughed out loud thinking about it. But that was the old Tamika. What would the new Tamika say? She hadn't even told her about France because she felt that she wasn't supposed to. Like there was an unwritten law entitled DUTCH, and she had to follow it, or else. She thought that knowing Dutch was alive would bring new meaning to her life, but he hadn't come into her life. In a way, she had followed him into this exiled form of death. She was no longer in love with a ghost...she had become one.

"Nina? You okay?"

Nina turned toward the unfamiliar voice to find Goldilocks had entered the garden. "I'm fine," she replied, a little too quickly, subconsciously brushing the hair from her face.

"Are you sure? You looked kinda...spaced," Goldilocks told her, approaching.

Nina and Goldilocks hadn't had any real dealings, but she knew who she was and that she was down with Angel. Nina didn't know what type of stuff she was on, so her defenses went up, just in case.

Goldilocks recognized the defenses and held her hands up with a smile. "Don't worry, I come in peace," she giggled. "I just saw you out here and I was bored to death, so I figured I'd come and see how you were doing."

"I thought you would've gone to the party, too."

"No chance of that. Angel wouldn't let me," Goldilocks lied, because she was the one who didn't want to go. "Believe me, a woman lover can be just as triflin' as a man."

Nina didn't know how to respond to that, so Goldilocks continued.

"I didn't mean to make you feel uncomfortable. You *did* know that Angel and I are...together...didn't you?"

"So I've heard," Nina replied, feeling a little self-conscious even talking about the subject. "But, hey...if that's how you get down, then cool...you know? To each his own and to me, mine," Nina said, letting her know by her tone that she was strictly dickly.

Goldilocks caught the hint and smiled to herself. "These are some really lovely flowers. I've never seen orange callalillies before."

"Yeah...these are my favorite."

"Listen, I know...like...you probably think I'm on that stuff Angels on, but I'm not. And really...it's not you. Angel's just real protective of her people, you know?" Goldilocks explained. "Well, anyway...since it looks like me and you are in the same boat, being left out of the loop, I just wanted you to know that if you ever wanna just kick it, I'm here."

Nina took her offer with a non-committal type of nod, and then Goldilocks walked away. She didn't know what made Goldilocks come to her like that, maybe it was because she too was *out of the loop*, like she said. Maybe it was more. Nina was skeptical, but inside, she really did need someone to talk to.

If she only knew...

** ** ** ** **

"I talked to Mommy."

"What she say? She comin'?"

"Yeah...but, umm..."

"But, what?"

"She wanna bring somebody..."

"Bring somebody?? Here?? Somebody like who??"

SILENCE

"Who?"

"She said...she was bringing your father."

** ** ** ** **

The antique brass headboard seemed to be her only refuge, so she gripped it tight with both hands. Nina didn't know how much more she could take. Spread out on all fours, Dutch had a firm grip on her hips, pounding her walls into submission. She had already come twice and she felt the inner surge of a third, steadily building inside of her.

"Please come," she whimpered between gasps, "come with me this time, baby."

His sexual grunts were Dutch's only reply.

Nina arched her back in spite of the pain, throwing the pussy back to him, gripping and ungripping her inner muscles, urging him to release himself inside of her. For Nina, it felt good, but it felt wrong. This wasn't making love, this wasn't even sexing...this was straight fucking. There were no kisses of passion, no freaky words that he always liked to whisper to her, turning her on more and sending her into sexual bliss. This was silent fucking. The only sounds were the squeaking of the bed, the slurp of her wetness and her orgasmic squeals.

"Owww...ow...wait, wait...oohhhh!!," Nina moaned, releasing her thick whitish cream all over Dutch's dick, but he still didn't come.

Nina collapsed to the bed, turning over to lie on her back, which made Dutch pull out of her. She reached up and stroked his sweaty chest.

"What's wrong, baby?"

Dutch smiled, but not his trademark smile - this one didn't reach his eyes. He gently took her hand and kissed it, but still, he did not reply. He got up and went over to the patio door, allowing the noonday sun to bathe him in her rays.

Nina looked at him from behind, waiting for him to speak. She had never noticed how rippled his whole body was. His dark skin sparkling with sweat, his slim, but muscular, frame rippled from his calves, his dimpled ass cheeks and cobra-v'd back. She had never noticed, because she had never seen his whole body, so rigid, so tense. He was so tense, that his dick was still hard when he turned around and came back to the bed.

"She lied to me, Nina. My...whole...fuckin'...life...she lied to me," he hissed between clenched teeth.

Dutch had already told Nina about what Craze had said – that the father he never knew, was on his way to meet him.

"Lied!" he stood and barked. "She told me that he was dead. Died in *their* war, but fightin' his own. Said he was at war wit' them crackers, you know? Died fightin'. So, I'm like, yeah...my Daddy. My Daddy didn't take no shit. Now...I fuckin' find out he's alive? After all these years? Where's he been?

The fuck! We never left Newark, my mother never changed her name, so it ain't like he couldn't find us, you know? Fuck 'dat nigguh. I should kill him myself, as soon as I lay eyes on him."

Nina didn't know what to say, she had never seen Dutch so furious...so full of rage. But, she didn't know his pain. He was thinking of all the years his mother struggled, days when there was no heat, nights when there was no food; and the whole time, his father never even showed up? For all that Dutch knew, he was out making babies, driving Cadillacs and living it up. But, he didn't know the half of it.

"Don't talk like that, Bernard. It –"

He cut her off, pointing a finger in her face, "Don't call me that...Don't ever...call me that again.I'm *Dutch*. I spit on that bastard's name."

The rage she saw in his eyes - the very same eyes she fell in love with – now gave her a different emotion...Fear.

Nina looked away, on the verge of tears. Seeing her about to cry, Dutch sat on the bed and took her in his arms. "I'm sorry, okay? I'm not snappin' on you, its just...I can't wear that name no more – now that I see what it means. It's fake, a coward, a liar – all the things I *ain't*, feel me? I named *myself* Dutch, and *that's* who I am."

Nina nodded her head, muffling her sobs.

"I remember you asked me once how I got that name. I never told you. You still wanna know?" he asked. She could hear the smile in his voice returning, so she looked up, wiping her eyes and nodded.

"Okay...this is kinda embarassin'. Craze's the only one that know other than you. When I was a shortie, everybody was runnin' around callin' theyself King this, Prince that or callin' each other Duke.

All those terms of royalty, you know? So, I don't know where I got the idea from, but I thought Dutch meant like a King or Duke or something, only bigger. So, when nigguhs was like, *I'm King, I'm the Don*, I was like *I'm the Dutch, the Don of Dons, the Prince of Princes*," he chuckled, shaking his head. "By the time I found out it meant payin' your own way, like going Dutch on a date, it was too late, 'cause it had stuck."

He laughed, and Nina felt relieved enough to giggle. "That's cute."

"Naw...that's dumb. But what did I know? I was a dumb kid."

Nina caressed the side of his face. "I could never imagine you dumb, baby. And, in a way, by who you are, you *gave* the word a new meaning. Look at you. You *did* pay your own way and you are more than a king. You're my man, and I love you. Your pain is mine, but, you gotta let me share...you gotta let me in...all the way," she told him softly, then kissing him gently, then deeper until she felt his manhood harden against her thigh. "Oh nooo,

82

don't even think about it. The kitty cat is sore," she snickered, pushing his head away, "like I been ridin' horses all day."

Dutch stood up, fully erect, "I told you, you was fuckin' with a thoroughbred," he boasted.

"Aaw...we talkin' shit now, huh? Okay, I got that ass...don't worry, you gonna get yours," she smirked, laying back on a pillow.

Dutch walked away, laughing, until Nina said, "Dutch," and he turned around. "I just wanted to say the name," she smiled.

Dutch got an instant sense of De'ja vu, he just couldn't immediately find the connection.

** ** ** ** **

After he showered and dressed, Dutch found Nina lying asleep across the bed with a smile on her face. Going outside to the main patio, he found Angel lain out in a biker's outfit and Dior sunglasses.

Rahman, Craze and Goldilocks were off in the distance riding horses. Deciding to share some time with Angel, he sat in the chez lounge next to the one she was chillin' in and took a sip of her lemonade, beginning to relax.

"So, we gonna have that talk now?" Angel asked, without looking at him.

"What talk?" he answered, question for question, but knowing exactly what she was talking about.

"You know exactly what the fuck I'm talkin' about. I *hate* when you do that," Angel replied.

"Do what?" he smirked, taking another sip of her lemonade.

"And *that*!" Angel stressed, snatching off her sunglasses and sitting up to face him. "Playing stupid and changin' the subject when you know damn well I'm talkin' about that *bitch* you in there laid up with and about to *marry* and we don't know her from Adam! She could be the fuckin' feds for all you know," Angel accused, not knowing that she had a snake in her own grass.

"Look, I don't need this right now, ai-ight?" he told her. Too much emotional shit was happening too fast for a man who prided himself on not dealing with them. "In a few days, Nina is gonna be my wife, so she here to stay. Find a way to get along wit' her."

Angel laid back and put her sunglasses back on. "We *are* getting' along…I'm lettin' her breathe ain't I?"

Dutch took a deep breath to tide his surging temper and got up from his chair. He towered over Angel and bent down so that they were almost face to face. "Dada, I love you, nothin' will ever change that. But, if I ever hear you speak ill of Nina again, then we got problems."

"Fuck you, do what you want. I don't give a fuck!" Angel bassed as Dutch walked away. She stood up and shouted after him as he walked away, "You hear me? Fuck you!"

** ** ** ** **

While Dutch and Angel were beefin', Craze was schemin'. Goldilocks was giving up entirely too much rhythm for him to ignore. Since they had met, she had been doing little things like holding eye contact a little too long or brushing up against him whenever Angel wasn't around or paying attention.

But now, while she was horseback riding with him and Roc, she was definitely letting him know what time it was.

The looks she gave him, eyeing him up and down while biting her lip or riding leaned forward in the saddle so Craze could see her average sized, but well shaped, ass bouncing against the saddle – giving him visions of her riding his dick.

He finally pulled Roc to the side and asked, "Yo, if I fuck Goldi, is that like I'm fuckin' Angel's girl?"

Roc just looked at him blankly.

"I mean like, it's your man and say his chick wanna fuck you. But, that's yo man, so you don't. But, like…is it the same with like…bitches?" Craze questioned. He didn't see two women as a real relationship. To him, it was just some freak shit. But, since Angel was fam', he wanted to get it straight.

"Man, I don't know nothin' about that, yo. Why you askin' me?"

"'Cause its like, what the fuck, its two bitches, right? But, I'm sayin'," Craze struggled to articulate himself.

Roc turned his horse around. "That's too deep for me. I'll see you back at the house," he said, galloping away.

Craze looked ahead and saw Goldilocks beckoning him to come to her. But, when he trotted his horse in her direction, she galloped hers off to a wooded area at the edge of the plateau. When he reached her in the woods, she had already dismounted and was tethering her horse to a tree.

"Ay, yo, believe me...I'm wit' whatever you got on your mind. But, I gotta know, what up wit' you and Angel?" Craze asked, feeling a little guilty. Had Angel been a man, he wouldn't have done it, but since she wasn't...

Goldilocks unzipped her black, knee length boots and stepped her bare feet out of them. "Me and Angel have an understandin'. She understand I want some dick every once in a while."

"So, she cool wit' dis? I mean, wit' me?"

Goldilocks giggled seductively, unzipping her form fitting, one-piece riding suit, revealing that she was totally naked underneath. "Angel doesn't own me, but I don't kiss and tell either," she told him while stripping down to her sexy butter toned nakedness.

That's all Craze had to hear. He began to dismount, but Goldilocks stopped him. "No...I'm comin' up."

She came over to the horse and mounted it, facing Craze. As soon as her ass hit the saddle, Craze caught the pungent aroma of a willing pussy. She reached for his zipper and released his rock hard dick..

"My pussy is sooo wet. Damn, I wanna fuck you," she moaned in his ear, biting the lobe, and then running her tongue along its ridge. "I know you got some candy for me."

"Candy?" Craze echoed, trying to pull his pants down to a comfortable level.

"Yeah...candy. Nose candy."

"Oh...no doubt. Craze keep that raw, shawtie," he assured her. He reached inside his saddle bag and pulled out a glass vial the size of a small deodorant bottle, snowy white flakes filling the container.

Goldilocks unscrewed the lid, which had a spoon attached to its center and gave herself a one on, then did the same for Craze. She put the spoon to her tongue for the freeze, and then tongued him down.

Craze felt how wet her thighs were from the juices flowing from her and couldn't wait to fuck her. He slid his dick in as she lifted up, sitting in his lap. Her pussy was tight, but her slickness helped accommodate Craze's thick girth.

"Shhhhiiittt," Goldilocks gasped, locking her arms around his neck. "Now...now, make it trot."

Craze put the horse in motion at a slow trot, but even that amount of movement had her jiggling in the saddle.

"Awww, yes...just like that, Craze...just like that. I want you to fuck me, Craze...you wanna fuck me?" she sighed, grinding her hips to his rhythm.

"I wanna fuck the shit out you," he replied, gripping her ass and the reins at the same time.

"Then, make it go faster."

Craze galloped the horse, making Goldilocks bounce and jiggle, coming off of and then back down on his dick, harder each time.

"Oohhh!! Its sooo good...hurts so good," she panted, lifting her legs onto the back of the horse and wrapping them around Craze's back.

Craze hardly had to stroke now, with the bounce of the horse, all he had to do was lay back and feel Goldilocks ride her way to her climax. She threw her head back, on the brink of frenzy, the horse's motion like a giant vibrator, guiding Craze's dick to just the right spots.

"Make...make...her st-stop, Craze...make her – " Goldilocks begged, feeling like she was about to explode.

Craze reigned the horse in, stopping the stallion just as Goldilocks leaned back against its mane, holding Craze's forearms and grinding his dick until she came. Feeling her pussy get extra soaked, Craze busted off right behind her. She laid there for a minute, panting and breathing hard, then she sat up, right on his lap.

"I bet you ain't never been fucked like that before."

"Naw," he replied, "but we can do it again whenever you ready."

Goldilocks kissed him again, wrapping her arms around his neck. She opened her hand to make sure the bottle was still intact, and then smiled to herself.

Chapter Five

Dutch watched the helicopter descend from the sky. All these years, thinking his father was dead…now it was like he was being hand delivered to him from heaven. But, the feeling he was having wasn't one of bliss or happiness – it was a feeling of subdued hostility. Whatever his father had been doing and wherever he had been, made no difference to him anymore. He had raised himself, made his own rules and enforced them. There was nothing really to be angry about, so he let his rage go and went downstairs to meet a stranger.

He and Nina descended the steps hand in hand, going out to meet the helicopter. Craze, Roc, Angel and Goldilocks were already there. Delores stepped off the plane with the assistance of Roc and Craze. She greeted all of them with a hug and kiss, and then she laid eyes on her son.

For a moment, mother and son looked at each other from a distance. Delores had picked up a little weight and the wisps of gray about her temples, Dutch hadn't remembered. But, she still looked good. He stepped forward with Nina at his side.

"Hello, Bernard. You look well," she commented, holding her emotions in check – something Dutch had inherited from her.

Dutch had grown some himself. Not necessarily in height or weight, but in stature. "I missed you, Ma," Dutch replied, calmly enveloping her in a warm embrace.

The hug began casual enough, like two friends who hadn't seen each other in weeks, instead of years. But, it intensified from there. Delores deplored what her son had become, but there was also a huge tinge of pride. They were all criminals in their own way. Delores' rebellion had been spontaneous – an almost involuntary response to the frustration that she felt inside and culminated in the torching of the store.

Bernard Sr.'s crime was more calculated, building steam as it went on like a locomotive out of control until it killed everyone, including the driver's son! But, in a way, they both had failed. Delores had gone on to work for the State she hated and Bernard had allowed the hate to fester too long, leaving cancerous-like tumors on the man he used to be. Dutch, on the other hand, had challenged the system head on and won. Now he stood, safe in his mother's arms, and it was his victory that she embraced, while the mother in her hugged her son.

When they broke the embrace, Nina greeted her. "Hello, Mrs. Murphy...how are you?"

It was then that Delores looked at Nina fully in the face. "Nina?" she called out, surprised, and Nina's smile confirmed what she already could see. Like herself, Nina hadn't given up.

It was while they embraced that Dutch saw the man who had just deboarded. He was standing behind and to the left of Delores. The two men stood, assessing one another, each clearly knowing exactly who the other was. There was no way of being mistaken. Had they passed each other on the street, there would've been cause for a double take, because they looked that much alike.

Bernard Sr. was maybe an inch shorter than Dutch's six-foot-two-inch frame, and was considerably heavier – well proportioned, but heavier. Delores had him looking his best with a snazzy suit from the Steve Harvey collection. He was dressed in a Zoot-Suit-styled black and white, pin-striped design with stark white cuff-linked dress shirt. He sported a black lacquered cane – not for show but – for support. Shaved and trimmed up, Bernard Sr. was looking very good. Too good for Dutch, and it only confirmed in his mind what he already wanted to believe. His father had been living it up all this time, and his attire only proved it.

Dutch could feel his surging anger returning as Bernard Sr. held out his hand and said, "Hello...son..."

Dutch stared him down coldly, and then turned and walked away.

** ** ** ** **

"I...I know that this is unexpected, but...it was unexpected to find out that you were still alive, Bernard," Delores tried to reason with a pleading quality to her tone.

They were in the spacious living room of the estate, just the three of them – father, mother and son.

Every time she called him by his father's name, it irked Dutch like crazy. But, he was trying to restore order to his world after all of the emotional disarray, so he was calm.

"Look, Ma, nothin' is a shock to me 'cause, Duke right *there* don't exist to me. You want him in *your* life, after all this time, then that's you. I'm just glad to see you made it for my wedding," Dutch told her, kissing her on the cheek.

"Don't be like that, Bernard, we –" "Ma," Dutch chuckled back his bubbling anger, "please call me Dutch. That name there don't apply to me," he expressed, looking his father dead in the eyes.

Bernard Sr. remained stoic, returning the gaze dispassionately.

"Call you what?" Delores questioned, her voice raised. "I swear by my *Lord*, I'll *never* call you that...name! Nigguh, don't forget *I* birthed you, *I* raised you, *I* named you! So if you don't respect nothin' else, you *will* respect *that*!" Delores was heated, but she took a deep breath and gently held Dutch by both his hands. "Baby, I know this is hard, but believe me, your father's been through a lot.

He's...He's real sick and he doesn't know –"

Dutch cut her off with a cold laugh. "Oohhh, now I see. Now its makin' sense," he said, turning to look at his father. "You sick now, huh? What, you got AIDS or somethin', some new exotic disease that only no good muhfuckas catch? And you want me to save you? Help you buy yo' life back? Nigguh, fuck you."

90

"Bernard, don't you talk to your father like that!"

"That's who he is? I coulda' sworn I ain't never seen this nigguh a day in my life!"

"Your father has –" Delores began to say, but Bernard Sr. cleared his throat to interrupt her.

"Naw, Baby girl, you ain't got to speak for me. Let the boy speak his mind." Bernard Sr.'s temper was just as lethal as his son's - even more so because he was the origin of it all. He had sat and let Dutch vent as long as he could, but there is only so much that any man can take.

"The only thing on my mind is my Mama and her happiness," Dutch told him, "So, if you and your thirty year old bullshit fits that description, so be it. You sick, she wanna save you…so be that too.

Just be careful…be careful, 'cause if you become the source of just one mo' tear –"

"You gonna what? Hmm? Kill me? You threatenin' me son?" Bernard Sr. asked him, trademark smile on his face.

Dutch took one look at the smile that he himself had mastered so well, and now knew why others felt it was so menacing, now that he was faced with it. "I don't make threats, I just establish understandings," Dutch calmly replied, then turned to walk away.

"Yeah, you sho' come a long way, gotta give you that. Yo' mama raised you well, can even tie your own shoe. A man…tie his own shoe, then stand on his own two."

That last statement stopped Dutch at the door. They were words he had known since he was a small child. Whenever he tied his shoe, he would remember what the man said, which helped him remember how to do it. Once he was older, the words were still with him. He lived by them because what it meant was being your own man. Dutch turned back and looked at Bernard Sr.

"Oh, you remember?" Bernard Sr. said, using his cane to get to his feet. "Just a little nappy headed nigguh. I remember everything about it…I remember because I was *there*."

Dutch re-entered the room, moving toward Bernard Sr. "Yeah, I remember you helped me tie 'em, but did you *buy* 'em? Was you there for *that*? Naw, you did what any stranger in the street probably would have done, then went on about they life…just like you did. Went back to whatever the fuck you was doin'…livin' your life. The only reason you remember is 'cause you know you shoulda' did *more*."

"You wanna know what I was doin, huh? Do you?" Bernard Sr. asked him.

"Naw, not really."

"I'ma show you what I was doin'," he told Dutch, taking off his suit jacket.

Dutch watched him, because he didn't know what he was doing. By the expression on his face and the removal of his jacket, Dutch thought that maybe the old nigguh wanted to fight. He shook his head, then looked at his mother, who was staring straight back at him.

Bernard Sr. rolled up both his shirt sleeves to his biceps and held his arms out, fists balled up.

"*This* is what I was doin'!"

Dutch looked at the various scars and discolorations that he knew came from shooting up.

"This is who I was! And you can call me a sorry muthafucka all you want, but I'd rather be a sorry muthafucka in the gutta' than to be a sorry muthafucka that took his family down with him!"

Dutch replied, "Then you really was better off dead."

"If so, guess who helped kill me," Bernard Sr. growled.

Dutch's eye twitch was the only sign that the accusation hit home.

"Yeah, I made my choice, ain't nobody put no gun to my head. But, every time I O.D.'d, every time they had ice to my nuts or forced milk down my throat, I could truly say that *my son got some good shit*. My *son*!" he emphasized, looking Dutch dead in the eyes.

It was the first time his own acts had ever hit that close to home. His thoughts didn't blame him, but he couldn't deny the irony of the situation. The father he thought had died fighting was really alive, dying. Dying, and Dutch was indirectly assisting in his demise. It was the closet he had come to questioning his own actions, but he quickly blocked it out with that trademark smile of his own.

"You was gonna spend that money somewhere," Dutch shrugged, "So, I guess I was wrong after all. You *did* buy my sneakers...thanks, *Dad*," Dutch said sarcastically, then turned and walked out.

A fuckin' dope addict, his thoughts cursed as he ascended the stairs to his bedroom. *Fuck 'em*. But, he couldn't just fuck him, because the image of *who* his father was, was very much a part of who *he* was.

In his mind, his father had died fighting his own war; therefore, he had won according to his own rules.

Dutch prided himself on living by his own rules; *how could he lose?* But, he had just seen how he could lose, standing in the living room. Now, on the brink of mastering what nigguhs by the buckets had died just trying to play, the thought wouldn't leave his mind.

How could you lose?

It was no longer an arrogantly rhetorical question, punctuated by a smirk – it was a searching inquiry into the nature of his own weaknesses. He entered the bedroom to find Nina sitting Indian-style on the bed, looking at a wedding magazine in one of his t-shirts, eating cookies and listening to a French instruction tape.

"Dutch, listen to this," she stated in a cheery tone, stopping the tape. "Permettez je...no, oh, wait...Permettez - moi de me presenter," she smiled. "I'm learning, right?"

He smiled through his thoughts, sitting next to her on the bed. "Oui, je pense qu'il est beau."

"What's that? I bet its something freaky, knowing you.'

"Naw, I said, *yes, I think it's beautiful*," he translated, kissing her shoulder where his shirt sagged on her.

"That's not as freaky as it sounded. When you gonna teach me the *freaky* stuff?" she flirted, and they both laughed. Nina flipped the page of her magazine and saw a beautiful dress. "Now, *that*, I love. What do you think?" she asked, holding up the magazine. When she looked at him and saw the distant look on his face though, she put it down. "Is everything okay? Is Miss Delores settled in?"

Dutch nodded. "She's ai-ight."

She wanted to ask about his father, but she wanted to wait until he was ready to discuss it.

"Remember when we first met?"

"Yes."

"What did you know about me?"

"Know about you?" she echoed. "You mean like, my first impression?"

"Naw, what you *heard* about me," he corrected her.

"Well, I really wasn't in the streets like that anymore. I had my job at the bank or whatever and was going to school, so I really didn't *know you*, know you. I knew your face, I knew the gambling spot was yours and you were supposed to be this big time hustla', but that's about it."

"And, when you put a face to the name?" he probed.

"I thought you were a really bad card player," she giggled, making him crack a smirk, "not to mention, fine. Oh, and persistent. You wouldn't take no for an answer, workin' my *last* nerve," she joked. "Why do you ask?"

Dutch took a deep breath and took her hand into his. "Yo...me and you are about to make the biggest move of our lives, you know? And I just...wanna make sure you know what you're gettin' into."

Nina searched his eyes for signs of having second thoughts, then breathed a sigh of relief when she saw none. "Baby, I know what you're sayin', believe me, and I thought about it. I know what you do, but I don't look at it as who you are. That's not what I love, that's *who* I love...the rest...it'll take care of itself."

"I'm a killer, Nina. These same hands that hold you, I've used to take lives with...*will* use to take lives with. Within a year, seventy-five percent of the world distribution of cocaine will carry my stamp.

In two, damn near a hundred percent will. Muthafuckas ain't gonna like it, they gonna want war, and I'ma give it to them. Then, I'ma come home to you and our children, trim the tree, massage your feet and grade homework. That's who I am, and I'm askin' you, is that who you want as the father of your children?" he questioned.

"If I didn't...I wouldn't be here," she assured him firmly. "All I ask is that you don't bring that into our home."

How can I not? he thought, but instead said, "Remember you showed me the mural of your brother?"

"Yes."

"You said he had been murdered?"

"Yeah, he was shot in front of our apartment," she painfully admitted, wishing Dutch hadn't dredged up that memory.

"What if I told you that I killed your brother?"

Her heart stopped.

His gaze was unflinching.

"Please," she begged in a whisper, "please don't tell me that."

"I'm not *tellin'* you anything. I'm *askin'* you. If I killed your brother, would you still love me, would you still just say *don't bring it into our home*," he questioned her.

Nina's whole body internally trembled. It was like she was seeing her dead brother, laying in his own blood with a death twitch and Dutch standing over him, smoking gun in hand, saying *I love you*.

"Did you kill my brother?" she asked, her eyes shut against what the truth might be.

"Would you still love me?"

"Did you...kill my *brother*?" her tone deepened.

"Would you still –"

"Answer me!" Nina exclaimed, lunging at him, but Dutch grabbed her by the wrists to restrain her.

"I need to know, Nina. I need to know, *would* you?" he asked firmly.

"Yes!" she blurted out through a torrent of sobs, "yes, I would still love you, but I would hate *myself*!" she admitted, feeling weakened by her admission.

Dutch pulled her to himself and cradled her against his body, "On my blood, Nina, I didn't kill your brother, I swear. It was just a question I needed an answer to. Nigguhs curse my name 'cause of the brothers I *did* kill, sisters I *did* slaughter...so I needed to know that even if it was your own, that what we have is true. I love you, Nina, my word...I love you," he expressed, never meaning it as much as he did right then.

Nina understood that the question was really a test – Dutch's test of loyalty – to see how deep her love truly went. But it was also a realization for her, as well. Once confronted with the love and loyalty she had for her dead brother, which played a significant role in her life, and the love she now had for Dutch, she knew that there was nothing that she wouldn't do for him. The truth of the matter was, the love she had for him was deeper than any she had felt in her life, and the realization of that fact, truly frightened her.

** ** ** ** **

Over the next few weeks, Nina threw herself into the planning of her wedding. Delores was very supportive, and because of that, the two women established a sincere friendship. Delores became like the mother she had left behind and the confidant that she truly needed. She also opened up to Goldilocks, who also helped with the planning. While Nina was planning her wedding, Dutch was tying up the loose ends of his plan.

"Ain't no way a muhfucka can read all these books," Angel commented, halfway up the ladder, perusing Ceylon's literary collection. "He got all this shit on ancient astronomy and shit. I don't trust nobody that fuck wit' the stars. You?" she asked Dutch, climbing down from the ladder.

She, Dutch and Roc were discussing the next phase of the plan. "We don't have to trust him, just understand him," Dutch smirked.

"But, who the hell is he?" Roc inquired, feeling the same way that Angel did. He still remembered their conversation on the yacht.

"Fat Tony hooked me up with him not long after the Kazami hit. Ceylon is a Turk. The Turks and the Italians have a long history together," Dutch replied.

"Meaning?"

"Back in World War II, Americans wanted to enter Europe through Italy, but to do that, they needed to secure the Isle of Sicily. So, President Roosevelt gets Lucky Luciano out of Alcatraz to help. American troops established a beach head in Sicily and then advanced into Europe through Italy."

97

"All's fair in love and war," Roc quipped, thinking of the hypocritical stance of such an alliance.

"No doubt and Lucky used it to his advantage. Once the troops moved into Italy, that opened the direct route back to the states. Turkey was big on heroin, so Lucky connected up wit' 'em. Turkey would control production and the Mafia would control distribution. That's why so many catz came back from the war strung out. Mainly Black catz," Dutch schooled them, thoughts of his father coming to mind.

"Anyway, the mob kept the reins of dope right up until the '70's, back when Fat Tony was still a foot soldier. He met Ceylon then, so once I came to him, the connect was a wrap."

"So, Fat Tony put you on to a connect...we the connect now, what we need him for?" Angel wanted to know.

"Because, politically, we about to step on a lot of toes and we need to make sure all the right palms get greased. What Fat Tony did for us in Newark, Ceylon is gonna do for us in the international underworld."

"But, you don't trust him, you said you understood him. What's the difference?" Roc probed.

"On this level of the game, Roc, all the trust you need is leverage. Turkey wants in on the European Union and one hundred percent control of the cocaine production in the world is enough to get 'em in. It ain't somethin' you'll read about in the paper, but its damn sure enough to keep the muhfuckas in Westminster, Germany and France on Turkey's dick. But, Turkey can't do it without our monopoly of the market. Leverage, Roc, is what counts among allies, trust only counts among friends," Dutch concluded.

Roc and Angel both nodded their understanding.

"Ex-excuse me, Monsieur," the butler interrupted, standing in the door.

"Yeah."

"The clothier is ready for you."

"Ai-ight, we'll be down," Dutch told him, then to Roc, "Let's go get fly, nigguh. This gonna be a day to remember."

He and Roc started out the room while Angel went back up the ladder.

"Ain't you comin' to pick out a dress?" Dutch asked.

"Why? I ain't goin'."

"So, its like that?"

"I should ask you the same thing."

"Fuck that 'posed to mean?"

"Nothin'," she replied, flipping open a book.

Dutch could only shake his head and walk out.

Chapter Six

The day was finally upon Nina and she couldn't have been more nervous. Delores kept her from becoming a total basket case with her stern advice, coupled with her motherly comfort.

"Miss Delores, I think the train is too long on this dress. Does it look right? See how it bunches up right here? Maybe I should've gone with the other one," Nina rambled, mixing questions and second guesses with a stream of various nervous gibberish.

The two French seamstresses scolded her in their native tongue as she fidgeted around in front of the full-length mirror.

"Nina, relax…you look beautiful, sweetheart," Delores assured her sincerely.

And she *was* beautiful. Her wedding gown was designed by Ralph Lauren in a crisp ivory white. It was tightly fitted to her torso, with the back cut out in a heart shape, the point just barely covering the crack of her ass. There were lace accents and hand sewn crystals decorating the bosom, which almost appeared to be on the verge of allowing her breasts to overflow. The train was ten feet long. Delores, who would act as Nina's maid of honor, was wearing a delicate Chanel gown, fitted to her frame like hand in glove, yet exquisitely tasteful.

"Are you sure? It *is* beautiful, but maybe I shouldn't have worn white," Nina giggled, selfconsciously.

Delores put her hand on Nina's shoulder and replied, "Love makes you pure, sweetheart.

Remember that. Don't you see how love makes you feel refreshed? Seeing the world in a whole new way? Love washes away all before it, so believe me…you're wearing the perfect color."

Nina smiled warmly, and then hugged Delores. "Thank you, Miss Delores. I never looked at it like that."

"And...don't you think it's about time you called me Mama? You about to be my daughter-inlaw," Delores told her, adding, "I know you wish your family could be here to share this day with you. But, it would be my honor if you allowed me to fill some of that void for you today."

"You already are, and believe me...I really do appreciate it."

"Which reminds me," Delores began, turning to one of the seamstresses. "Excuse me, could you-"

"Oui, Mademoiselle?" she asked.

"Can you go get Bernard Sr. please?"

"Qu'est – ce que vous avez dit?"

"Can you...never mind," Delores sighed. "I'll get him my damn self," she huffed out of exasperation and left the room.

Nina looked at herself in the mirror and took a deep breath. There was no doubt in her mind as to what she was about to do. She truly loved Dutch with all her heart. It was something she had fought for so long, but once she acquiesced, she abandoned herself to it totally.

She remembered the conversation she and Dutch had, and she prayed that she wasn't being naïve. She knew what he did, but, she wondered, *when did what a person does become a part of who they are?*

For years, she made no separation between the two, but from the first time she looked into Dutch's baby brown eyes and saw that smile, *mostly the smile*, it was no longer about what he *did*, but what he did *for her*. And, like Delores said, at that moment, on the threshold of their union, she did indeed feel refreshed. "I do," she said to the mirror, looking herself in the eyes.

Delores led Bernard Sr. into the room as he was saying, "I thought it was bad luck to see the bride before the wedding?"

"Only for the groom," Delores corrected him.

Nina looked at him with admiration. He was dressed in a traditional black tuxedo with satin stripes down the legs, a pure white cummerbund, as well as matching handkerchief and gloves with a pair of brand new, uncreased, Stacey Adams dress shoes – black with white toes, looking extremely dapper. Just looking at him, she could see what Dutch would look like in about twenty years. And, if so…Lord, Lord, Lord…

"Miss Lady, I know that me and my boy ain't found common ground yet, maybe not ever, but…a beautiful, loving wife is the greatest gift a man could ever have, and since I ain't never gave him nothing, if I could walk you down the aisle, I'd be givin' him that greatest gift on Earth," Bernard proposed.

Nina was touched by his sentiment, which was apparent in the tears flowing from her eyes. "Of course, Mr. James…I'd really like that."

** ** ** ** **

Dutch, Roc and Craze were getting dressed - they were all wearing white-on-white tailed tuxedos. The only touches of color were the gold ties and cummerbunds.

Dutch stood in front of the mirror, adjusting his cuffs, a self-satisfied smirk accenting his dimples. He was on top of the world – almost literally. If his had been a corporation, there had never been a takeover so hostile; had he been a general, no army had successfully won a war with nary a shot fired.

And now, he would have the icing on his cake. For every Napoleon, there is a Josephine…for every Malcolm, a Betty…and for every Dutch, there is a Nina.

But, she wasn't just some kind of trophy wife in his mind. Nina had sparked him the way no woman ever had. At first, he was open to the fact that she was elusive, and the chase was nothing that a man of his stature wasn't used to. But as he got to know her, all the chicks he was smashing couldn't compete. He was nonchalant, he

102

was laid back, but he was hooked. Now, four years later, she was about to become his wife, and he couldn't front; he was nervous, too.

"Ay, yo Duke, you been in front of the mirror for twenty fuckin' minutes adjustin' ties and shit.

Let me find out you on some *Oh, my God, I'm gettin' married* shit!" Craze cracked, imitating a White girl's voice. He and Roc cracked up and Dutch couldn't help but to laugh. Craze gave Roc a dap, and then wiped his nose.

"Yo, I know this nigguh ain't laughin'," Dutch replied, referring to Roc. "Yo, Chris, remember when this nigguh first got married? He was runnin' around on some Shug Avery shit. *I's married now!*"

Dutch joked as Craze and Roc continued to bug out.

"And I also remember *you* said you wasn't never getting married," Roc reminded Dutch.

"I said that?"

"*You* said that."

"Word," Craze seconded, "Matter of fact, your exact words was, '*I'm already married to the game, I ain't never marryin' no broad!*'"

"Naw, I don't remember that," Dutch lied.

"Oh, nigguh, you remember," Roc replied "Admit it. Never say never."

"Well *I* can say never. Ain't no *way* I'm layin' up wit' one chick night after night wit' all this free pussy bitches beggin' to give away," Craze bragged, running his hands over his head full of waves, then wiping his nose.

Dutch noticed that Craze kept wiping his nose. He turned to Craze and looked him in his red, glazed over eyes. "Look at this nigguh, Roc. You high ain't you?" he asked, abruptly turning serious.

"Man, go 'head wit' that bullshit," Craze tried to brush it off.

Dutch smacked Craze, not hard, but hard enough to get his attention. "Look at me...yeah...you high. You always fuckin' high. You turnin' into a straight up chickenhead," Dutch told him, calling him the Newark name for a cokehead.

"I ain't no fuckin' chickenhead, nigguh; fuck you. I get high, so what? I'm ai-ight," Craze huffed.

The festive mood of the moment was gone as Dutch surveyed his old friend. Craze had always done some type of drug – starting out with blunts back in the day. Now, with his fast paced, jet-set hustler lifestyle, he was becoming a more frequent user of narcotics – especially cocaine – and Dutch hated it. Had they still been on the street end of the game, he would've had no choice but to cut Craze off. Now, he could afford to relegate him to the background. But, he wondered if even *that* was a good idea, considering what was at stake.

A light knock at the door diverted Dutch's attention.

"Yeah?"

"Sir, are you ready to proceed?"

Dutch looked at Craze and answered, "Yeah," then to Craze, "After I get back, we gonna talk. Ya' hear me? Your shit is gettin' real raggedy. Tighten up," Dutch warned him.

"Yeah, whatever," Craze responded, like it was no big deal, but the look in Dutch's eyes let him know that it was indeed a big deal.
** ** ** ** **

The field of roses and lavender had been perfectly landscaped for the occasion. A few rows had been harvested to make way for a red-carpeted lane that led up to a clearing, where a large gazebo, trimmed in flowers and decorated with intricate design, had been placed. The minister, a middle-aged White man of the cloth stood just inside the gazebo, on the second platform. On the first platform, Dutch stood, while Roc and Craze stood to his left and Delores on the other side, to his right, stood on ground level.

To the left of the party, was a 12-piece orchestra of string instruments and delicate flutes playing Toccata in D minor, by Bach. Next to the orchestra, was Ceylon and a group of several, very distinguished, older European men, along with two younger ones and Goldilocks. The wedding would be a combination of a small, private affair, with the lavishness of a larger, more traditional one. The servants were scattered around, awaiting the commencement of the nuptials.

On cue, the orchestra faded out Bach and began the harmony that accompanies the wedding march.

Nina emerged from the house, looking radiant and being escorted by Bernard Sr.. Dutch was so mesmerized by her beauty that it took a minute before he realized who was escorting her. He and his father's eyes met, and Dutch conceded him a smirk. He was too into the moment to let it bother him. He focused his attention on Nina, slowly approaching him.

They always say that if you love someone and have to let them go, know that if they come back to you, then it was meant to be, because it was your destiny. For Dutch, that's what Nina represented…his destiny.

Nina reached the gazebo and took her place beside Dutch after the couple exchanged loving smiles. The minister cleared his throat and spoke with a light, French accent.

"We are gathered here, today, to witness this man, Bernard James, and this woman, Nina Martin, as they join one another in holy matrimony. If anyone opposes this marriage, speak now, or forever hold your peace."

Angel silently opposed from her bedroom, where she was watching the ceremony, seething.

"Now," the minister continued, smiling benevolently, "traditionally, I would now ask Mr. James and Miss Martin the *do you take* questions, but the couple has requested that they themselves do the asking. Mr. James, you may proceed."

Dutch took a deep breath, took both of Nina's hands in his, and began. "Some people say you never miss what you have until its gone. But, for me, it was the opposite, because I didn't know what I was missing until I met you. Before you, life to me was about winning, the goal...but you've shown me that there's meaning in the journey...in the simple things that so many take for granted. You make me appreciate them. So...I vow to honor you as my Queen, cherish you as my woman and never ever forget to be your lover," he smiled. "I love you, and I'm asking you, Nina Celeste Martin, to take me, Bernard James, to be your lawfully wedded husband...to have and to hold, through sickness and in health...as long as we both shall live?"

"I do," Nina answered with all her heart and tears of joy lining her face. Roc handed Dutch the ring and he slid it on her finger. If she thought the engagement ring was exquisite, it paled in comparison to the wedding band. It was packed with quarter carat diamonds surrounding a single carat yellow diamond. She looked at it in awe, then into Dutch's eyes.

"Uhhh...Miss Martin," the minister prompted her.

"My heart is beating so fast," she said through a breathless giggle. She took a deep breath.

"Okay...Bernard James, I love you so much that...no matter the words, they can't express how I feel about you. If I could sing like Mariah, my love would raise the octaves to shatter glass, or like Mahalia, so deep down in your soul, its like a prayer. But, what I can do is give you all that I am as a woman, as a person and as a soul. I vow to cherish every moment we share, may it be a day or a hundred years, and from the moment I gave my heart to you, until now, and forever more, I vow to love you like no other," she stopped and took another deep breath.

"Take your time, baby," Delores consoled her.

"So, I'm asking you, Bernard James, to take me, Nina Celeste Martin, as your lawfully wedded wife...to have and to hold, through sickness and in health, for as long as we both shall live."

"I do," Dutch replied.

Nina took the ring from Delores and slipped it on Dutch's finger, then they both turned to the minister.

"Then, by the powers vested in me by the Province of Marseille, I now pronounce you man and wife," the minister announced, but, Dutch needed no permission to kiss the bride.

He lifted Nina's veil and pulled her into his kiss and embrace. The orchestra began to play *Capriccio Italien*, as two servants behind the gazebo released ninety nine doves into the air. The doves had been dyed an array or colors, from red, yellow and orange, to blue and pink. The Humane Society would've pitched a fit, but the visual of the colorful birds rising into the air had a truly magical effect.

The wedding party, and guests, moved into the ballroom of the estate, where the food was to be served. Several tables were set up around the perimeter of the spacious hall for the few guests. Along one wall, was a row of tables where the food was to be self-served, buffet style.

Nina, Dutch, Delores and Bernard Sr. moved out into the open area to dance. Dutch started to lead her, but he felt awkward. The sterile harmony of the classical music felt fake...soulless.

"Ay, yo, its okay to get married to this shit, but I can't step to it," Dutch chuckled.

"Hold up. Step...step...side to...side..." Nina joked, trying to step to the dragging rhythm. "I think you're right."

"Excuse me...yo, Craze! Craze, come 'ere!"

Craze walked over, meeting Dutch halfway.

"Go get the stereo and bring the speakers in here, ai-ight?

"I got you."

Craze jogged off and Dutch went back over to Nina. As he approached, Bernard Sr. came over to the couple.

"I …uhhh…just wanna say, congratulations," Bernard Sr. offered, his hand extended.

Dutch looked at the hand first, then directly at his father, who continued to extend it, and then Dutch shook it firmly.

"Yeah…thank you," Dutch replied stoically.

The orchestra's blandness was drowned out by the soulful sounds of M.F.S.B.'s "Love is the message." The ancient architecture of the estate vibrated from the percussion.

"If you don't mind," Bernard Sr. said, "can I have this dance?" he asked, but took Nina's hand with the assuredness of consent.

Dutch stepped back, mockingly holding up his hands, palms out. Bernard Sr. led Nina a few steps away and then began to lead her in a basic stepping routine. Ceylon approached Dutch and leaned in to his ear.

"Congratulations, my young friend. And may your first born be a masculine child," Ceylon smirked, imitating the Godfather without affectations. "As you see, our scientists are here for their… compensation."

Dutch smiled his infamous grin. "Yeah, compensation…tell 'em I'm ready to cut the check."

Ceylon walked away and Dutch went over to Roc.

After Dutch leaned in and whispered in his ear, Roc shrugged, sipping his fruit punch. "Ai-ight, fuck it. Me and you can handle it."

Dutch led the way and Roc followed him through the house, and then down the stairs into the wine cellar. The cellar was dimly lit, and musty with mold. A row of barrels stood against one wall with several wine racks in the center.

Ceylon and the two scientists stood near the racks. Roc looked at the two young men. They were both young, in their mid-twenties. One of them resembled Joaquin Phoenix, except he had sandy brown hair. The other looked like a straight nerd, like a big eared Bill Gates.

"If you'll excuse me, I must see our guests out," Ceylon said, excusing himself before ascending the stone steps.

Dutch turned to the two scientists. "Roc, allow me to introduce you to the brains of the outfit," he chuckled, putting the men at ease. "M.I.T. catz, Roc - top of the line. This is Edward Bennett...and this is Michael Burkes, correct?"

They both nodded in agreement.

"These are the geniuses we owe it all to, ain't that right?" Dutch asked, approaching the two in a non-threatening manner.

"Well, you know, I wouldn't exactly say that," Edward commented, trying to be humble. "If you hadn't invested so much money —"

Dutch cut him off by putting an arm around him. "Yeah, but ya'll did all the work. How much did we agree on?"

"Two million each and one percent of the yearly gross," Michael replied, like an accountant.

"Two million up front, right? Like right now?" Dutch asked, and then looked at Roc. "Roc, these guys wanna get paid. I respect that; you?"

Roc looked at Dutch and understood what he was asking of him. He knew why he had brought him into the situation — to kill the two men for him. Dutch wanted him to commit himself, prove that he was truly ready to get down for the crown.

"Leverage," Roc remembered Dutch as saying, and by eliminating the only two men who knew the synthetic's formula, that leverage would be absolutely increased.

The two men started to sense that something was wrong – that they had walked into a trap. But being unfamiliar to the ways of gangstas, they had been led like lambs to slaughter.

"Mr...Mr James. If the two –" Michael began to stammer, but the single gunshot that burst through the back of his head, silenced him before slumping him to the floor. The shot was deafening in the low ceilinged enclosure, making Edward jump.

Dutch held a gun at his side and Edward broke down into tears. "My God...My God...My God..." Edward sobbed. "Please don't kill me."

Dutch looked at Roc, but he spoke to Edward. "You shoulda got your money from jump, at least you would've had a chance to spend some of it." Dutch pushed a screaming Edward to his knees.

"Noooo....nooo..."

Dutch handed the gun to Roc. "Don't worry about cleanin' up...it'll be taken care of."

Roc looked at the nickel plated .38 in his palm, and then at Dutch. There were no emotions in Dutch's eyes, only the subtle hint of a question...*Well?*

Roc looked at the blubbering Edward on his knees, who looked like he was praying. In Islam, killing a man in cold blood is a heinous sin – it goes against the moral fiber of any society. But Roc knew he had made a deal, and what he would be able to do for so many in the ghetto had been his reason for it.

This was only one man, he reasoned, and *didn't the benefit of many outweigh the sacrifice of a few?* Then, he remembered the Qur'an:

> *If anyone killed a person (i.e. – in cold blood)... it would Be as if he killed all of mankind.*

Dutch walked up the steps. By the time he reached the top, he heard the single gunshot and the pleas were no more. He smiled to himself, and then went back to the party.

** ** ** ** **

Craze was at the food table, fixing himself a plate. He felt a presence approach, but paid it no mind until he felt a hand grab his dick from behind.

"Could you fix me a plate of this?" Goldilocks whispered seductively in his ear.

Craze moved her hand and turned to face her. He looked around to make sure that no one was looking, and then said, "Ay, yo…we gonna have to chill wit' this shit, ai-ight," he scolded, feeling guilty for ever having begun the torrid affair.

He had fucked her twice since the horseback episode, and each time, he felt more and more like he was betraying Angel. "I don't know how this pussy lickin' shit go, but ya'll gotta be somethin' to one another if she brought you to France wit' her," Craze reasoned.

"I like the way her pussy taste," Goldilocks replied with a shrug.

"So, why can't we tell Angel what's up then?"

"Come on, Craze," she purred, "just one more time, pleeeeaasse," she moaned, grabbing his dick again. She could tell by its hardness that he was already convinced.

Craze sighed extra hard, like he was annoyed, but he was only frontin'. There was no way he was turning shortie down, but to appease his conscience, he promised himself that he'd tell Angel the deal.

"I gotta go to the bathroom," he said, finishing his drink – she knew it meant to come behind him.

Dutch didn't pass Craze, but he passed Goldilocks on her way out of the room. She gave him that look like he could get it too, and then brushed past him. He paid no mind as he crossed the floor to where Nina was sitting with Delores and Bernard Sr. Anita

111

Baker's, *Good Love*, was just going off as he walked up and Donnie Hathaway's, *To You*, was coming on.

I've been so many places, in my life and time…
I've sung a lot of songs…

"I was startin' to get lonely," Nina remarked with playful sass.

Dutch held out his hand and escorted her to the dance floor. The only other people in the room were Bernard Sr. and Delores. "As beautiful as you are, you left here, lonely? What fool would ever do that?" Dutch smirked, "I'm sure every man in here would love to be in his shoes."

"Maybe," Nina replied, playing along, "but I'm sure none can fill 'em."

"Is that right?"

"That's right."

"Well, how am I doing?"

She shrugged. "You'll do."

They shared a laugh, swaying to the music.

I love you in a place where there's no space or time
I love you! You're a friend of mine…

"You ready for the honeymoon?" Dutch asked.

"Where do you honeymoon when you livin' in Paradise?"

Dutch smiled. "I love *you*, Mrs. James."

"I love you, Mr. James." Nina started to put her head on his shoulder when she noticed a speck on his lapel. It looked red, and then, on closer inspection, reddish-brown. When she realized what it was, her whole body shuddered – it was blood.

"You okay? You chilly or somethin'?" Dutch inquired, because he'd felt her shudder.

"N-no…" Nina replied, "I'm fine."

There was no doubt what it was, and no doubt that it hadn't been there earlier. Wherever it came from, whoever it came from, it was fresh. Nina didn't even want to imagine how it got there, so she closed her eyes, put her head on his shoulder and pretended that it wasn't there.

I know your image of me
is what I hope to be...

** ** ** ** **

Craze sucked in his breath, and then exhaled with a grunt. Goldilocks' head game was crazy. Her deep throat techniques made her mouth feel as wet and as hot as her pussy. She had him up against the bathroom wall, damn near on his toes, with his pants down around his ankles.

Goldilocks was on her knees, steadily devouring his thick meat, keeping that lust filled eye contact that had Craze fighting his urges so he could enjoy the pleasure that much longer. She bobbed on him, deep throating his shaft, and then bringing it all the way back to the head and slurping it like it was a blow pop, and then slid it back in her mouth. He grabbed the back of her dreads, ready to burst, so she knew she had to work fast.

Goldilocks slid a glass vial of cocaine from under her dress, reaching down with her free hand to Craze's pants. She fumbled momentarily, until she felt something hard inside the right, front pocket.

Pulling it out, she felt it, knowing that it was another vial – slightly smaller, but she prayed that he didn't know the difference – then she made the switch.

Each of the times she had fucked him, she peeped his coke stash - where he kept it and what he kept it in. She had it down pat by now because, again, her head game was crazy. Goldilocks slid the vial she'd just taken from his pocket under her dress just as Craze nutted hard, coating the back of her throat.

He was huffing and puffing like he had just run a marathon. Goldilocks rose up from her knees, smoothing out her dress and wiping away what little nut she'd missed with her pinky.

"Damn, Ma, you make a muhfucka wanna call out *your* name," Craze said, catching his breath.

"That's because I'm definitely tryin' to blow your mind," Goldilocks purred, with more meaning than Craze could understand.

Her head game ... was crazy.

** ** ** ** **

After taking some wedding pictures – Dutch even posed for one with Delores and Bernard, Sr.

Dutch and Nina were ready to leave for their honeymoon in Paris. Dutch pulled Roc aside and told him, "That meeting we discussed is gonna be in Paris. Ceylon is setting it up, and all the O.G.'s are flying in within a few days. You remember what we discussed?"

"Yeah, I remember," Roc replied flatly.

"Ceylon will make sure you get around. I'll be in Paris, too, just in case you need me, ai-ight?"

"Yeah."

"You okay?"

"I'm good," Roc lied. The truth is, he couldn't get the murder he'd just committed out of his mind. Dutch knew what was wrong, but he knew Roc would handle business like a true general.

"Ai-ight, I'm goin' to play newlywed. Any problems wit' them nigguhs, you get at me."

"Won't be no problems," Roc assured him.

Dutch gave Roc a hug and a pound, and then headed off to the helicopter where Nina was awaiting him, already inside.

Angel sat in her darkened room, a sliver of moonlight cutting across her face. As she watched the helicopter ascend into the sky, a lone tear tricked down her face.

"Congratulations..." she mumbled.

Chapter Seven
The Take Over

I'll be your lollipop...
You can lick me everywhere...

"You ticklish?"

"Naw."

"Then, why you squirmin'?"

Nina started at his feet, and then continued kissing up along the sides of his calves and running her tongue up the inside of his thigh. The smell of scented candles and the sounds of Mtume's *Juicy Fruit* filled the suite and Dutch laid back, allowing Nina to freak him.

She wanted to kiss and lick every inch of him, taking her time and enjoying being in control for once. She grabbed his erection, massaging and running her hand along its length while she French-kissed all around the head in tantalizing swirls, tasting his pre-cum.

Her pussy was on fire and she wanted to just hop on his dick and go buck, but she enjoyed teasing herself as much as teasing him. Nina ran her tongue along his shaft, tracing the throbbing veins down to his nuts, and then sucked them both, one at a time. Dutch's moans became grunts once Nina slipped her lips around the head and began to bob on it, taking more and more into her mouth with each bob.

Cherry blossom kiss is what you're givin'
Makes my body rock, keeps me sizzlin'...

She continued to cover him with kisses, along his pelvis, then to the nipples on his chest. By the time she was at his lips, sucking on the bottom one, she could feel his erection rubbing against her clit. The foreplay had made her whole body sensitive to the slightest touch, so she was on the verge of cumming, just feeling his dick between her lips. She lifted her hips, gripped him and slid him inside of her, taking the whole length in one stroke. Nina leaned forward with her titties in Dutch's face, sliding herself up and down his length until she could sit up vertically on him.

I've had a few, but not that many

But you're the only one, that gives me good and plenty...

Nina rode him hard, cumming twice before Dutch rolled her over, cocking her legs over his shoulder, spreading-eagle style. He angled her body until he found the soft, spongy center inside of her that made Nina talk in tongues with every stroke.

"Ohhh...Dutch...right, there! Right there! I love you!" she squealed, breathlessly. She could feel another climax building, so she wrapped her legs around Dutch's back, while arching her own. Feeling him release his load inside of her, made her release her own, until they both lay spent.

They shared the first day and a half in their luxurious suite and, the way Nina was putting it on him, Dutch was content with seeing Paris from their balcony. For him, honeymooning in Paris was like being from Harlem and honeymooning in Midtown. But, his circumstances wouldn't permit anywhere else.

Nina, on the other hand, was amped. Going to St. Tropez was one thing, but she had always dreamed about being in the international City of Love. So Dutch consented and gave her a whirlwind tour. He knew the city like he back of his hand, so whatever she could think of, he led the way.

They dined at the Café d'Eiffel, the beautiful restaurant at the base of the Eiffel Tower. Then, they ascended its three levels and took in its panoramic view of Paris. He took her to the famous Musee Du Louvre, which is known to natives simply as The Louvre and Nina got to see the Venus de Milo and the Mona Lisa.

"On the real, DaVinci was a hell of a painter. But damn...Mona Lisa? That's one ugly bitch," Dutch joked, Nina shushing him and looking around to see if anyone had heard him, although, she had to laugh, too.

"She's not really ugly, just…plain," Nina replied.

"You know DaVinci was a faggot, right? Some historians say that he painted himself basically in drag and pawned it off as a woman. So, millions of dudes around the world singing her praises…and the bitch might be a man!" Dutch laughed.

They walked along Quai de Louvre, which becomes Quai de Tuileries and borders the Seine, the river that runs through France, and entered Jardin du Tuleries. Jardin du Tuleries includes the Bois de Boulogne, a park so vast that it contains ornamental lakes, flower gardens, cafés, two race tracks and a children's amusement park.

Nina was enchanted by all of the sights and sounds; even her French was improving, but her feet hurt something awful from all the walking. She and Dutch sat down on the grass, watching children play, while he massaged her feet.

"Thank you," she told him.

"For what? This?" he asked, referring to the foot massage, "Oh, this ain't free. I'll be expectin' payment as soon as we get back to the hotel."

Nina giggled. "No, not that…this…all of this…for loving me."

Dutch smiled his reply.

"Can I ask you something?" she began to ask.

"Anything."

"What if I hadn't been on that flight? What would you have done?" she finished, thinking about how close she had come to not getting on that plane to France.

Dutch shrugged. "I woulda' had you kidnapped," he replied, without a smile.

Nina studied his face, starting to think that he was serious until he winked and cracked a smirk.

"Naw, baby…I'm kiddin'."

She heard him, but she still wondered if he *was* kidding.

Nina's feet feeling better, they decided to take the bus to the Latin Quarter. She noticed upon boarding that certain seats were marked RESERVED. At first, it reminded her of what she read about Rosa Parks and the way buses were segregated, but when Dutch translated the signs to her, she appreciated the rule fully - on any train, bus or metro – subway – there are a certain number of seats reserved for disabled veterans, handicapped persons, pregnant women and persons with children under the age of four years old. It was a noble gesture, but she couldn't see it working well in the United States, with the insensitivity of commuters.

Nina loved their days in Paris, but she was open from their nights, when the city came alive.

They hit all the hot spots, like le Gibus, la Coupole and L'etage. They even hit up Atlantis and le Titan, for the ill reggae and African rhythms.

"J'ai envie de danser," Nina told Dutch, saying that she felt like dancing.

They were at L'etage, where it seemed as if everyone knew Dutch. Even Joey Starr sent him a bottle of bubbly, which Dutch acknowledged by nodding Joey's way from their corner booth.

"Who's that?" Nina asked, because Joey seemed to be attracting celebrity status attention.

"That's a kid named Joey Starr…he's a French M.C.. He been in the game for a minute, so he has like Jay-Z status over here," Dutch explained. "But, back to you. You say you feel like dancin'? Shall we?"

Nina led the way to the dance floor. She may not have understood what the music was saying, but she definitely understood the rhythm. She was enjoying one of the best nights of her life, dancing that blood stain right out of her mind.

** ** ** ** **

While Dutch and Nina were enjoying the tourist side of Paris, Roc was arriving on the side that the cameras don't show – like Midtown to Uptown.

The ghettos of France were identical in every way to the ones in the states. Paris City is divided into twenty districts, and the last three of them are real ghetto. But the hardest, most crime ridden areas are called Banlieues and are divided into seven departments. Although these banlieues have rich sections, they also have a side of town that any ghetto head can identify with.

"This place looks like Newark," Roc commented, riding in the back seat of an old green Ranault.

Seated next to him was his contact, M'Baye. He was Senegalese and French mixed, and resembled Tyrese. The only difference was that his smooth black skin was interrupted by the scars of street life.

"It should. The same dude that designed most of the inner city projects in New York and shit, designed these fuckin' rat traps," he explained, his English flawless.

"Word?"

M'Baye nodded, lighting a cigarette. "Le Corbusier," M'Baye replied with sarcasm in his pronunciation, "he considers it a tower in the park, his Radiant City. Do this shit look radiant to you?" he quipped.

Roc looked out at the graffiti covered walls, the rubble left behind from condemned buildings and the hard grills of the young corner huggers. "The world is a ghetto," Roc remarked.

"We can't get jobs, everybody broke, half of the spots tourists go to, we can't even get in and we born here?" M'Baye blew out his frustration in a cloud of smoke. "French born, but not French bred is how they see us. Fuck 'em. Qu'est ce Qu'on attend."

"Kee who?" Roc inquired.

"Qu'est ce Qu'on attend...it means, What are we waitin' for? Or how you American catz say it?

When we gonna set it?"

Roc smiled because he could definitely understand that phrase. In fact, settin' it was the reason he was in Paris for the meeting.

They were riding through Clichy-sous-Bois on the northern outskirts of Paris, where the meeting was to be held. All of the American gangs would be represented in this meeting – the Bloods, Crips, Jamaicans, Gangster Disciples, Black Guerilla Family, Vice Lords, The Folk Nation and the Hispanic gangs like La Familia, Latin Kings and the Mexican Mafia. It was what Dutch called leverage, but what Roc understood as consolidation. They had used it to lock down the oil distribution on the East Coast, but they had never implemented it with this type of magnitude.

They pulled into a housing project that reminded Roc of Fort Greene Housing Projects in Brooklyn, New York. The high rise apartment buildings were separated by parking lots and surrounded by courtyards. It was a cloudy day, but the projects were still packed with playfully screaming children, French women gossiping in rapid-fire French and booming systems playing everything from American and French hip-hop to African music and reggae - a cacophony of rhythms.

Roc and M'Baye stepped out of the cab and M'Baye was immediately swarmed by little children with their hands out, representing all descents, from Black to Arab and Asian. "M'Baye! M'Baye!" they squealed excitedly, asking him for a few francs.

M'Baye chuckled, reaching into his pocket and handing out silver coins that were valued at five francs a piece. "C'est ca. C'est ca," he laughed, saying *that's it*, in French.

The children scampered off as he and Roc headed towards the building. Roc could tell that M'Baye was the man around there from the way the kids came at him to the differential treatment the hard rocks gave him as they passed, and especially the way the shorties eyed him, calling out his name flirtatiously.

"Sometimes I think the first word children around here learn is my name," he snickered as they entered the building, "but, I don't mind. Black, Arab, Asian, they're all my children...some might even *really* be my children."

Roc laughed. He liked M'Baye's style. He was a Don with heart, but definitely a Don in the way that he barked orders to a few catz in the lobby. The pair took the stairs because, as Roc guessed, the elevator didn't work, and it was then, that he knew French projects dwellers had the same style as American projects dwellers, because the stairway was filthy!

The next similarity Roc noticed were the looks on the faces of the fiends they passed. They harassed M'Baye as they ascended, but he brushed past them with obvious disdain, calling them *La' Morte*, or the dead, even though it was off of their francs that he lived. M'Baye had the same contradictions as the American hustler, but Roc could still feel where he was coming from.

They reached the tenth floor, with Roc a little winded, but M'Baye maintained his swagger. He pulled out a set of keys and unlocked one of the apartment doors at the end of the hall. Once they entered the apartment, the ghetto ended and the luxury began. M'Baye's apartment was laced with all the amenities of a ghetto superstar.

"This is where you're staying...with me. Go ahead and make yourself at home." M'Baye walked down the hallway that led to the bedrooms while Roc went into the living room. The T.V. was blaring, but he didn't understand until he saw that the plasma television hung against the far wall was turned to a soccer game. The room was cloudy from weed being smoked by two scantily clad Black chicks lounging on the couch and armchair. Both were a soft, sensual brown and had shapely physiques. They were wearing no more than boy shorts and sports bras, and neither moved an inch as they looked Roc up and down, exchanging giggles and French whispers.

"You must be, Roc," the one holding the blunt surmised. "I'm Monique...that's Laila."

"What's up?" Roc nodded, keeping his eyes off of their brown sugar and on the television.

"What's up indeed," Monique flirted, looking him up and down, and then offered him the blunt.

Roc shook his head no, so she shrugged and kept on puffing.

M'Baye came into the living room smiling, but the smile disappeared when he saw the two females. "Sortez!" He stated firmly, causing the two chicks to get up without hesitation and go into a back room.

M'Baye and Roc then sat down. "I apologize, Dutch told me you are a Muslim. Sunni or Shia?" he inquired.

"Just Muslim. M. Qur'an and Sunnah," Roc replied.

"Ah...Sunni...I know a lot of Muslims. Anyway, like I said, I apologize for their lack of etiquette.

They're...how ya'll say it...ghetto chicks, 'eh?"

Roc snickered, "Yeah, I can see that."

"What I was gonna tell you is that everything is set up for tomorrow, when the rest of the group is scheduled to arrive. Until then," he turned to the T.V., "do you like football?"

"You mean, soccer?"

"No, its really called football...only Americans call it soccer."

"Oh...I never really sat down and watched," Roc admitted.

Roc and M'Baye casually conversed during the course of the game. He found out one of M'Baye's hustles was bootlegging. He had a large network set up in several of the banliues that moved everything from C.D.'s and D.V.D.'s to clothing and sneakers. His ghetto monopoly kept him in constant beef with rivals, but his main hustles were cocaine and ecstasy. Dutch had set M'Baye up and the young man never looked back.

"Dutch did a lot for me, Roc. Believe me, whatever he needs, and I can do it or get it, it's done or got," M'Baye vowed. "Shit, I got Dutch more shooters in France than the Foreign Legion."

Roc could tell that the young Frenchman looked up to Dutch because he asked Roc so many questions about how they had come up. He already knew Craze and had heard a lot about Angel.

"Is she comin' to Paris?" M'Baye wanted to know.

By the time Roc looked up, it was dark. They had talked for hours, but Roc got up because it was time for salat. He prayed with a strange feeling of distance from his prayer. M'Baye had brought back memories and feelings he had forgotten, or tried hard to forget. But, now, they were back and pumping through his veins. As he finished, Roc realized it was the first time he had ever offered salat and felt nothing…and that really scared him.

** ** ** ** **

While Dutch was honeymooning and Roc was ghetto politikin', Craze was doing what he did best – fucking and getting high. He was lounging at his little hideaway beach spot in Cannes – a place where he liked to play hard because of the annual film festival.

His personal goal was to fuck the hottest bitch in Hollywood every year, and this year was no exception. He had scooped a famous White actress, known for her sleepy bedroom eyes, thick lips and freakish ways. Craze put all three to the test.

They were laid up in his Jacuzzi T650 La Scala, watching Mr. and Mrs. Smith and sniffing coke.

"Yo, Ma, where the fuck you cop this bullshit?" he asked, screwing up his face and examining the product. "This some straight garbage."

She shrugged, putting a cigarette between her sexy ass lips. "How the fuck should I know? Call it schwag. I tell my people to

123

get coke...they get coke," she replied in a rapid fire neurotic fashion.

Craze dumped the shit in the Jacuzzi, and then got out and went over to his drawer. He pulled out a large glass vial and brought the contents back to the Jacuzzi.

She watched his manhood swing as he walked and uttered, "You're so fucking beautiful...my God...I wanna fuck you until I can taste my own blood!"

Damn, these Hollywood bitches fucked up in the head, he thought to himself, amazed at what she'd said, as he got back into the Jacuzzi. "Now this is that bomb-zee! Craze got that fish scale, nah mean!" he boasted, unscrewing the lid. "Trust me, this will blow your mind," he smiled, not knowing how truly accurate that statement was.

** ** ** ** **

Five black Benz's cut through the narrow streets of Clichy-sous-Bois like a diplomatic procession, the fog lights on each vehicle cutting through the misty French afternoon. Pedestrian heads turned, watching the tinted windowed convoy pass by. They reached a small club and pulled into the vacant lot that served as a parking lot beside it.

The European drivers got out to open the door for their African-American and Latino passengers.

Each Benz carried two men, each representing the ghetto armies that gangs really are. Looking around, each dressed like grown men, but ghetto fabulous nonetheless – diamond earrings and encrusted bezels adorned ears and wrists. These were not the top dogs of the organizations, but they were high enough in the hierarchies to carry the weight of decisions and give orders based on them.

One of M'Baye's soldiers stood by the side door and beckoned for the men to enter. Once inside, he closed the door, he himself, remaining outside. Inside, M'Baye and Roc greeted and shook each man's hand, and then took them to the back room where a large round table had been set up.

Three extremely attractive women came around, took their orders for drinks, filled them and then left the room. A few catz lit cigarettes, one a cigar, creating a wafting haze that hung low in the room. Roc sat at the table with M'Baye to his right and the representative for the Latin Kings to his left.

"I'm glad to see that everyone we invited came through – Respect. I know the different routes ya'll took seemed to take you around the block to get next door, so to speak, but I'm sure ya'll know Dutch's situation," Roc began.

"That there goes without saying," the representative of the Gangster Disciples replied with an arrogant air, "but, now that *we* here, why ain't he?"

"Same reason none of the founders are here, brother," Roc shot right back, forcefully, but not challenging. He knew that there was a lot of testosterone at the table, but he also had nuts, too. "Any type way the Feds, the CIA or Interpol knew this meeting was takin' place, the fuckin' U.N. would be surrounding the building."

A few catz chuckled lightly, raising the tension a decibel.

"Every man in here represents a nation within a nation. Armies, corporations, ghetto governments, all rolled into one. J. Edgar Hoover started Cointelpro. Just because we put on berets and pumped our fists, what the fuck you think they'd do if they knew we were at the same table?" Roc asked, putting his hand, palm down, on the table firmly. "Now, for years, we been at each other's throats, merckin' nigguhs left and right. Don't matter the set, or the color, you claim, 'cause when it comes right down to it, the color is green, the power is gold and the price we paid was red, our own."

Roc looked around the table for signs of disagreement, but all the faces wore poker expressions.

"Now, the way we brought ya'll here by two's had a purpose. Blood rode with Crip, Disciple with Lord, and so on and so forth. No one objected because you had a common destiny – this meeting.

The ride represented the means, and this is the ends. We've been fighting over means, brothers…when we've all wanted the same ends."

"So, what's this," Crip sniped, with a distinctive Cali drawl, "some type of gang truce you talkin'? What, Farrakhan gonna step from behind them curtains and lead us in prayer?"

A few catz laughed, but Roc silenced them swiftly.

"Naw, bruh…we here to take a lot of money, real fast."

"How much you talkin'?"

"One hundred million dollars."

"A hundred? Man, it's ten catz up in here. That ain't but –"

"*Each*…one hundred million *each*."

All laughter ceased.

"Check it out, Homes, that's a lot of dough. I mean, we know Dutch was doin' it big, but a hundred million each comes to –"

"A billion dollars," Roc calculated for him, with a smirk. "And that's only the first year. As our percentage increases, so does yours."

"Your percentage of what?" the Black Guerilla Family wanted to know.

"Cocaine distribution. Our people have created a hybrid of coke and heroin…there's never been anything like it before. Its coke, pure and simple, but with the addictive quality of heroin. You can cut it a hundred times, and if someone smokes enough, not even the rawest amount of regular coke can replace it," Roc explained.

"And you're gonna pay us to sell it, Papi? What's the catch?"

"The catch is, we're *not* sellin' it. The cartels are gonna pay *us* not to," Roc answered the Latin Kings.

The men took it in, looking from one to another and mumbling thoughts.

"Extortion 'eh, Esse?" the Mexican Mafia smirked. "You're gonna extort the cartels not to market your product...that's war."

"That's what we need you for" Roc told the Mexican Mafia, looking him in his eyes. He knew that going to war with the cartels, if it came to that, would mean many Hispanics would have to war with their own people. "All of you...but, if they choose war, they lose on all fronts. They'd have to take on all of us in our own hoods, which is fuckin' suicide and they lose their entire market share because if we market ours through your organizations, their product will be obsolete."

"So, why not say fuck the cartels and put it out for self?" the Folk Nation wanted to know.

Because, in war, you always leave your opponent a way out," Roc jeweled him, "never make him fight to the death, because then they have nothing to lose. Besides, the cartels are established with the U.S. government in ways it would take us years to build, if ever. Naw, bruh, its enough money to go around."

"So, what's the hundred mil' for?" Blood questioned, "You said you need us for war, but you ain't really expectin' one...so what you askin' of us?"

Roc leaned forward and counted off on his fingers as he spoke. "One, our arms in America, coast to coast. Two, you'll be the prime distributors in your prospective areas, either through the cartels or us.

Nothing gets sold in your area unless it's through you. That way, we can screen who's who and keep a lot of potential snitches from gettin' on. Three, you will leave one area, drug free, gun free, bullshit free, specifically for Muslim control. And, four, this table may be round, but it does come full circle and stops here with me.

127

Any problems you can't solve amongst yourselves, we arbitrate and ours is the final say."

Grumbles went around the table.

"I don't see no problem with the first three, but four…you basically askin' us to pledge allegiance to yo' flag, so to speak, which in a way, means drop our own. And, I'm sure I speak for the majority when I say, its been a lot of bloodshed between families and even though a hundred large is helluva grip, I can't say its enough to pay for the past," Vice Lords commented.

"'Ear me now," Jamaica began, squinting trough his blunt smoke, "What da breden say, its reasoning, ya understan'. Who a– dem 'ere nah a-bust 'dem gun? Dem massives, Black Rose, House O' Dread, we 'ave nuff guns, ya understand, Don' pon Don down yard fightin' each other, keelin' dem likkle yout'," Jamaica raved, then leaned forward, "but at da end of da day, me see Seaga, me see Marley 'ave everythin'…we 'are nothin'. Dem nah care 'bout PNP of JLP, dem a care about m-o-nee, you understan'…money!"

The group chuckled at Dread's lyrical reasoning, but nodded their understanding.

"Same thin' in America, bredren, same thin'. Bush keep you Blood, keep you – a Crip, him not tink 'bout dat, him just see a dead nigguh! Me not wan war wit' you, seen, we come together, make a lot of money, get pussy, blow da ganja like ancient kings. Respect!" The dread leaned back, puffing the but head spliff until it glared orange.

"Yo, I hear what Dread is sayin', and I'm feelin' Dutch's plan. But I don't think this is somethin' to be decided in one sit down, ya feel me?" Gangster Disciples told Roc. "I need to run this by a few catz, then we take it from there."

Roc nodded.

"But, if we do agree, when do we get the hundred large?" La Familia asked.

"Just then…when we agreed," Roc assured.

M'Baye saw that the meeting was concluded and said, "Until then, you're all my guests, 'eh? From your hood, to my hood. Let's go eat and enjoy the life we work hard to have. But yo, I gotta warn you, American chicks are okay…but French pussy is creamier!" he joked, and the table shook with laughter.

Everyone filed out, getting back into their respective vehicles. Roc got into M'Baye's platinum toned Jaguar XK convertible. With one foot in the car, he saw a Muslim sister walking home with her husband and daughter. He viewed the simple smiles of happiness on their faces and thought of calling Ayesha, but quickly dismissed it, because he couldn't think of what to say. She had made her decision and he felt like he had finally made his.

Chapter Eight

"Our marriage is a lie."

Reality was beginning to sear through to Nina's heart. It had started out simple enough. She and Dutch had spent the day in Masne-La-Vallee, where Euro Disney is located. Nina had enjoyed herself, especially seeing all of the children in different stages of development – from infants to toddlers, from their terrible twos to lptheir inquisitive sixes. Their conversation had naturally turned to the topic of their own children to be.

"Boy."

"Girl."

"Twins."

Laughter.

Names they would name them, and traits they both hoped they had.

"Your nose."

"Your eyes."

"Your smile...definitely your smile."

Like the day, their banter was sunny and warm. That is, until they got back to the suite and Dutch showed her their marriage certificate. Nina didn't know what to say. There was no mention of Nina Celeste Martin or a Bernard James. Where it said, Ma Femme – wife – and Le Mari – husband – the names Thelma Lewis and Jonathan Green stood out in bold, black ink.

"Who is this?" she asked, searching his eyes for the joke.

"That's umm...the marriage certificate. We just gotta sign –"

"But, they got the names wrong...look," she pointed out, hoping that maybe they had the wrong one. But she knew it was no mistake by the look on his face.

"That's us. Its nothing, yo, just our aliases," he reasoned.

"Nothing? Baby, this *is* our marriage certificate. I mean, I understand what's going on, but out marriage certificate?" Nina questioned him, hoping he'd see her point.

Dutch gently gripped her by the arms and replied, "Nina, listen...don't sweat it, okay, its just a piece of paper, nothing more, nothing less. Like a fake I.D., don't tell me you ain't never have one of those," he tried to joke, but Nina wasn't in a joking mood.

"What about the kids?" she probed, trying to go back to their earlier topic. "Will they be Lewis or Green?" she asked, tone dripping with sarcasm. "I mean, when we go to my mother's for Christmas, or...or your mother's for Thanksgiving...who do we say they are?"

Dutch sighed. "We won't be goin' to see your mother any time soon."

She stared at him, hoping that she hadn't heard him right.

"Not now, Nina. It'll be a long time before we can go back to the states," he broke to her.

"Let me get this straight...we're married, right, but not on paper? Because on paper, I'm really not Nina and you're really not Bernard, and our kids won't really be our kids, except on paper, because they'll be Lewis-Green or Green-Green or whoever, right?"

Dutch rubbed his head.

"Right?" she repeated, "and whoever the hell we are or ain't don't matter, because we can't go and share who we are with the family?" she shook her head, recognizing the solidity of reality searing through her heart. "Our marriage is a lie."

Dutch picked up the marriage certificate and tore it up, trying to maintain his composure.

"Happy now? Forget Lewis, forget Green...its me and you... Nina and Dutch...us. See?" he asked, holding up the pieces of the certificate. "Do you feel any less married, huh? Them rocks on your finger feel any less real?"

"Don't even go there," Nina warned him.

"I ain't sayin it like that…I'm sayin' paper don't make us, okay? It don't. I -," he replied, when his cell phone rung with the sound of a cocking gun ring tone. "All I know, Ma, is that I love you and that ain't a lie," he told her, sincerely.

The phone continued to cock, so he answered it, walking out on the open balcony.

"Yeah…Angel?…what's wrong?…wha…," he took the phone from his ear and rubbed his face.

Nina could tell by his demeanor that something was terribly wrong. Dutch slowly put the phone back to his ear.

"Don't…tell me that…please…don't…FUCK!!!" he bellowed, then hurled the phone down into the streets of Paris.

"Dutch…what's wrong?" Nina went to him, holding him, but his whole body was rigid and unbending.

"We gotta go," was all he said, pulling away from her and going back into the room.

Tears lined Nina's face because she was scared of his silence. "Please, tell me what's wrong, baby."

He looked at her as if seeing her face for the first time, and then answered, "Craze is dead…he O.D.'d …we gotta go home."

Craze dead? She thought, feeling her man's pain. It all seemed to be happening so fast - too fast.

Her head was spinning as she quickly packed for home, wondering if they really had a home.

Despite the beauty of France, she was slowly realizing that it was their virtual prison. If so, then this couldn't be heaven, so those weren't pearly gates in her dreams, they were really bars.

** ** ** ** **

"Oh, Dutch...I'm so sorry," Goldilocks wept, wrapping her arms around Dutch, "I know how much you loved Craze," she continued.

Dutch returned her hug weakly, and then stepped past her. She turned and gave Nina a hug.

"Are you okay?"

"I – I'm okay," Nina responded, appreciating what she saw as concern.

"How is he?" Goldilocks inquired about Dutch.

Nina lowered her eyes. "I...don't know...its like...distant, you know? Like he won't let me in," Nina admitted. She and Goldilocks had established a relationship during the planning of the wedding, so she felt comfortable in confiding in her to an extent. Besides, Goldilocks was the closest she had to a friend...or so she thought.

They were at a small funeral home near the estate. It was owned by John Mallwitz, an associate of Ceylon. He had arranged for the bodies to be taken there, to avoid the media and the local authorities.

Dutch entered the room, trailed by Nina and Goldilocks. He saw the two sheeted bodies in the middle of the room. Angel was in the corner. She sat in a chair, leaned forward, her elbows on her knees, rocking on the balls of her feet. She hadn't seen or heard Dutch come in, she just stared at Craze's sheeted body.

"Angel," Dutch spoke to her, but she didn't respond. "Angel," he repeated, and then went over and crouched in front of her.

"He's gone, B," she said, almost in a whisper. "I kept callin' him to get up. Get up. Get up, Chris. But, he was gone. I keep callin'..."

Dutch hugged her for a moment before she realized she was being held, and then she grasped onto him like she was drowning.

John Mallwitz, a tall, barrel-chested White man in a white smock walked in. "Mr. James? Omar told me you were on your way."

Dutch stood up, but Angel stayed with him, with her arms around his neck. Dutch shook Mallwitz's hand. "I appreciate what you're doing."

Mallwitz nodded. "I know this is difficult for you, Omar said he was a close friend, but did you...also know the woman?"

"Who?"

Mallwitz pulled back both sheets so he could see Craze and the dead actress. Angel turned her face and buried it in Dutch's shoulder. Nina looked away as well, but Goldilocks' eyes gleamed as she viewed her dirty work. She wondered to herself how it must've felt to sniff cocaine and crushed glass: the combination of the euphoric rush and the excruciating pain of having your brain sliced to pieces.

Dutch studied Craze's dead face. His butter pecan skin tone had begun to take on an ashen gray quality, and there was dried blood coming from both his mouth and nose. He glanced at the woman, who was already turning a bluish purple. She also had dried blood on her face. Dutch recognized her from some of her films, she was one of Hollywood's starlets. Dutch nodded for Mallwitz to cover the faces back up.

"Omar said to talk to you about the arrangements," Mallwitz said.

Dutch knew he couldn't send the body back to Jersey – he couldn't send Craze back to be buried by his mother – it was too risky. Once the Feds found out Craze's body was back, it would be nothing to trace it back to France. Shipping the body was out. As much as he hated it, he knew there was only one solution.

"Can you...cremate the body here?"

134

Angel's head shot up and she looked at Dutch. "Dutch, nooo ...we can't burn Chris," she begged.

"It ain't Chris no more, Dada, he gone. We can't send him home, it'll be too easy to trace."

"Bury him here somewhere, just don't burn him," Angel's eyes pleaded, but she knew he was right.

Dutch kissed her on the forehead, and then turned to Mallwitz. "Just give us a few minutes."

Mallwitz understood and walked out as Dutch uncovered Craze's face one more time.

"So, this is it, huh? This is how it ends?" he shook his head and took a deep breath. "Chris," Dutch spoke, then kissed him on the forehead.

Angel's face was beet red, like it was about to explode, but it hurt too much to cry. She crossed herself and then kissed Craze on the lips, "Te Quiero, Papi...siempre."

Dutch urged her to come with him and they all headed for the door as Mallwitz came back in.

"Okay," Dutch told him.

"Both of them, I presume?"

"Yeah."

"When shall you return for the ashes?"

"I won't ."

They walked out.

Nina and Dutch rode back to the estate in silence. The only sound was the hum of the Bentley GTC's engine. Nina still felt awkward on the left side of the car. She always got the feeling like she was in the driver's seat, but she wasn't in control. It reminded her of her life. She didn't think with a gangster's mind, so she didn't understand Dutch's decision to cremate Craze. She didn't want to understand it, nor did she want to question it. But, what she

135

did want to know was, "If something happened to me…would you burn me too?"

There was no sarcasm in her voice, nor did it carry a judgmental tone. Dutch glanced over at her and asked, "Why would you even say somethin' like that?"

"I'm not trying to question your decisions, I know you did what you felt was best for everybody."

"Yeah, I did."

"So, what makes me any different?" Nina tried to hold back the tears and speak calmly. "I know that you loved Chris…You've known him since you were little and…I know this is hard for you. But, a lot of things lately have been hard for me. I just feel like a lot of doors are just closing in my face and I need to know that at least one isn't closing. If something happens to me –"

"Nothing's gonna happen to you."

"– I want to know that you'll send me home," her voice cracked on the word *home*, and a tear escaped her eye.

"Nothing's gonna happen to you, okay?" Dutch tried to console her, holding her hand tightly.

"Just promise me."

Dutch looked at her solemnly. "I promise."

** ** ** ** **

"Joseph."

"It's been a long time."

"He's dead."

"Who?"

"Craze, Dutch's partner. Next…I will take his heart."

"Excellent."

"And Joseph? I think you need to speak with the Turk, Ceylon. What Dutch is planning…can make *us* both very, very rich."

** ** ** ** **

136

That night, Roc came back from Paris. He was just finishing his night salat when he noticed that Angel was standing in the door.

"Did you pray for Craze?" she asked.

"I prayed for all of us," Roc replied, folding up his rug.

"Me, too?"

"No doubt."

Angel smiled and dropped her eyes. "Thanks, man, I ain't prayed in a long time," she admitted, pulling out a Newport and lighting it.

"I ain't seen you smoke since we been here. I thought you quit?"

"I did, too," Angel chuckled, blowing a stream of smoke out. She allowed herself to slide down the wall, until she was in a sitting position, with her knees to her chest. "Why'd he have to die, Roc? Man, why?" she pulled hard on the cigarette, "what we gonna do now?"

"I don't know."

They sat in silence for a few minutes while Angel French inhaled the smoke. "You know what I remember most about Craze? He was a funny nigguh, yo. Even when he was irkin' my nerves, he could still make me laugh!"

Roc smiled at the memory, because he remembered Craze's humor, too.

"I mean, like, Dutch is all B.I.," she continued, "fuckin' Black Caesar right, and you, Shock and Zoom was on that RaRa, that Prince Street bullshit. But Craze was the bug out. Don't get me wrong, he got down for the crown, but me and him used to get drunk, blow some charm and bug the fuck out," she smiled, inhaling the memory through the smoke. "Wit' his stupid laugh, te-he-a heyaa heya."

Yeah…that's what I remember, yo, his laugh."

"Member when we hit the Port? You shoulda heard how many ways he described yo' ass afterward," Roc laughed.

Angel smirked. "Fuckin' pervert," she looked to the ceiling and yelled, "Craze, you still a fuckin' pervert!'"

They both laughed and Angel put the cigarette butt out on the floor and then stood up. "And, Roc, I know you type caught up right now, you know. This ain't your thing no more, but you really wanna help the people, I respect that."

Roc dropped his head, not knowing if he still deserved that respect. "Allah knows best."

"Your heart's in the right place, not like these so-called leaders out here livin' off the people like T.D. Jakes and Creflo Dollar. A preacher named Dollar? Tha' fuck? Godddamn fakes…anyway, don't be too hard on yourself. I mean, who else is gonna pray for this she devilizzes," she winked, and then left the room.

Angel walked down the hall towards her bedroom. On the way, she saw Dutch's bedroom door opened, so she walked over and saw Nina, sitting in the edge of the bed, looking at her and Dutch's wedding portrait. Delores had given it to them as a wedding gift. Whoever had painted it was a master of realism, because it looked just like the actual photo. Dutch and Nina were embracing one another, both smiling towards the camera.

Nina felt someone in the door and looked up to see Angel. Angel just stood there, gazing at her, but subtly scrutinizing her. Nina didn't back away, nor did she break the gaze. The silent animosity had been building and festering since the day they met, so Nina felt like it needed to come to an end, one way or another.

"Where's Dutch?" Angel asked, her voice neither challenging, nor warm – neutral.

Nina shrugged her shoulders and went back to looking at the portrait.

"You know, he's not going to admit it," Angel stated.

"Admit what?"

"What he's feeling right now. Not to you, not to me, nobody...not even himself. Pain is weakness, and to Dutch, that makes you vulnerable, you know, leaves you open," Angel explained.

"But, nobody's invincible," Nina retorted.

"Naw, but you *can* be impenetrable. That's his edge, because, believe me, mad catz done died by showing they weren't," she told her, thinking of Kazami's weakness for Simone and Quan's weakness for her. She wondered if Dutch had now done the same thing because of Nina.

"Why are you telling me this, Angel? We're both grown women, okay...and its no secret that you don't like me, or whatever. So, why do you feel the need to tell me about my man?" Nina probed. She felt jealous of Angel's intimate knowledge of Dutch, but she couldn't deny its accuracy. She had seen it herself. She had experienced the stone inside him, which his emotions were held behind but she felt powerless to move it.

"I don't like you?" Angel snickered. "Is that what you think? Since we're both grown women, as you say, let me put it to you like this...if I didn't *like* you, you wouldn't be *breathin'*...period. But...I could never hurt something Dutch loved," Angel admitted, momentarily dropping her gaze, "and since I know that he loves you...he needs you right now. I just wanted you to know how he needed."

Nina didn't take Angel's comment on her life lightly, but she let it go. "Believe me, Angel, I know what my *husband* needs, okay?" she retorted, flinging her marriage in Angel's face.

Angel smiled and shrugged nonchalantly. "Maybe you're right, Nina, maybe you're right. But, ahhh...if so...then why ain't he here wit' you right now?"

Nina watched her walk away, and she hated to admit it, but that was the question in her mind as well.

139

** ** ** ** **

Dutch sat under the full moon, alone, except for the bottle of Hennessy he was clutching. He wasn't a drinker, even though he could hold his liquor, he just hated to be off point. But, his head was bad and he felt the only way to make it right was to make it worse.

Craze was gone, and there was nothing he could do about that. He remembered the early days, the first car he stole, the first cat he robbed...Craze was always right there by his side. Every ring on the game's ladder he had climbed, Craze had been there to hold him down. The tiny voice of conscience that he still possessed questioned *whether he had held Craze down?* He had always warned him about fucking with drugs, but maybe he hadn't been forceful enough, persistent enough or hard enough on him.

But Craze was a grown man, his steel will countered, and people will do what they want, regardless of consequences. A doctor tells a man, *Stop drinking or you'll be dead in a month,* and that man will probably go out and *double* his drinking just to celebrate his last thirty days.

Dutch took a shot of Henney to the neck and grunted, "Fuck 'em," trying to convince himself to internalize the sentiment. Craze had become weak, and that's what weak nigguhs get. That was why he didn't bury Craze in France. He couldn't ship him home, but he could have buried him. He didn't, because Dutch refused to eulogize what Craze had become, so he burned him to remind himself of what happens to weakness. Still, he couldn't deny that, with Craze gone, he had burned a part of himself along with him.

"You gonna drink all that to the head, or can an old player get some instead?"

Dutch looked up into the smirking face of Bernard Sr.. He eyed him for a minute, and then extended the bottle to him. Bernard Sr. propped his cane against the seat next to Dutch's and sat down.

"Don't tell yo' mother. She'll kill me, she catch me drinkin'," Bernard Sr. admitted, turning the bottle up.

"You a grown man," Dutch responded, remembering his earlier analogy of the doctor.

"Yeah, but yo' mama's will ain't one to oppose," Bernard Sr. chuckled, passing the bottle back to Dutch.

"Yeah, you right about 'dat," Dutch agreed.

They sat for a moment, both looking at the moon, passing the bottle back and forth.

"I'm sorry to hear about your friend. Your mama say ya'll was real close."

"Like brothers."

Bernard Sr. lit up a Kool. "I had a friend like that once. Back in 'Nam. Ole' country ass nigguh named Eddie. Think he come from Mississippi...blue-black motherfucka, strong as a bull and meaner than a boatload of mean motherfuckas!"

Dutch laughed along with Bernard Sr.

"...And didn't take shit off them crackers. Knock one down just as soon as one look at 'em. He didn't know what I was doin', but I reckoned he guessed somethin' was fishy because every time one of them crackers died, he looked at me real sly-like and say, *Cracka ain't safe in them jungles like he is in the states, huh?* But, I never let on," he said, inhaling the cigarette smoke. "Well, one day, our platoon got caught in an ambush, real bad one, too. I had already said the Lord's Prayer on my soul when a land mine exploded behind me, and then I heard a man holler. Now, I done heard many a man holler, and its something you never get used to, but it happened. But, this time, it was Eddie. I run back to see if I could do something and I find him with damn near his whole bottom half blown off."

Dutch listened, imagining the story as he went.

"Truth be told, if I could get him to the medic, he woulda' lived, no doubt in my mind. But, to do that, I woulda' had to carry him…and like I said, this ambush was bad. If I carry him, we both dead…or I could leave him to die," Bernard Sr. said, blowing out smoke.

"So, what you do?"

"I shot him myself," Bernard Sr. told him, then took another sip from the bottle. "One shot…I wasn't gonna leave him to suffer, and I couldn't carry him wit' me…so I killed him. Now, you might say that was cold, that he was my friend. But, I say, I woulda' wanted him to do the same thing if it woulda' been me. I had my own war to fight, son, and I'll be goddamned if I was gonna die fightin' for somebody else's…but that's me. Now, I don't know what you got goin' on over here, but I know who you are and what you do. My point is, son, dead friends make for good memories, but love…don't win wars."

** ** ** ** **

Goldilocks was feeling herself…killing Craze had been easier than she'd thought. He had been so careless, and she had been flawless. There would be no autopsy, so no one would ever suspect that it was the crushed glass that he had really O.D.'d on, and even if they did, who would suspect her?

She was feeling herself…literally.

She watched herself spread eagle on the bed, through the floor length mirror. The twelve-inch dildo, with the girth of a good sized cucumber had her legs trembling and feeling as if her pussy was being ripped apart. Still, she wanted more…she wanted to be able to take the whole length.

Power made her horny, and she truly felt powerful, confident in her plan. She would weaken Dutch emotionally, taking away everyone he cared for – Roc, Nina, his mother, his father…Angel. There was no denying her feelings for Angel. In the beginning, she felt positive that after all was said and done, Angel would roll with her, but after seeing her around Dutch, she wasn't so sure. Plus, Angel hadn't been attentive to her like she had been back in Newark. Still, she hoped that Angel would make the right decision when the time came...or...

Goldilocks had all of the twelve-inch dildo shoved inside of her. The sight of it between her soft, pink lips, turned her on. Seeing her own French pedicure hoisted in the air turned her on...the feeling of her own power and sexuality drove her crazy as she grinded and shook until the dildo was covered in her foamy, white.

Angel came in and saw Goldilocks on the bed, moaning to herself. The smell of her sex filled the room and mildly repulsed Angel for reasons she couldn't quite grasp.

"I made you a lollipop, wanna lick?" Goldilocks asked enticingly, licking her own juices from the dildo.

"I'm just gonna take a shower and go to bed," Angel answered, heading for the bathroom.

Goldilocks knew her advances were being thwarted, but she was confident in her powers of persuasion. "Can I come?" she flirted, but Angel didn't answer. Still, she followed her into the bathroom.

Goldilocks watched Angel slip out of her Roc-A-Fella sweat suit and Sean Jean boxers. Goldilocks admired her Egyptian-bronze skin tone, the firmness of her breasts and suppleness of her hips and thighs. She moved into Angel's arms, pressing her own nakedness against Angel's.

Angel allowed Goldilocks to kiss her, tasting her juices on her tongue. The flavor sparked a tinge of desire in Angel, but not enough to overcome everything on her mind.

"Not tonight, Mami, I'm tired. Go 'head to bed, I'll be there in a minute," Angel told her, but Goldilocks persisted.

"Come on, baby, my pussy needs a tongue massage," Goldilocks purred, licking along Angel's neck.

Angel untangled Goldilocks' arms from her neck and repeated more firmly, "I said, not tonight, okay? I just lost my brother!" she reminded her in a tone like, *what the fuck?*

Goldilocks stepped back and folded her arms across her bare breasts as Angel got in the shower.

"Yes, I know…and I'm sorry. But, what about last night…or the night before that? You've barely touched me since we got here. I wonder if that has anything to do with Dutch," she quipped sarcastically.

"You talkin' stupid," Angel mumbled, her back to her, letting the water run over her body.

"Am I? You must really think that I don't see the way you look at him! Yeah, I'm stupid alright. Stupid for being here with you…stupid for loving you. I *told* you this would happen…didn't I?" Goldilocks huffed.

Angel turned to her. She knew she hadn't been affectionate with Goldilocks and it made her feel guilty. But, like Roc's religious dilemma, Angel's dilemma went to the very core of who she was.

Trapped between the two people she loved…she was torn, so she knew she wasn't being fair with Goldilocks.

"You right, yo, I been buggin'…so check it, let me take this shower and when I get out, we can –"

"Oh…so we charity fuckin' now? Let me lick this bitch so she'll shut up now? You know what? Fuck you, Angel, how 'bout 'dat?! Fuck you! You ain't gonna keep treatin' me like this, I swear you ain't!" Goldilocks warned, heading for the door.

"Goldi!" Angel called after her, but she didn't respond. "I love you," she mumbled, putting her hands on the wall and letting the water run over her confused mind.

** ** ** ** **

The next morning, after breakfast, Dutch and Nina took a walk through the field of lilies.

"This reminds me of *The Color Purple*," Nina remarked, inhaling the sweet fragrances of the flowers.

"I may be Black...I may be po', hell, I may even be ugly...but I'm still here!" Dutch exclaimed, mocking Celie's southern accent.

Nina laughed, bumping him playfully. "You so silly...and, Baby, I'm sorry about saying that our marriage is a lie. I was just...reacting. I've never felt anything more real than what I feel when I'm with you. So, I'm proud to be your Thelma Louise," she joked.

"Thelma Lewis," he cracked.

She stopped and held his hand. "No, Thelma *and* Louise. I wanna be a part of every aspect of our life. Believe me, I'm no stranger to the streets. I could be your ride or die chick," she sang, teasingly.

Dutch smiled at her naivety, but appreciated her comment all the same.

"Plus, since I used to work at the bank, I know lots of ways to financially duck the Feds," she told him, like she was applying for a job.

"Yeah? That just may come in handy," he humored her, "I'll keep that in mind."

"Don't patronize me, Dutch," she replied sourly, her voice wilting.

"I'm not patronizing you, I'm serious. Maybe you could be the financial guru of this outfit."

"Or, you could teach me what Angel does."

Dutch understood where it was coming from and looked at her seriously. "You know, you might be right. But, I'm sayin', you sure this is what you want?"

"I'm sure."

"And you ain't gonna back out or nut up under pressure?"

"Anything, Baby, I'm wit' you."

"Okay…listen. This is what I need," he began, placing his hands on both sides of her cheeks, framing her face. "I'ma need you to have my back through thick and thin, okay, give me beautiful little girls that look just like you and bad ass little boys that bop like me, feel me? But, above all, I need you to love me with all that you are. Can you handle that?"

"I already do that, but –"

"Hey," he crooned, "listen to me. You don't have to compete wit' nobody, you hear; your spot's a lock, okay?"

She nodded, feeling her jealousy for Angel being lifted from her heart.

"Okay?" he repeated, "You the Dutchess," he smiled, the smirk that made her drip. "And believe me, lovin' me is a handful."

"Or, a mouthful," she retorted, kissing him gently and then lowering herself slowly to her knees…

Chapter Nine

Roc returned to Paris along with Angel. He knew that there was a racial divide between the gangs, one he wished to bridge with Angel's presence. Plus, she needed to become familiar with the group for future reference.

Angel welcomed the trip because it gave her a chance to get away from her Goldilocks/Dutch emotional dilemma and let her get back to familiar territory – getting money.

As Roc pushed the black Mclaren SLR through the streets of Clichy-sous-Bois, Angel was going through the same thing he had, seeing the seedy side of Paris.

"What the fuck? This Paris?" she asked, looking out at the Parisian slums.

Roc nodded.

They drove to M'Baye's project building and parked next to his Jaguar. M'Baye was on the basketball court with a few of the representatives and his crew, playing five on five. M'Baye had his shirt off, revealing his tribal tattoos.

When he saw them pull up, he made his way over to the car and gave Roc a ghetto hug and then set his gaze on Angel. Seeing her for the first time, it was hard to picture such a gorgeous creature committing the heinous acts he had heard about.

"Let me guess…Angel, right?" M'Baye surmised, extending his hand for Angel to shake.

"Yeah, and you must be M'Baye," she replied, shaking his hand and drinking her bottled water.

"I didn't know Paris had projects, let alone gangsta nigguhs like Dutch say you is."

"Say 'ello to 'da bad guy," M'Baye remarked, with a perfect Scarface accent, arms open and staggering.

Angel chuckled. "I like you, dude," she told him, offering him some of her water.

"I like you, too," he said, looking her up and down, imagining what was under that baggy sweat suit. He took the water, looked at it, then quipped, "you sure its safe?"

She winked. "I only do that to enemies, you mi familia."

He held up the bottle for an impromptu toast. "Mon Famille," he echoed in French, drinking the water. "And, yo, speakin' of family, I'm sorry to hear about Craze. I didn't know him well, still, he will be missed."

"What up wit' them?" Roc asked, referring to the few representatives on the court.

M'Baye shrugged, handing the bottle back to Angel. "Lot of calls made, a lot received, but other than that, ballin' in the city, nothin' for sure."

"They stallin'," Roc surmised, "waitin' to see who is and who ain't. Cool. Get 'em all together in your apartment."

"Gimme a minute to round up everybody."

Roc and Angel went up to the apartment to wait. It took about forty-five minutes before everyone arrived at M'Baye's apartment. Some sat, some stood, while Angel sat in the armchair, right in the middle of it all and Roc stood across the room.

"Who's she?" Gangster Disciples asked.

"I'm the maid. Anybody want a drink?" she asked sarcastically.

Only La Familia got the joke, being familiar with the tri-state area. He laughed and shook his head. "Naw, Mami, not for me. Your reputation proceeds you, Angel."

Angel nodded La Familia greetings. "As does yours, Squeeze. Give Chino my love."

Roc saw how every man in the room was getting distracted by Angel's arresting beauty, so he cleared his throat and got down to business.

"Ya'll all had a few days to contemplate our offer. What's the deal?"

"Roc, man, I'ma be honest wit' you," Blood began, "me and my peoples a little skeptical…it sound too good to be true."

A few murmurs of agreement went through the group.

"Okay, let's be honest," Roc countered. "Honestly, some of ya'll think if we can afford to give you a hundred, we can give you *two* hundred. Why? Because you think we *need* you, so, you wanna juice it for all its worth."

Angel looked around the room, reading the faces of those she knew Roc was speaking of.

"I can dig it, and its only half true. We do need you, but not *all* of you. We want us all to work together, but, bottom line…the majority will agree and a few will hold out – maybe two or three – then, we will *crush* you," Roc looked around the room sternly and could almost see the testosterone rising.

"Now we can get into a lot of chest beating and nut grabbin', but ain't no way two or three of you can take on all of us, especially since you won't stand together. We ain't takin' nothing from you, we can only gain."

Black Guerilla Family sat back on the couch, right leg over left, smirking. "These last few days ballin' at Dutch's expense, I done got to know a lot of these catz. Now, I ain't got nothin' against nobody in the room personally, I think it's a beautiful thang, if it can happen. But nigguhs will put out the fire in hell, ya understand, they fuck everything up. We stand for different thangs."

"Do we?" Roc inquired. "Naw, Bruh, I don't agree. Whether we bang up under the five point or the six point, whatever your flag, who don't profess knowledge, wisdom or peace or equality? We been fightin' in the streets we don't own, wit' guns we didn't make and makin' another muhfucka rich!

Lawyers, police, politicians, car dealers, even Jacob the Jeweler is pimpin' us, Bruh! Straight up. Wit' this, we flip the script. It don't come in our hood unless *we* control it. We establish

149

ourselves, so in years to come our kids ain't gotta stand on no corners. You think the Mafia kids on corners? The Jews? The Irish?

Been there, done that, now they kids in Harvard, on the Supreme Court benches and runnin' corporations. So, like my man, M'Baye, said...how you say it, *What are we waitin' for?*"

"Qu'est ce qu'on attend," M'Baye bellowed.

The tide was turning Roc's way, but there was one last obstacle.

"I feel you, homes," the Mexican Mafia said, "its basically a ghetto U.N., a urban commission."

"True."

"But, why do you get the final say? You puttin' up the dough, cool, but if we workin' together, ain't no big I's and little U's."

Roc nodded. "listen...I pledge allegiance to no man's flag, only Allah's cause. Everything this stands for goes against what I believe, but I'm here. I'm here to make a better day for the babies, for the sisters and brothers who *ain't* in the game. I'm here for them, even if it costs me my soul. Ya'll are the blood of our union, all I ask is that you leave the soul to me."

The room fell silent for a moment while everyone thought about what had been said. La Familia spoke first.

"So...how do we get the money?"

Angel explained. "We have accounts for each of you in the Caymans, under dummy corporations. Each of you will be given the name of your corporation and the name of a banker, who will make any and all transfers between accounts related to your corporation. Once you receive the account number, its all yours, and you can do with it what you will.

"And let every man be as good as his word, and let his word represent the honor of his family. Whoever violates, let his blood run in the streets," Roc vowed, and then - one by one - each organization voiced their acceptance and agreement.

As Roc looked around the room at all the smiling faces and shaking hands, he appreciated the fact that unity had begun. What kind of unity, he dreaded to think of its implication, but at least it was unity, and he knew, it had to start somewhere.

** ** ** ** **

"Nina, you ride like a pro," Goldilocks complimented her as they brought their horses to a stop, overlooking the valley below.

"Thank you."

"No wonder you got them equestrian thighs," Goldilocks giggled.

Nina didn't know how to take that compliment, considering who it was coming from.

"No, I'm not trying to come onto you, if that's what you're thinking. Just a compliment from one beautiful Black woman to another," Goldilocks explained.

"In that case, thank you again," Nina replied, with an awkward snicker. They both looked out at the picturesque landscape laid out before them - the distant mountaintops, seemingly poking right into the sky to the valley below.

"This is so beautiful," Goldilocks sighed.

"Yeah, a long way from the projects," Nina agreed.

"Did you ever think that you would be this rich?" Goldilocks looked at Nina.

"You sound like R. Kelly."

"Not just money, but everything. A beautiful wedding, a chateau in France, a gorgeous, loving husband...with some thug in 'em and, of course, the money don't hurt," Goldilocks joked, and they both laughed.

"Yeah," Nina responded with a hint of melancholy, "it's almost too good to be true."

This bitch, Goldilocks thought. She wanted to hear Nina's happiness, to enjoy the fact that she was about to take it all away from her. Everything...including her life.

"You know what I feel like doing?" Goldilocks said.

"What?"

"Shopping. I haven't had a chance to really ball out since we've been here; you?

"A little, while we were in Paris, Dutch took me to a Black designer's fashion show."

Goldilocks turned to her enthusiastically, "Let's go!"

"You mean, now? I don't –"

"Yeah, now...why not now? Come on, girl! It ain't like you on a budget, and I know these great places near Cannes! It'll be fun," Goldilocks urged her.

Nina thought about it. Things were a little boring when Dutch wasn't there, and she *did* love to shop. "What the hell, you only live once, right?"

Goldilocks smiled devilishly, "Exactly."

** ** ** ** **

"That was Rahman. He says that the streets are ready," Dutch informed Ceylon as he hung up the phone. He and Ceylon were just entering St. Tropez. They were being chauffeured in Ceylon's Phantom heading for the Zanzibar, where the meeting with the cartels was to be held.

"I understand the need for preparations, Dutch, but I hope you will allow me to deal with the Italians and the Russians... diplomatically," Ceylon offered.

Dutch lit his cigar. "C, you handle the politics, let me handle the streets. You make the law wit' these paper gangstas and I'll deal wit' the real ones, okay?"

"So, shall we anticipate another bloodbath, after the month of murder?" Ceylon probed.

Dutch smirked, "Power only respects power, C, you know that."

"But violence is like salt...too much, spoils the dish. Believe me, my young friend, I understand the use of force, but you have proven yourself a formidable ally. You have the unofficial backing of France and Turkey, mongst men who play the world like chess," Ceylon explained. It wasn't that Ceylon disagreed with Dutch's intentions; he just loved to test the minds of men.

"Yeah, but on the streets, the Italians won't budge. Russians are like machines...once we solidify the cartels, they won't give up. So now, we take it to *them*. We take it to Bensonhurst, we take it to their Catholic churches, we take it to their *homes*, wives and kids until they *fully* understand that nothing moves in the hoods, unless its through our commission, *period*. We been puppets in our hood for too long, it's time to cut the strings," Dutch growled, flicking his ashes from his cigar.

"How ironic, when it was the Italians who supported you in the beginning," Ceylon quipped.

Dutch turned to him, eyes ablaze, until he saw the smirk on Ceylon's face and he knew he was trying to get a rise out of him. "I owe them nothing, not even Fat Tony. I appreciate everything he did, but I owe him nothin'. I saw an opportunity and I took it. Isn't that what you did wit' me to keep the Nigerians out of the game?" Dutch smirked.

Ceylon nodded, "Indeed."

"Then," Dutch said, looking Ceylon in his eyes, "I'd say, all debts are paid, no?"

Ceylon grinned, "Certainly, my young friend, all debts are indeed paid"

Dutch held Ceylon's gaze a moment longer, until he was satisfied that he was understood. Dutch owed him nothing either. Regardless of circumstance, they needed each other and Dutch would make sure that Ceylon wouldn't forget.

Ceylon on the other hand, had already received word that the Nigerians wanted to speak with him, a message to which he had yet to respond. The outcome of the meeting would tell which way the pendulum would swing.

** ** ** ** **

Dutch watched the limousines of the cartels arrive, nine in total. He stood on the third deck of the Zanzibar watching the men get out of their cars, all complete with one or two bodyguards. The nine men were the heads of the largest cocaine cartels in the world. The majority of them were dressed in pastel colored casual suits and appeared to be in their fifties and sixties. Dutch marveled at the fact that so few men controlled an industry that generated trillions of dollars throughout the last twenty years. Since the eighties, street level soldiers had been their chief power, scrambling for a piece of the pie, only to be set up, locked up and straight up murdered by the same federal authorities that made deals with these very men to flood the country.

But, it was just business, and Dutch wasn't mad or bitter. Business was business. Today would be business as well. Like Jay said, *I'm overchargin' nigguhs for what they did to the Cold Crush…*

Dutch provided a bevy of women for the elite entourage, many of which were topless or totally nude, sunbathing on the lower deck. As the yacht sailed out into Cote d'Azure, Ceylon introduced Dutch to each man, personally. They ate lunch and then reconvened deck side to conduct their meeting over drinks and cigars.

"Gentlemen, I trust you enjoyed your meal?" Ceylon inquired.

"Eh," the head of the Arellano cartel grunted, a heavyset man in his early sixties. "the French, they eat like mice, itty bitty. Hardly a meal for men, eh?"

154

"The French believe in moderation, Manuel. Too much of a good thing spoils a man."

The man waved his hand dismissively. "I'll worry about moderation when I'm dead," he huffed, his chubby finger wrapped around his cigar.

"Omar, the meal was, as the French say, magnifique, but the women are even better," the head of the Camorra cartel praised. He was in his forties and resembled the singer, Marc Anthony, in his style and manner.

"That's the dessert," Dutch remarked without smiling, but the group found it amusing.

Dutch looked from face to face, sizing up the men in attendance. Many of the men appeared soft.

He wondered how they got to the positions they had, because very few possessed the cold glint of a killer's eye. The only one who did, was also the youngest – Jorge Quintero.

At thirty-six, he was already the head of the Medellin cartel. Columbian born, but no stranger to the streets of Miami and New York. He remained straight faced, but cordial. He didn't mingle with the women. Dutch had watched, and could tell he was ready to get down to business.

"Gentlemen, I realize that your time is money, so is mine," Dutch said, sipping his drink. "The nine of you together represent 85% of the cocaine distribution in the world. Ceylon and his people facilitate and maintain a large percentage of its distribution. And I...will represent the man that can put you all out of business," Dutch smirked, meeting Jorge's gaze long enough to make his point.

The rest of the group grumbled their dissent.

"What Mr. James meant," Ceylon interjected, trying to smooth ruffled feathers, "is that he and I wish to be *in* business with you, so we summoned you here in hopes that we could negotiate the terms."

"Omar, is this some type of joke? I fail to find it funny," said the head of the Cali cartel.

"Who is this man that threatens my business?!" Manuel barked with a glimmer of a killer in his eyes.

"I assure you, gentlemen, it is no joke, nor is it meant as a threat," Ceylon assured them. "Please hear him out, because we can all benefit from the proposal."

Dutch leaned forward, resting his elbows on his knees, the sun glistening off of is diamond bezel.

"In this business, it makes no difference to me. I mean no one any disrespect, but I want to be clear that there is only one way...my way. Otherwise, let the chips fall where they may," Dutch said, pulling a small zip-lock bag full of cocaine from his pocket and handing it to the closest man to his right. "Please, pass that around."

Dutch waited while the bag went around. Some tasted it, some just examined it, while others dismissed it arrogantly. Jorge received it, turning it over in his hands.

"It's cocaine," shrugged the head of the Camorra cartel.

"Yes and no," Dutch corrected him, its cocaine, but not like you've ever seen it. It's a hybrid of the coca and the poppy. Smoked, shot or sniffed...it's a cocaine high, but within three days, it packs a heroin addiction. One hit of this and no other coke'll do."

The men spoke in Spanish in mumbles to one another.

"By *no other coke*, you mean our coke, no?" Asked the Marc Anthony looking cat.

Dutch's reply was his smile.

"Omar?" Stammered Manuel.

"Yes, gentlemen, what my young friend states, is true," Ceylon answered the unasked question.

"How much?"

"Forty billion," Dutch replied.

"Forty what?! Es loco!" Manuel exclaimed.

"I'm not askin' forty of each of you, no," Dutch corrected him calmly. "Although I could, and you'd either pay, or go out of business, but –"

"Or go to *war* mi amigo, and settle it in steel," growled the head of the N'drangheta' cartel.

"Then what?" Dutch countered. "Once it hits the streets, your cocaine will be obsolete. But, I'm not tryin' to start a war. The forty billion will be paid in quarters for the first year, collectively. Eleven percent from each of you, which is 4.4 billion the first year. For every four ounces you produce, you add one of mine, a quarter to every kilo. Not only will you save money, you will also make more in the end."

"How so?"

"You cut back production relative to what you use of my product, and at the same time, raise prices at the wholesale level. With mine, you can cut as much as you like, and it won't lose its addictive kick. The quality of coke will suffer, but the fiend will still be hooked. Once the streets see this, they'll decrease street level volume, thereby decreasing their demand from you. You save on both ends," Dutch smirked, then sat back and let the men discuss it.

"Omar," Manuel began, "surely you understand, this is a decision that will take time –"

"No, it's a deal you must not refuse," Dutch cut him off firmly, "or I'll put it out at 65%, starting in Miami and New York. We will agree collectively *today*, or you can find out if steel could take back the tidal wave of change."

"I have no doubt that this is what you say," Jorge spoke up, "nor that you won't do what you say. It would be foolish to go to war, not when you're offering me a chance to get rich. I will pay."

The other men looked at Jorge in amazement. Feverish Spanish whispers blew ear to ear like the French breeze.

"When do we pay first quarter?" Manuel wanted to know.

"Within exactly seven days. Anyone falters and..." Dutch let his voice trail off, insinuating the consequences.

"Gentlemen, consider what my young friend is proposing. It is not an ultimatum, merely an ingenious plan to monopolize the market. Besides, Mr. Quintero has already voiced his support."

The men knew young Quintero would pay what he had to in order to join Dutch in effectively bankrupting their operations. They had no choice, and many saw the potential as well. One by one, they voiced their consent and Dutch stood up.

"I hope there are no hard feelings between us," he began, holding up his drink, "a toast, if you will."

The men stood with him and raised their glasses.

"To success...by any means necessary."

Not many understood the significance of Dutch's toast, but Jorge certainly did.

"Now, for dessert," Manuel remarked lustfully, licking his lips at all the eye candy.

The group broke up to mingle with the women and only Jorge remained. He walked up to Dutch with his hand extended and Dutch shook it.

"You and I are very much alike, no? We're both young, know what we want, and nothing will stop us from getting it. I will pay 2.5," Jorge stated, sipping his drink.

Dutch just looked at him.

"Believe me, Dutch, without me, we would've never reached an agreement. The Spanish don't like ultimatums."

Dutch nodded. "Ultimatums should never make a man refuse a profitable deal. Four even."

"War would cost us both a lot of time and money. You wanted it no more than we. Three even."

"But, you had more to lose. 3.5 or 4.4," Dutch smirked.

Jorge shrugged, good naturedly. "Beggars can't be choosey, 'eh?" They shook hands on the reduced price and Jorge added, "I like you Dutch. We will talk again soon."

Jorge started to walk away, but Dutch called him back. "Quintero," he said, "3.3 and we'll *definitely* talk again." Dutch knew that an ally on the inside would come in handy, and so, as always, he saw an opportunity, so he took it.

** ** ** ** **

"Nina, are you ready? The drivers waitin' for us," Goldilocks called out from the living room. She then turned to Delores. "You sure you don't want to go shopping with us?"

"Naw, Baby...Bernard ain't feelin' too well, so I better stick around. Maybe next time."

Goldilocks would've loved to literally kill two birds with one stone, but Delores wouldn't bite.

Goldilocks mentally shrugged it off, because she already had other plans for Delores.

Nina came downstairs, clipping on her earrings, with her purse under her arm. "I had to find my purse."

"Cannes, here we come, Maybe we'll get to see some stars," Goldilocks teased.

"I know, right, maybe I should bring my camera," Nina chuckled.

Outside, the driver waited beside the back door of the vintage Rolls Royce. He tipped his hat as the two young women approached. Goldilocks' cell phone went off, playing the sounds of

50 Cent's Window Shopper and she held up a finger, then stepped away from Nina.

"Hello?"

"You called me?" Angel asked, riding with M'Baye.

"Yes," Goldilocks spoke lowly, "When are you coming back? We really need to talk."

Goldilocks had called Angel a few minutes earlier and paged her via voicemail. She just needed her phone to ring, so the conversation was really of no significance.

"Soon."

"How soon?"

"Soon as I'm finished."

CLICK

Goldilocks closed her phone and went back to the car. Nina was already inside, and the driver continued to hold the door open.

"Bad news, girl," Goldilocks simpered.

"Is everything okay?"

"Oh, yeah, nothing like that. But Angel's on her way and she needs me to go with her to handle something. I'm gonna have to stay behind," she explained, trying her best to sound disappointed.

"Oohh, but I don't want to go by myself. I'll just stay –"

"No, no...don't let this monkey stop your show," Goldilocks giggled. "Go on and enjoy yourself."

"But, I don't know nothing about no Cannes."

"You're familiar with Cannes, aren't you?" Goldilocks asked the driver.

"Very," he assured her.

"And you'll take good care of my girl?"

"The best," he smiled.

"Then, its settled. Go ball out," she said, adding in a sultry whisper, "Buy something sexy for your husband."

Nina sighed. "Maybe I will."

The driver closed the door and the thud sounded like the closing of a coffin to Goldilocks. She had no intentions of getting into that car – not after having cut the brake line. She was an expert in sabotage and brake lines were child's play. She had severed it almost completely, knowing that the steep decline to the road below would take care of the rest.

She watched as the driver pulled off. The last thing she saw was Nina's smiling face, waving good-bye.

** ** ** ** **

"I took the liberty of having the deposits spread out between the Caymans and Switzerland," Ceylon told Dutch.

"Cool. But if we ain't clickin' forty in seven days, then I'll need distribution into Miami," Dutch replied. He was dead serious on the deadline.

"Not a problem."

"And make sure everything is straight with the gang's accounts. I wanna make sure I keep my word."

Dutch looked out at the passing landscape. They were only a few miles from the estate and he couldn't wait to get back and celebrate with his wife.

** ** ** ** **

"I hope I can find a sexy bustier and thong set, Dutch will love to come home and see me in that," she mused to herself, a glowing smile on her face. It was a beautiful day and the view from the mountain path was breathtaking. But it seemed like something was wrong.

The path was narrow and steep, but the driver seemed to be treating it like the Autobahn – they were going too fast. The driver had already noticed, but when he went to press the brake, his foot went clean to the floor.

** ** ** ** **

"Who's Quintero?" Dutch wanted to know.

"Quite simply, a very dangerous man. He assumed control of the cartel after his father's assassination. Many believe that it was Jorge himself that pulled the trigger. He's a Columbian national and travels with a diplomatic passport, therefore, he is virtually untouchable."

"I like him already."

** ** ** ** **

Nina was too scared to scream. The driver fought the winding curves desperately, but, faced with a solid wall of stone and a hundred foot drop, his chances of controlling the automobile were slim to none. Nina reached for the door handle on the left side of the car and pushed the door open, only to have it slammed back shut as the Rolls Royce slammed into the side of the rocky mountain wall. The window shattered and sprayed back in her face, causing her to close her eyes.

It was then that she felt the car fishtail hard to the right, sending it onto its side. She felt her body slam up against the floor of the car, which was now vertical, sliding uncontrollably toward the edge of the path. She knew when she no longer felt the car bumping and twisting, when she no longer heard the pelt of the gravel against the steel body of the automobile exactly what had happened – the car was now airborne.

There was an eerie silence as the wind whistled in through the busted window. The door, now free to open, flapped in the air like a wounded wing. Nina prepared herself, knowing that in seconds, the impact of the ordeal was inevitable.

Her stomach fluttered, like falling in a dream and she wished she could open her eyes once more, see the sun just one more time, see Dutch smile one last time…but it wasn't to be. In those last few moments, she regretted nothing, not even the choice she had made, which ultimately led to this.

She had chosen to love, and in more ways than she could've imagined, chose to give up the only life she had ever known. Her last thoughts were a prayer for peace, and her last words were a whispered, "I love you," that she knew would reach Dutch's heart.

** ** ** ** **

"We have a few weeks before any sustained activity. I have a villa in Bordeaux, I offer you, and your lovely wife," Ceylon smiled.

"I accept. Maybe then I can work on that masculine child you spoke about," Dutch chuckled.

"Enjoy your life, my young friend. We only get one."

"I intend to."

Dutch and Ceylon were almost upon the estate. He could see the majestic chateau atop its mountain plateau. Below, he saw the multicolored valley…and smoke.

A frown creased his brow, and then grew deeper as they came closer and he could see the mangled remains of the Rolls Royce. It had landed on it roof with such impact, that all of the windows had shattered, and one door sat open and off its hinges.

"Stop the car," he hoarsely voiced, then repeated, "Stop the fuckin' car!"

Something was wrong. Something was terribly wrong and his gut instinct only confirmed it.

Ceylon noticed the wrecked automobile as the driver skidded to a stop and Dutch leaped out.

From the roadside, the valley was only about a ten foot drop, but with a comfortable decline.

Dutch hurried down through the thickets of bramble, thinking nothing of his outfit as he slipped and slid his way up to the smoking car. He saw the driver, literally stuck to the windshield, eyes opened, but sightless – in a death gaze. He quickly scanned the back seat, hoping, praying and demanding that it not be…that's when he saw her.

The one that was different…the one that had stolen his heart because he had to earn her presence…the one he had pledged his love to, meant to spend the rest of his life with, and despite who he was and all he money he had, or could ever make, there she was…dead.

Her body was contorted in such a grotesque position that he had to look away from the sight.

Her beauty was bruised, bloody and battered. Her neck had broken on impact. Dutch's whole body went numb and his mind froze.

He looked up at Ceylon, who looked down at him. He wanted to ask Dutch if everything was alright, but the look on Dutch's face told him that it wasn't and he dropped his head. Dutch turned back to the car, rapidly blinking his eyes, trying to regain focus, wondering why the world all around him became blurred. Then he realized that his blurred vision came from the tears in his eyes and he did nothing to stop them from silently falling to the ground.

** ** ** ** **

"Joseph."

"His heart?"

"Shattered on the valley floor."

"Crush him…slow."

"I intend to. And, by next Mother's Day, he will have nothing to celebrate.

** ** ** ** **

Halle Berry didn't have shit on Goldilocks' Academy Award winning performance. When the news came back to her of the successful assassination, she didn't cry, she didn't scream and wail…she simply fainted. Right there - before Ceylon, Dutch, Delores, Bernard Sr. and a few of the servants.

"Oh my God! Goldilocks, are you okay?" Delores exclaimed hysterically. "Someone, please get her some water…get her to the couch!"

Two servants carried her to the couch where Delores cradled her head in her lap until she regained consciousness. Goldilocks was a master at manipulation, so she knew that to approach Dutch with her grief directly would be counterproductive. Despite the weakness she was creating in him, she knew he was still a very dangerous man, cobra-like in his strike of lethalness, so the volatility she had brought out could go either way – for or against her. So instead, she worked on Dutch's solace and where he'd naturally seek solace – his mother.

"No, no…don't get up, baby…relax. My God, my God, what happened, Bernard?" she questioned Dutch, but he was beyond words, sitting blankly in the armchair – no tears, no expression, nothing.

"Why, Miss Delores?" Goldilocks sobbed into her bosom. "Why? Sh-she was so *happy?* So…so…" her voice broke up in sobs, "if she didn't deserve happiness, then who does?" she asked with a double meaning to her question.

Dutch didn't respond, but he heard. He got up from his chair and headed for the stairs.

"Bernard…where are you going?" Delores asked. "Please, Baby, talk to me."

Dutch went up the stairs, drained of his usual swagger. Dutch was a logical man who understood the balance of relativities, but the world can sometimes be cruel to a man of cold, calculating logic. He could understand cause and effect, action and reaction and friends and enemies.

His whole reign had been based on the accurate assessment of his enemies and his swift merciless response. Any losses he suffered, he had inflicted doubly, but in *this* loss – one so full of meaning – *who could he inflict? What enemy could he single out for blame, and therefore unleash his painful rage?* There was no one, so his rage became guilt. He blamed himself because Dutch believed in the fact that he was maker of his own destiny so, if he took credit in victory, it was only logical that he bear the brunt of the loss.

He had seduced Nina, not with ill intent, but the most sincere of intentions – to make her his wife. Now, she was dead and her blood was on his hands…and that hurt the most.

It is said that it is better to have loved and lost than to never have loved at all. For men like Dutch, the opposite was true. For those who aspire to be notorious - the ruthless and cold – it is better to have never experienced the life energy called love, because its absence leaves a void. That void is inevitably filled with confusion, then an acute bitterness, and finally, a hardening of hate. Great men have been destroyed by the cancer of love and Dutch inwardly struggled not to become one of them.

He sat on the bed, hands tented beneath his chin, looking at the wedding portrait of he and Nina when he heard a light knock on the opened door. He looked up to the doorway and saw that it was Goldilocks, her face red and puffy, in her hand a cell phone.

"It…its, Dada. She wants to speak to you."

He wanted to be alone, but he knew that if he didn't take the call, she would just keep calling, so he took the phone.

"Me and Roc are on our way," was the first thing she said.

"No, stay there, I'm ai-ight," Dutch lied.

"Bullshit," she spat. "Besides, it's on fire out here. I'll tell you the rest later," she added. Paris was about to become combustible. Dutch remained silent, so she concluded, "It's cool if M'Baye comes, too?"

"Whatever," Dutch replied, then hung up. Though he would never admit it, it felt good to have family at a time like this. He turned around to find Goldilocks still standing in the door and gave her back the cell phone.

"I...I just wanted to say that," she stammered, nervously wringing her hands, "I understand what you're going through, because I once...I once lost someone close to me," she finally got out, looking up and into his eyes. "Not like a spouse, but they...they meant a lot to me, a lot to the people I love. It still hurts," Goldilocks confessed, a tear of deception trickling down her cheek. "So, I know you are hurting. I just wanted you to know I'm...I'm sorry."

It would be the closest Goldilocks could come to concealing the truth of her presence, but she had to look him in the eyes and justify her actions – to claim her victory even if only one of them understood.

Dutch took it in stride, thanking her with a nod of his head, then turning away from her and refocusing his gaze on the portrait. Goldilocks smiled behind his turned back and then went back downstairs.

Chapter Ten

From M'Baye's tenth floor apartment, Roc could see the lights of Paris. To the south stood the Eiffel Tower. He could also see Sacre' Couer Church atop Mont Marte, its lights theatrical in brilliance. The elegance of Paris City's illumination was in direct contrast to the inferno that Clichy-sous-Bois had become. The poverty, degradation and frustration had finally ignited n the Parisian ghettos, sparked by the same thing that had sparked many American riots – the police.

Like Watts, Newark and Detroit, the riots were the result of the death of Zyed Benna and Bouna Traore. They had been electrocuted after climbing into an electrical substation, being chased by the police. The riot took off from there and the projects exploded like a time bomb. Roc and M'Baye had been in the streets witnessing the destruction first hand.

Cars were set ablaze all along the streets like huge metal torches, lighting the path into madness.

Molotov cocktails exploded all around them, igniting the police precinct and police cars. Fires danced in the windows of buildings that the youth held in contempt. Even shots had been fired at the confused and retreating police.

In retaliation, the police had tear-gassed a local masjid. Roc was infuriated. They helped the few individuals inside to safety and then, on instinct, Roc let off a clip on a passing police car. The driver's side window was smashed and the bullets barely missed the policeman's head.

"Come my brother, we have to get off the streets," M'Baye warned him, but Roc wanted a war.

He understood the mentality of the riot. To outsiders, it seemed as if they were destroying their own neighborhoods and their own communities. But, in many ways, they weren't *their* communities, they merely lived there. They didn't own the shops and malls, they

168

weren't employed there, so they burned them. They didn't work at Renault, so they burned it. They may have belonged to Clichy-sous-Bois, but Clichy-sous-Bois didn't belong to them and so, they burned it.

In coming days, the riots would spread to other areas, as far as Bordeaux and Lyon. Paris was now, truly a city of lights.

But, for M'Baye, it was dangerous. Being known as a top ranking shot caller in the banlieue, the police would be sure to come after him, question him and maybe worse. So, by extension, Roc, Angel and the heads of the American gangs were in danger. Fortunately, the gang reps were staying in the luxury of Paris City, so they would be safe to return to America. Meanwhile, Roc, Angel and M'Baye had to get out of Clichy-sous-Bois. It was like Escape from New York, with all the police and helicopters swarming the area.

"We can't take my car," M'Baye informed them, "the police will be all over it."

They still had the McLaren, but, it would also draw attention.

Angel shrugged, lighting a cigarette. "Anybody got a snatch car?" she smiled.

Once M'Baye got hold of one from a local mechanic, it wasn't long before they were on their way out of the district in a "throw-up green" '71 BMW - it was half rusted along the body, but it would get them back to the estate.

"Did you time me, Roc? Oh, my fault, it was probably too quick," she bragged; she still had her car thief touch.

M'Baye drove, puffing hard on his cigarette. "It is sad that a man must burn his own home to be heard, yet even then, he is called crazy," he shook his head in disgust. "I will tell you what is crazy…for a man to be humiliated daily, socially spat upon, but he is supposed to bear it with dignity? That is crazy! Then, when this man runs raving out into the streets, beating and killing and torching, then *that* is sanity – the only sanity left for a true man of dignity!"

"When freedom is outlawed, only outlaws will be free," Roc added, quoting Bonz Malone.

"Exactly," M'Baye concurred, "the outlaws, like us, with cunning and cooperation, thwart their absolute power, until such time as we have amassed our own. Then we can join society with honor, but on our terms."

Roc couldn't agree more. Governments the world over had proven that they weren't for the people, and they used the police to not only enforce their laws, but their code of ethics as well. How else could the people get justice if they didn't create their own? Even if that meant selling drugs, so be it.

After all, it took cow shit as fertilizer to grow the food that fed millions. If he hadn't been before, the riot convinced Roc of the justice of Dutch's operation. To him, it was simple, people don't burn buildings if they own them.

The estate was in a state of mourning. Cries were sniffled like everyone had a cold. First, Craze, and now Nina, back to back, therefore a blanket of grief crept into everyone's hearts. When Angel, Roc and M'Baye arrived, they went up to Dutch's bedroom where they found him clutching the half empty wine bottle that was to be his and Nina's tenth anniversary gift to themselves. Since it would never be, Dutch used it to try and drown out the feelings festering inside him.

M'Baye and Roc gave him their condolences, but Angel refused to acknowledge the tragedy.

Instead, she said "You look like a fuckin' drunk."

Dutch glared at her over the rim of the bottle while he took a hard swig.

Angel flipped on the 40 inch wall unit to see the reports of the raging French riots. "Yo, have you seen this shit! Fuckin' France is on fire!" she exclaimed.

"Let in burn," Dutch mumbled, his voice thick and slightly slurred.

"Fuck you mean, let it burn? The last thing we needed in Clichy-sous-Bois was a riot, yo. Its cops everywhere. We barely got everybody outta there. How we gonna use that spot as our base of operations and coordinate our moves back in the states? We damn sure can't do it from here," Angel reminded him.

Even in his inebriated state, Dutch understood the validity of her point. Clichy and the surrounding ghettos were important to the success of the operation. But he couldn't get his mind out of the haze, so he shrugged it off. "Then, we just can't."

"You slippin', D," Angel retorted, "shit can't wait, Roc needs to go back to the states and handle it from there until we can move back into Clichy."

Dutch was sluggish with his assessment, but he agreed with Angel. "Yeah, okay. You and Roc go back and –"

"I'm stayin'," she cut him off.

"Naw, you goin'," Dutch replied, his resolve firm, but his voice not carrying the same aire of authority. "Roc gonna need you."

"So, M'Baye can go. M'Baye…you wit' it?" Angel asked.

"I'm a soldier, Angel. If Dutch say go, then, it's cool wit' me," he told her, careful not to side with Angel because he could see the tension between the two building.

Angel sucked her teeth. "Look at this muhfucka, he fucked up in the head right now. You think I'ma take orders –"

That was all she got out before Dutch grabbed her by the throat and slammed her hard into the wall unit.

"Bitch, don't you ever question my authority…you got that?! Do you?!" Dutch hissed, his grasp on her throat like a steel vise.

Angel gasped for air, clawing at his hand, until Roc moved in to physically intervene.

"Chill, yo. You know how she is, let her go…its cool," Roc told him.

Dutch slowly released her and Angel's body sagged against the wall, her hands on her knees for support. Dutch glared down at her until she looked up and he saw that she was smiling. It was then that he realized what she had been doing.

Angel refused to acknowledge his grief or give condolences to his inebriated state of mind. She knew how to bring him back and it wasn't with hugs and kisses, but with the fire inside that fueled them both. Now that she could see it back in his eyes, her smile confirmed her intentions.

"I still ain't goin'," Angel repeated, her voice dry. "Why shouldn't M'Baye go? If he a link, then he need to know the whole chain, right?" she questioned.

Dutch couldn't deny her logic because it was his own. Angel had been around him so long that she reflected his thought pattern in almost every way. He took another long swig from the bottle, and then slouched down in the chair. "Fuck it, you wanna be boss…be boss."

"Gladly," she retorted, and then turned to Roc and M'Baye. "Ya'll gotta go back to the states for awhile, until Clichy quiets down…make sure the gangs stay on course. Dutch said he gave the cartels seven days, and that's that. If they front and try to throw block, muhfuckas die…period. We got an army now," she smirked. "Que quierele?"

"Dutch?" Roc asked, looking for Dutch's confirmation.

Angel looked over her shoulder at him with a knowing look that knew she'd said what he would've said. He grumbled his agreement, brushing them off as she drunk from the bottle.

Roc and M'Baye nodded and then headed to the door, followed by Angel.

"Angel," Dutch called her, and she turned around, "come here."

She walked over to him.

"Sit down."

Angel sat on the edge of the bed, almost knee to knee with Dutch in the armchair. He eyed her for a moment, then leaned his head back and closed his eyes. They had known each other for so long and been through so much together that words weren't necessary, the presence was comforting enough.

Angel looked at the T.V. screen, watching the fires of the riot blaze in high definition. She lay back, letting the strain of the day be released from her body. Deep inside, she worried about Dutch and how Nina's death would affect him. She had never known him to show his emotions the way he had since seeing him with her, and emotions were dangerous in the high-stakes world in which they dwelled. After all, *hadn't she also fought her own emotions for the time?*

Her mind drifted off, relieving it of the burden of contemplation and she felt the bed compress on the right side. Before she knew it, Dutch's face was so close to hers that she could smell the wine on his breath and his body up against hers.

"Du –" she started to protest, but he pressed his finger to her lips.

"Shhh...remember, I'm the only man you wanted to fuck?" his lips met hers and her protesting became confusion which showed in the rigidness of her kiss. She didn't return it, wanted to fight it, but feeling his hand under her shirt, caressing her stomach, and then up to her breasts, quickened her breath and melted her resistance. She allowed herself to kiss him back, wrapping her arms around his neck and feeling the pleasure of his hand caressing her body.

173

Dutch began to slip his hand into her sweatpants, guiding his fingers towards the garden no man had ever explored. She parted her moistened thighs so he could finally feel...

Her body jolted and she sat upright, breathing hard and looking around. Dutch was still sitting in the chair, asleep. The wine bottle had slipped from his hand and spilled out onto the floor.

It was all a dream...

But, her rapidly beating heart wasn't, nor was the wetness between her legs. She ran her hand through her hair, trying to get her head together, and then she stood to leave. Angel looked back at Dutch, asleep, and then headed to her own room; the dream still vivid in her mind. It was a dream that she hadn't had in awhile, but had many times before.

Before Diamond had turned her out, and Dutch was locked up, she imagined him coming home, she being there to greet him with her virginity. But, at that time, she hadn't fully recovered from the molestation, so she distrusted a man's touch, except in her dreams. Then, once Diamond turned her out on the taste of pussy, she found her release, her intimate satisfaction, something she thought she'd never be able to share with a man.

Then, Dutch came home and it seemed like he treated her just like one of the guys. Like he saw her as a dyke and that was that. So, what she felt, she tried to bury...love became loyalty and her dreams became dormant...until now.

Angel entered her bedroom and found Goldilocks asleep in the bed laying on her stomach, clothed only by the thin silk sheet. Angel stood and listened to her breathe lightly. Goldilocks was indeed beautiful to her. Angel sat on the bed next to Goldilocks, stroking her back gently. She purred lightly, and then rolled over onto her back and looked into Angel's eyes. She saw the lusty quality and welcomed it with a smile.

"I missed you," she whispered to Angel, taking her hand and guiding it down between her legs.

Angel leaned down to kiss her, wrapping her tongue around Goldi's, but it wasn't the same. She went through the act, but her mind was somewhere else.

** ** ** ** **

Roc and M'Baye went to America while Dutch held a private funeral for Nina, which he alone attended. Ceylon gave him permission to bury her in the family graveyard of the estate. Angel disagreed, but she did so silently. She felt that if Craze had been cremated, then so should Nina. But Dutch refused to break his promise to her, feeling like he owed her at least that much. He visited her grave daily, bringing fresh flowers each time. During his period of mourning, Angel handled the business communications with M'Baye and the cartels.

Goldilocks – emboldened by her two successful assassinations - set her sights on the third, and final, murder…Delores.

Since she and Angel's relationship had seemed to solidify, even though it had mellowed, she planned on bringing Angel over to her side once this was all over. To her, it was simple – death, or take over where Dutch had left off with his multi-billion dollar plan.

Delores gave Dutch ample space, trying to be there for him, but not quite knowing how. She had never been very emotionally supportive of her only child. Emotions were something she had to control for so long because of Bernard Sr.'s absence. Since she had to be strong, she had taught Dutch to be strong. Strength was a valuable asset to the James' – an asset she truly regretted instilling in Dutch so much. Seeing him struggle to maintain the strength now, in the face of such a tragic loss, was painful to her, but she truly didn't know how to comfort him.

But Delores also believed in what the old folks say about death coming in threes so, even though Dutch had gotten Bernard Sr. the best doctors on call, she still felt that it was time to go home. She watched the last of the riots on T.V. and the scenes brought back memories of the riot that freed her so many years before. She could still remember the smell of the soot as the store she torched burned to the ground. How truly liberating it felt, so she could understand how the French youth felt.

Despair was a word that every language had an expression for. Although she didn't understand the French reporter, she understood the feeling. But she also knew that when it was all said and done, after all the political promises for more jobs, more activities and more dialogue, that the cycle would just continue. As long as the poor were treated like beasts of burden, they would always resist those shackles with beastly rage.

"Miss Delores," she heard her name being called behind her and it startled her out of her thoughts. She turned to find Goldilocks standing in the door of the living room.

"Oh, I'm sorry, I hope I didn't scare you," Goldilocks apologized.

"Oh, no chile, just lost in my own thoughts," she replied, turning back to the screen. "It's just a shame what folks gotta do to be treated like somebody in this world."

Goldilocks looked at the T.V. screen as well. "I know. It really is sad," she replied, but inside she felt like, *let them eat cake.*

"Back in my day, James Brown had a song where he said, *I don't want nobody givin' me nothin'. Just open the door and I'll get it myself.* That's how them folks is feelin', 'cept they openin' the door for *theyself*, she snickered.

"I heard there were a lot of riots back in the 60's and stuff. Sounds like you know first hand.

That was many years ago, baby…many, *many* years. I'm old and disillusioned now," Delores replied wistfully.

Goldilocks nodded. "Well, I was just about to fix me some tea. Would you like a spot?" she asked, mocking an English accent.

"Tea sounds nice," Delores accepted, "now how do we say it in French for these servants? I know they speak some English, actin' like they don't," Delores huffed good naturedly.

"Don't worry, I'll get it," Goldilocks gladly offered, heading for the kitchen.

Inside, she found one of the maids cleaning the counter.

"Would you go and check on Miss Delores, in the living room? Ask her does she want sugar."

The maid nodded, then left the kitchen, leaving Goldilocks alone to carry out her plan. She knew she had to work quickly, but she moved with the air of confidence of a seasoned professional. She poured the water over the two tea bags in bone colored teacups. In the palm of her hand was a vial of the same poison Angel had used at Rell's party, and she smiled at the memory. Once Miss Delores drank it, Goldilocks would be sure to excuse herself and head off towards the horse stables, where her gun was stashed.

Angel would surely recognize the greenish bile that Delores would spew, but the time had come, so if she did, then so be it. Goldilocks untwisted the lid, looking around one last time before she dumped the poison into Delores' cup.

"Goldi."

Goldilocks froze in place, then looked up to see Angel standing in the door.

"What you doin'?" she asked, with just a hint of suspicion in her voice, brow furled. She had come in and seen Goldilocks taking furtive glances, and that sent off a tiny alarm in her instincts.

Goldilocks masked her surprise while she palmed the vial, hoping that Angel hadn't seen it.

"Oh, I was just fixing me and Miss Delores some tea. Want some?" she offered, trying to read Angel's expression, her calculating mind racing.

Angel was usually armed, out of habit, even on the estate. If she saw her with the vial, Goldilocks knew that one of them would have to die right there.

Angel looked at her curiously and something deep down told her that something wasn't right, but there was nothing to connect her suspicions to. "Naw," she said slowly, "I'm cool. Why you ain't get the maid to do it?"

Goldilocks picked up the tray and approached Angel. Now that she was in striking distance, she felt more confident about controlling the situation, should one arise. "Because, my French ain't good enough," she giggled, "Besides, I didn't mind," she shrugged, then moved past Angel, heading for the living room.

Angel walked behind her, so there was no way that she could empty the vial into Delores' teacup. So, she simply set the vial on the table, then handed Delores a cup.

"Thank you, baby," Delores said, taking the cup from her.

"My pleasure," Goldilocks responded, thinking *You one lucky bitch. There must really be a God.'*

"Oh, hello, Angel. How are you today?"

"Fine, Miss Delores," Angel smiled, her gaze returning to Goldilocks once more.

"And my son?" Delores asked, because she knew that Angel was the chief liaison while Dutch got his head together.

Angel shrugged, "He'll be okay. He just need a few days to shake it off."

Delores sipped her tea and Goldilocks silently cursed, wishing that she could see the look on her face as the life drained from it.

"Do me a favor, baby...tell him that I need to see him," Delores asked Angel.

"Goldi, go get Dutch," Angel told her.

"No problem," Goldilocks said, then left the room.

Delores studied Angel over the rim of her cup. The silence was awkward for Angel, so she turned her attention to the T.V..

"I'm glad...Bernard has someone like you at a time like this," Delores commented. As a woman, she could see the devotion Angel had to Dutch and she also knew how Angel felt about Nina and the marriage.

"We family, he'd do the same thing for me," Angel replied, still not meeting Delores' gaze.

"Family would've come to the wedding," Delores quipped, with a smirk.

Angel shot her a look, ready to justify her position, but Delores continued.

"Now, I'm not signifyin' or tryin' to imply nothin' about you, sugar, but woman to woman...I know, so I'm simply expressing my gratitude for the position you play in my son's life."

An expression flickered in Angel's eyes, but before she could express it, Dutch entered the room.

"Ma...you wanted to see me?"

Angel excused herself, so they could be alone.

"Sit down, Bernard."

Dutch took a seat next to his mother on the couch, glancing at the T.V. screen while Delores studied his profile. His smooth, dark brown skin stretched taut over his strong jaw line, which flexed rigidly when he was upset. His presence exuded authority and power so she knew that he had been willing himself not to feel. She knew, because it was what she had taught him. Now, as she reached out her hand to comfort him, the contact felt awkward and strange.

"How you feelin', Bernard?"

He cocked his head to the side with a shrug. "I just lost my man and my wife, back to back…I'm still tryin' to figure out what I feel, Ma, for real."

"Yes, Chris was like a son to me. He will be truly missed."

"Yeah, no doubt."

"And Nina…I really liked Nina. She was a beautiful person and she loved you so much."

Dutch nodded solemnly. "Believe me, Ma, I felt the same way. I mean, I had always told myself that females…relationships…they just wasn't worth it. I used to see catz in prison waitin' on mail call like they life depended on it. Seen chicks feed their man to the sharks," he shook his head, thinking of the treacherous Simone, "but, when I met Nina, it was never like that kind of vibe, man…never…she made me think, you know? Havin' a family… kids…the whole nine. Then, things happened. It got hot and I had to bounce, but I never forgot about her. Now, she's gone and I don't understand," Dutch admitted, leaning forward and tenting his hands under his chin.

"By *things happened*, do you mean your trial?" Delores inquired.

Dutch nodded.

"That…that was a hard time for me as well, Bernard," Delores spoke with her head lowered, then looked up at him, "and I don't know why you did, but…do you regret it?" she asked?

"Do I regret it? Regret what? Should I regret that a man too cowardly to face me in my world turned me over to his?" he said, referring to Frankie Bonno's deal with the D.A., "or should I regret that cracka' bastard in that black robe tryin' to play God wit' my life, like they do nigguhs seven days a week? Or should I regret those twelve people in the box waitin'…itchin' to take my life…my freedom?

180

Naw, Ma, I don't regret it. I don't regret it worth a damn," Dutch stated firmly as he stood up.

"Is that what you think? That you're free? You're not free, Bernard. Look around you. You can't even send Chris home to be buried by his mother because then, they may know where you are," Delores pointed out. "And what about Nina? Her mother will never know what happened to her own child. You call that free? You may not be locked up in one of their prisons, but you're still enslaved to their system."

"Yeah, well...I got a lovely view from my cell," he retorted sarcastically. "I got St. Tropez as a rec yard and five star chefs in the chow hall. A free man should be so lucky."

Delores got up and slowly went over to him. "And a dead best friend and a dead wife to visit you...don't forget that...because, when it's all said and done, that's what you'll remember most. Not what you had, but what you lost," she told him gently.

"Ma...I don't want to argue with you –"

"Nor I with you, Bernard, I just want you to take a long, hard look at your life and ask yourself one thing...is it worth it? Is what you've gained worth what you've lost...because if it is, you're bound to lose more. But, if it isn't, then all you'll have is regrets," she kissed him on his cheek. "I love you, Bernard, but I can't be a part of this anymore. Your father and I are ready to go home."

"Whatever, Ma. If that's what you want, I'll make the arrangements right away," Dutch replied reluctantly. Deep inside, he felt that his mother was abandoning him like she did during his prison bid.

"Thank you, Bernard." She answered with regret in her tone. She knew her son was too headstrong to understand the wisdom in her words. She knew something wasn't right and she hated that Dutch refused to see it.

** ** ** ** **

When Goldilocks found out that Delores and Bernard Sr. were leaving, she cursed herself for letting them get away. His mother would've been the icing on her torturous cake. She could just imagine the anguish Dutch would've felt, the look on his face once he knew it had been her who had taken it all from him, and then she would claim his head in revenge for Kazami.

Although she didn't kill Delores, she was still pleased with the fact that she was leaving him, which seemed to be causing him another kind of pain, and that, brought her an enormous amount of pleasure - the type of pleasure that a black widow must feel watching her mate crawl into her web.

Dutch would die, for that was her mission, but she would taste him first, because that would be her pleasure. Power turned her on and powerful men made her cream, especially when she had them at her mercy, and that's where she felt she had Dutch.

** ** ** ** **

Dutch relaxed in his large, oval shaped bathtub in his spacious bathroom. Now that his mother and Bernard Sr. were gone, he tried to block their absence out of his mind. She had never been a truly emotional part of his life, so it wasn't hard to do. Still, he had hoped that they could start fresh. He had wanted her to be a part of his and Nina's life, give her grandkids and maybe establish that family life that had always eluded him.

Then, he found out that his father was alive and coming along with her, straining their reunion and ruining any chances of creating a stronger bond, because she was trying to forge another bond between the two men that she loved. Resisting Bernard Sr. was like resisting her, and so all of Dutch's intentions had been turned in reverse, creating more distance than closing it.

But, one thing had come out of it all – he had met his father. At first, he resented his presence, and then hated him as a man. But watching him with his mother, the few talks they'd had and his smooth style, he came to have a grudging respect for the man, even giving him a manly hug before they left in the helicopter. He planned on seeing them again after the operation got established.

His thoughts turned to the forty billion dollars and brought a smile to his face. The cartels had only a few days left to comply with his ultimatum. He had become more than a drug boss or drug lord, Dutch had become a drug terrorist. His plan of extortion was ingenious, and his political backing with Ceylon, uncontested. With Roc and M'Baye securing his street alliance, the day would come where he'd be the Pope of the underworld, either with Ceylon's approval, or without it. With all his pieces and pawns in order, his position was secured and a total checkmate was inevitable.

He heard a knock at the door, but before he could ask who it was, Angel came into the bathroom.

"I'm glad you wasn't shittin', yo," she cracked, walking over and sitting on the edge of the tub.

Dutch shook his head. "Fuck you bother to knock for if you just gonna bust in?" he smirked.

"Common courtesy. I just spoke with Roc. They still in Miami and shit is cool," she informed him.

"Some of the cartels already paid up. Three more days, if it ain't all accounted for, then we flood Miami."

Angel agreed.

"What you know about a cat named Quintero?"

"Pedro Quintero? He did run the Medellin cartel, but he got mercked."

"Yeah, by his son, Jorge…that's the cat I'm talkin' about."

"What about him?"

"I like Duke. He's hungry –"

"Or greedy…"

"Same difference," Dutch smirked. "He pulled some slick shit at the meeting with the cartels. Nothin' foul, but I dig his approach. Plus, he's got connects to make shit happen. I think we should put a bug in his ear, you feel me...set up a one on one and see where his head is at."

Angel nodded, reaching her hand into the water and scooping up a handful of bubbles. "But, we can't forget the Cali cartel, because they are the oldest and best established of all of 'em. Whatever we say to Quintero, we need to say to them, too. Even money...then let them create the odds," she suggested, blowing the bubbles softly and watching them rise into the air.

"True indeed," Dutch replied, "you gettin' pretty sharp."

"I learned from the best," she winked.

Having Angel by his side in the game, relaxed his mind. Even the greatest strategist needed a devil's advocate, every Don a consiglieri...and, with Craze gone, Angel was doing a good job taking up the role.

He liked talking to her, because the conversation flowed so smoothly. Their minds were so much alike and they lived in the same world. Talking to Angel was like talking to himself.

"But, how are you gonna trust the gangs in all of this? A hundred million is damn sure enough to get 'em in line, but how do we keep 'em in line? Play 'em against one another, too?" she asked.

Dutch shook his head. "They our allies, not potential enemies. Naw, we maintain the balance at the top, but we control the sets at the base."

"Meaning?"

"The same way we controlled Jersey," he smiled, like it should've been obvious. "*You*...put a team of these high roller chicks together across the map. Scour the big events, All Star weekend, Super Bowl, the Grammy's...shit like that. Remember, control the pussy, control the game. And, when it comes to pussy, you got a helluva tongue game," Dutch said, complimenting her, but Angel didn't take it as one and subtly frowned. "What's wrong?"

"Nothin'," she lied.

"Hand me that towel, yo," he requested.

Angel walked over to the towel rack, removed a heavy burgundy towel and then tossed it to Dutch. He stood up from the tub and began to dry himself off and Angel turned her back to him.

"What's wrong wit' you?" he chuckled, "you seen me naked a thousand times, yo."

"I'm just sayin', man, hurry up and get dressed...mannish muhfucka," she retorted.

"Who you callin' mannish?" Dutch joked, rolling the towel up into a rat tail and snapping Angel on the ass with it.

She didn't see it coming, so she jumped from the surprise. "Owww! Dumb ass! Stop playin'!" she huffed, going into the bedroom.

Dutch came behind her and snapped the towel again, but Angel jumped out of the way and faced him. She tried to keep her eyes from roaming his body, but couldn't keep the blood from rushing to her cheeks.

"I said, stop playin', yo," she repeated more firmly.

Dutch could tell by her tone that she had something on her mind. He wrapped the towel around himself and asked, "What's wrong, Dada?"

"Nothin. I couldn't sleep."

Dutch smiled.

"What's so funny?" she questioned.

"I just ain't heard that in a long time, you know? I remember you used to have them nightmares and shit and you'd come and get in my bed. Cock blockin' on my pussy...I remember that, too."

She smirked, remembering the same. She just never told Dutch that it wasn't always nightmares, sometimes they were ones about him.

"Where was our apartment, Hawthorne Avenue?"

"Naw, Renner..."

"Oh, yeah. I always get it mixed up with the first stash house, remember that? We'd count a hundred thousand and think we was the Rockefellers!" He laughed and she laughed with him.

"Word, right...and Zoom would take all the one dollar bills and throw 'em out the window to the little kids," she added.

"Little kids?? Shit, Craze be runnin' down there, too, callin' Zoom all kind of stupid muhfuckas, talkin' 'bout *that's sneaker money*," Dutch laughed. He shook his head, laughter fading, "That's when we was all together. Family, man...now, it ain't the same."

Angel lowered her gaze, because she felt the same way.

"Yo, you think its worth it? Everything we are now, compared to then...is it worth it?" he questioned her, echoing his mother's words.

"It seem like every time we take it to another level, we lose a piece. First Shock, then Zoom, now Craze and Roc...Roc he wit' us, but he ain't wit' us, you know? He got his cause now...I don't know if its worth it, man. I guess we won't know until the end," she told him.

Dutch gazed at the wedding portrait. "Sometimes I feel like its me against the world, yo."

Angel came over to him and turned his face from the portrait. "Naw, Papi, its *us* against the world...believe that," she assured him.

Neither one of them were aware of the intimate overtures because they were in that place where the platonic lines were blurred.

"I'm not gonna lose, Ma, no matter the cost."

"Then, I'ma play it wit' you...no matter the cost." Angel wrapped her arms around him and hugged him tightly, the blurred lines slowly ebbing completely away. Her head rested on his shoulders, her hands against the wetness of his back.

The embrace lasted longer than one shared between friends, even lifelong friends. The awkwardness of that transitional moment brought Angel's lips to his neck, softly at first, and then, increased in its intensity.

"Dada...wha-" Dutch tried to speak, but Angel silenced him with her lips against his.

⸺ It felt so natural, nothing forced, so she kept her eyes open and on him so that whatever needed to be said, could be expressed with a gaze. Dutch ran his hands up her back, bringing them around to cradle her face. Angel untied the towel from around his waist and let it drop to the floor, pressing herself against his nakedness, his stiffening erection giving her stomach quivers.

Dutch held her face in his hands, checking the certainty of her emotions. *"The only one I wanna fuck..."* He hadn't forgotten those words either.

Angel backed up to the bed, pulling Dutch down on top of her. She was nervous and her body trembled because she was 33 years old and still a virgin, despite the molestation as a child, her hymen was still intact.

Even though Angel had seen Dutch naked many times, Dutch had never seen her naked, so the vision had his complete attention. Her Egyptian bronze tone was flawless, her thick, toned thighs to the crest of her curvaceous hips, her erect nipples the color of black cherries. Dutch looked around their sensitive circumference, then gently bit them, making Angel let out soft whimpers of approval.

"Harder," she breathed.

He bit down harder, squeezing the nipple between his teeth, making her suck in her breath through clenched teeth. Angel planted her feet flat on the bed and guided Dutch between her legs, the scent of her willing wetness beginning to fill the room. She wanted to finally feel him inside of her, the years of dreams hadn't satisfied her need for the tender caresses of foreplay.

Dutch positioned himself over her and she instinctively raised her left leg and rested it on his hip as he guided himself inside of her. Her pussy was so tight that the first few inches made her cry out with passionate anguish. Her virginity felt like the softest place on Earth as Dutch penetrated deeper and deeper, turning her high pitched exclamations into breathless gasps.

Her mouth was open, but nothing would come out. The pain made her want to beg him to stop, but the pleasure wouldn't dare let her until she felt her cherry burst, and then the pain gave way to a pleasure that made her feel like she would lose her mind. Angel propped her right leg up on his hip and began to grind Dutch back until her clit felt swollen, getting fuller and fuller until she exploded, soaking the sheets with her blood and her juices.

** ** ** ** **

Goldilocks was paralyzed, a mixture of rage and pain rooted her to the spot where she stood. They were oblivious to Goldilocks' presence. The cries of passion had brought her from the room she shared with Angel to witness what she called betrayal.

Despite her lies and deception, the truth was, that she really loved Angel, but she had underestimated the bond that Dutch and Angel shared. She thought the emotional influence she had over Angel would be enough to break the bond, but what she was witnessing told her that she had been naïve and foolish.

She convinced herself that Angel had never loved her, that she had only loved Dutch. Now that place in her heart, reserved for Angel, hardened like stone. She decided that Angel would share the same fate as everyone else Dutch loved, but it would be slow and Angel would know who was taking her life.

Then she'd have Dutch all to herself.

Chapter Eleven

M'Baye was in love with Miami – the beautiful weather and the glamorous decadence of the atmosphere. The French Riviera had the same type appeal – the gorgeous females strutting around naked or damn near – but the French Riviera couldn't compare to Miami for one reason alone: the Black women.

M'Baye had a thugged Frenchness that attracted many kinds of females. He had been with beautiful Greek, Italian and German model type chicks, but none of them could hold a candle to the beauty and style of the Black woman. Their thick curvaceousness from thighs to hips, coming through in thongs and strings, attitudes and struts, sexy, sassy – ain't enough silicone been implanted to bring White women into any type of competition.

M'Baye wanted to sample every flavor, and when they found out he was a French nigguh pushing a yellow Ferrari Scaglietti 612 – the high gloss shine blending so well with his chocolate skin tone – they were more than willing to sit on his plate.

"You from Paris, for real?" a thick redbone out of D.C. asked.

"You sho' do tawk funny" said a petite Georgia peach with sweet country grammer.

"Say somethin' in French," a caramel covered Creole out of the N'awlins challenged him, because she spoke it, too.

"Voulez-vous jouer? Je vous attendrai devant l'hotel – Do you want to play? I'll wait for you in front of the hotel.

Creole caramel winked her *Oui*, while the other girls harassed her with their frustration.

"Ohhh, what he say girl?"

"I bet she don't even know."

"Whatever it was, he a nigguh, so I know it had somethin' to do wit' pussy."

M'Baye played the night life hard, frequenting clubs like BED, Club Rollexx and Jimmy'z. Roc dug young M'Baye, but he was worried about his caliber. He knew Dutch wouldn't have put M'Baye on if he wasn't some kind of thoroughbred, but this wasn't Paris, and he truly wondered if the young man could get down for the crown. He seemed too preoccupied with the flash and bling and, in America that could be a problem.

Roc made sure everything was a go in Miami, spending most of his time with Mikelson LaPlanche, a Haitian smuggler out of lil' Haiti. If the cartels didn't comply, then Laplanche's people were going to get Dutch's product over from Europe, once it reached Jamaica, the dread representative from the meeting being on the Jamaican end. The two hundred pound shipment was just a sample, because it would be used on a 3 to 1 ratio with the Jamaican supply, then distributed in the streets of Miami to low level dealers. That alone would be enough to turn Miami out and cause a major loss to any other coke in the city.

But, it didn't come to that. All nine cartels met their first quarter debt of $1 billion dollars each.

Angel told Roc it was all good, so he headed to Newark to check on his own burgeoning oil monopoly.

They had a few days before the real street cleanings would begin, so M'Baye opted to stay in Miami, and then go to Newark later.

"You sure, M? Don't worry, they got clubs in New York, too," Roc remarked sarcastically.

M'Baye caught it, but smirked it off. "No, really...I have business I need to attend to. Three days..."

"Two," Roc countered, holding up two fingers, "Two days!"

M'Baye nodded, then shook his hand. As M'Baye screeched out in the Ferrari, Roc decided to speak to Angel about his sensual appetites. Roc wasn't about doing business with tricks.

** ** ** ** **

191

The Akon and Young Jeezy joint bumped through the exquisite Italian sound system. M'Baye didn't know Young Jeezy, but he knew about Akon. Once he heard that he was Sengalese too, it was all that he played. He'd have to get C. Miller to connect him with Akon.

C. Miller was who he was going to meet at the Solid Gold strip club. He had met him in the V.I.P. section of Club Blue where C. Miller had overheard him speaking French, and being from New Orleans, he'd understood it. They struck up a conversation and a mutual respect.

M'Baye was interested in the rap scene in America. He had a hand in the French scene, dealing with catz like Joey Star, Solaar and Disiz LaPeste. He wanted to build a bridge between the two scenes and figured C. Miller could help.

Once he arrived at Solid Gold, he made his way through the throngs of ballers and would-be's-if-they-could-be's, the jiggling breasts of the lap dancers and waitresses, then entered V.I.P. to find C. Miller laid in the cut, corner booth, surrounded by purple smoke, Moet and three dime chicks.

"Sac pase'," C. Miller greeted him in Creole, shaking his hand and passing him the purple.

"Kap bole'," M'Baye responded, accepting the purple and the once over by the chicks in attendance. He didn't have to say a word to them because his shine spoke for him.

The sounds of Juvenile's *Rodeo Show* gyrated the succulent bodies of the strippers. M'Baye loved the atmosphere of a strip club because it was like being a kid in a candy store.

"I hollered at my peoples about you, ya' heard me? They say you fuck wit' LaPlanche, so you gots to be good people if that mean ass Haitian vouch for ya'," C. Miller joked.

M'Baye inhaled the charm and smirked.

"So, how long you gonna be in the states?" C. Miller inquired.

"A few months, maybe less," M'Baye replied, purposefully remaining vague. "But, while I'm here, I wanna use this opportunity to get connected with the rap scene. Believe me, C, its a lot of money to be made with international distribution, but the way that Def Jam Germany and all them are going about it, is all wrong."

"I feel you, dog...I see a lot of opportunity myself across the water. But ahhh, this ain't the time or place to get into particulars, ya heard me? I just wanted to let you know that you good wit' me, and to hit you wit' my personal cell and two-way."

M'Baye nodded as C. Miller slipped him his card. They talked a while longer about the similarities between New Orleans and France, then C. Miller got a call.

He looked at the number displayed on the Caller ID and then at M'Baye, "Dig, whody, I gotta take this, but you be sho' to get at me. And, if you got a minute, come on through and we'll talk some mo'," C. Miller said as he stood up.

They shook hands, and then C. Miller and the chicks left. M'Baye turned his attention to the two chicks that had kept steady eye contact throughout his conversation with C. Miller. The pair had Angelic faces and bodies of pure temptation. They flirted with gestures and innuendos, making it hard for him to concentrate on what he was talking about.

Once C. Miller had gone, the two chicks rose from their table and made their way over to him.

The closer they got, the hotter they looked. One chick was honey complexioned and almost six feet tall with her six inch, glass bottomed heels. Her tiny mini skirt barely covered her ass and her 38 D's swayed seductively in her bikini top. Shortie had on less clothes than some of the strippers. Her partner was shorter and darker and, where she lacked in the tittie department, she more than made up for in the ass department, giving Buffy a run for her money. By the time they made it over and sat down at M'Baye's booth, he was already mesmerized and rock hard.

The taller chick licked her lips suggestively, revealing her diamond studded tongue ring. "I know you don't mind if we join you."

"Not at all," M'Baye replied. He dug how straight forward and aggressive American chicks could be.

"I'm Tamara, and she's Kiki," the tall chick introduced. "We woulda' come over sooner, but we saw you with C. Miller and them chicks, and we ain't want you to think we on some groupie shit. Plus, we ain't know if you was either."

"Has anybody told you that you look like Tyrese?" Kiki asked, "and I looove me some Tyrese," she purred.

"Tyrese?" he questioned, because he had never heard of him.

His pronunciation of the name prompted Kiki to conclude, "You not from here, are you? You Haitian or somethin'?"

"I'm French, but I'm also somethin' else, if you're not afraid to find out," he gamed with a smirk.

"Well, we're not from around here either," Tamara answered, "and we lookin' to get into a little somethin' like you," she teased.

"Yeah…'cause we speak French, too…menage' trios."

M'Baye snickered smoothly. "Just like that? That's how you do it in America?"

Tamara smirked. "Why waste time when you know what you want? Besides…it's just sex, right?"

"Exactly," he concurred, rising from the booth. "Shall we?"

"We shall," Kiki giggled.

The three of them made their way out of the club and to the parking lot. M'Baye walked them over to a red Nissan Z and Tamara chirped the alarm.

"I'm in the yellow Ferrari," M'Baye told them, gesturing to his whip, several spaces away.

"We know," Kiki replied, "we been checkin' for you all night," she winked.

"Follow us. We got a room, not far from here. That cool wit' you?"

"Lead the way," M'Baye grinned, and then headed for his car.

He followed them to a motel off of I-95. They pulled up into the parking lot, exited their vehicles and proceeded to ascend the stairs to the second floor walkway and entered a room. Inside, the room was spotless, like it had just been cleaned and there were no signs of luggage anywhere. M'Baye didn't notice that though, because he was too busy noticing Kiki and Tamara.

M'Baye went over to, and relaxed himself on the bed while Kiki moved into Tamara's arms, tonguing her down and pulling up her skirt to grip her bare ass. Tamara unfastened Kiki's extra tight booty shorts, running her hand between Kiki's legs and making her whole body shiver. They undressed one another, rubbing their erect nipples against one another while M'Baye laid back and enjoyed the show.

"You're welcome to join us," Tamara purred, licking Kiki's juices from her fingers.

"You welcome to join *me*," M'Baye replied, slipping his gun under the pillow from the small of his back.

The two chicks crawled up on the bed like twin panthers, stalking their prey with insatiable gazes. They moved up beside M'Baye and took turns kissing him. Kiki removed his shirt, while Tamara removed his jean shorts and then smiled at his erection, which stood as tall as a French flagpole. Tamara squeezed and massaged his dick, running her tongue over her lips.

"Damn, you got a big dick," she moaned, like the sight of it alone was making her cream.

She ran the tip of her tongue around it in swirls, then stuck her tongue ring in the eye of his dick head. M'Baye grunted and his toes curled. Kiki kissed him down his chest, and then joined Tamara down below his waist. They took turns licking along the length of his shaft, from his balls to the bell of his head, until Kiki slid his dick in her mouth. She didn't have a tongue ring, but she definitely had a deep throat.

M'Baye thought he'd go cross-eyed and started to shut them, but out of his peripheral, he saw two shadows move quickly past the room's window and his instincts took over. His eyes darted to the door knob and saw that it was turning, slowly. He quickly sat up, turning for his gun and causing Kiki's mouth to slip off of his dick with a wet, slurping sound.

As the door opened, he didn't give whoever was on the other side a chance to even enter the room. He let off three shots in quick succession, blowing quarter sized holes in the door and filled the room with the booming roar of his .40 caliber. An agonizing cry let him know that at least one of his shots had found its target.

The girls screamed and dropped down between the bed and the wall. A shot was returned, but it sounded like a fire cracker compared to the boom of M'Baye's pistol. He saw a man run across the window and he opened up, shattering the window. He saw the shadow twist violently, throwing itself so wrecklessly against the breezeway's railing that it flipped over it.

M'Baye snatched the door open to find a dude clutching his stomach, curled up in the fetal position. M'Baye fired once, splitting his head until it oozed blood, skull and gray matter.

M'Baye knew he had been set up, so he turned his rage onto the girls. He stormed across the room, dick still hard, because his murderous adrenaline was pumping through it. He snatched a blubbering Tamara up by her hair and put the gun to her head.

"Who sent you?" his voice barked.

"No...nobody," she sobbed hysterically.

M'Baye only asked once, then pulled the trigger, blowing her brains all over the wall and a nearly senseless Kiki, who he snatched up by the throat and pinned to the wall.

"I said...who sent you?" he hissed so coldly that it chilled her from head to toe.

"Fonzo! Fonzo sent us! Please don't kill me, please...I got three kids, please!" she begged with all her heart and soul.

"Who is Fonzo?"

"Th...this dude I know. He...he seen your jewels and wanted to set you up. Get you up here and rob you...I swear...I'm sorry...please...please..." That's as far as she got.

M'Baye shoved the gun in her mouth so hard that it broke two of her front teeth and made her gag on the steel, and then blew the back of her head all over the wall and part of the ceiling. He let her body drop as he snatched up his clothes, only stopping long enough to put on his shoes as he ran out, butt naked.

Lights had come on in other rooms and a few people had stepped outside their rooms but, as soon as they saw the nude Black man with a gun, they hurried up and shut themselves in behind closed doors.

Once M'Baye reached the ground floor, he saw that the other stickup kid had landed on someone's car hood, dead. M'Baye jumped in the Ferrari and took off, heading for the nearest entrance to Interstate 95 North.

He never would've thought that bitches could be so treacherous, but he saw that not only did he have to learn the American way, but the Americans would also have to learn *his* way as well.

** ** ** ** **

"The Prophet, peace be upon him, said, *'he who has the perfect faith is he who has the best character',*" Imam Ahmad said, addressing the hundreds of Muslims sitting on the thick carpeted floor before him. He wore a green jalabiyya, the Islamic garment that looked like an extra long shirt that reached to the knees, and a pair of matching green trousers. On his head, he wore a black kufi trimmed in green. He was an older brother with a full salt and pepper beard, piercing eyes full of perception, and a light brown skin tone. Half Dominican and half black, he was the spiritual leader of the largest community of Muslims in Newark.

Roc sat a few rows back, amongst all of the other brothers listening to Imam Ahmad giving his Friday Jumaah Khutbah speech. It felt good to be home. Back in Newark, back on Bradford Place and back amongst the brothers and sisters that believed as he did, and therefore, shared his perspective. But what they didn't share was how he felt. The tranquil sereneness of the masjid lulled his senses and relaxed his frazzled mind. But, at the same time, the quietude of the gathering made the voice of guilt within him easier to hear.

The street life was becoming harder to resist, more tempting with each foray into its midst. In Miami, he dealt in the gangsta circles with catz that moved with the assurances that fear and respect gave the confident. He looked at the state of the street game - the overindulgence, the laziness, the disorganization and overall novice of the so-called player.

Roc knew that, if he wanted, he could crush them, and that knowledge bolstered his arrogance.

When he recognized it, he ran from it. As soon as things were clear in Miami, he jetted back to Newark, trying to distance himself from himself.

"No matter where you go, there you are," Dutch had said, and that statement rang true because that arrogance continued to fester inside of him.

Roc refocused on the Khutbah, trying to glean a shard of a jewel of wisdom by which to strengthen his resolve.

"...and I understand the need to build strong communities...that is Islam. But, we must also remember to build strong *inner* communities, within ourselves, and that is Iman, faith," Imam Ahmad bellowed. "Because what is good fasting...if it doesn't increase our spirituality? If right after the fast, we gorge ourselves with huge, elaborate feasts? The prophet, peace be unto him, said, *'fast, and all they get is hunger and thirst.'* You see? What good is our salat if we don't make our lives a prayer? An extension of our salat in our walk and character, you see? Yes...yes...we need that. Now, don't get me wrong, the form is just as important as the spirit, because without form, the spirit loses its boundaries. Spirituality becomes sensuality, and a search for stimulation as opposed to spriritualization. But, form without spirit, is just as dangerous. Religion becomes rigid, empty...soulless. We must have both, brothers and sisters. Adherence to the path of Allah and inculcate the principles of this path within us. Character manifest destiny. As Salaam Alaykum."

The crowd greeted him back with boisterous harmony, then readied themselves for the prayer.

Standing in the row, shoulder to shoulder with other Muslims, Roc felt invigorated, but he knew that he was leaning on them, as opposed to truly standing with them and he wondered what would happen if the crutch was removed.

After the prayer, Roc greeted many brothers he hadn't seen in a while with smiles and Salaams.

When he reached Imam Ahmad, they embraced each other warmly.

"As Salaamm Alaiykum, Rahman! Good to see you!" Imam Ahmad said cheerfully.

"Wa Alaiykum As Salaam," he returned, "good to see you, too."

"You got time for an old friend...and may I emphasize *old*, as in *elder*?" Imam Ahmad winked, but still made his point.

Rahman smiled. Imam Ahmad was the jovial type leader of men, which made his orders seem more like friendly requests, therefore, more readily accepted.

"Sure, Ock…you know I do."

Roc and Imam Ahmad went to his office and, instead of sitting behind his desk, Imam Ahmad sat in one of two chairs in front of his desk, and Roc chose the other and they smiled in silence at one another for a moment.

"So, all praises are due to Allah. Hanif tells me that your oil business is doing extremely well," Imam Ahmad congratulated him. "Since I haven't seen you, I figured you were away on business."

"Alhamdulillah," Roc responded, "Hanif's really handling that, I've kinda been out of the country."

"Oh?" Imam Ahmad expressed, "Yes, Ayesha said that you were. I didn't ask where, and she didn't say."

On the mention of Ayesha's name, Roc grew silent.

"She and her father came to see me. I think you know why?"

Roc nodded. "Khul divorce."

"Well, yes and no. You know, both parties have to be present in any type of divorce, no matter who initiates it. But that was the main topic of the discussion."

Roc silently seethed. He knew that what Ayesha had done was appropriate, still he hated the fact that someone else knew of his family problems.

"Believe me, Rahman, I really don't think that this is what she wants. That wasn't the impression that she gave me. She didn't go into the issues, but you know me, Ock, I'm 57 years old, and have three wives myself. I know a woman's strength is her subtlety. This can be reconciled."

"Yeah, but I don't know if I *want* to reconcile, you know? Maybe divorce is the best thing."

"Divorce is never the best thing. Allah hates divorce, but it is available as a last resort."

Roc knew the Islamic divorce process and it was indeed disliked. Both parties must do all that is possible to reconcile, but if it couldn't be, then both parties went their separate ways in peace. Roc didn't really feel he had done all that he could, but he was getting tired of figuring out what he should do.

"I'm just tired of trying to be in two places at one time."

"Is that what you feel Ayesha is asking of you?"

"Naw," Roc chuckled, "she just wants me home."

"So, it's you who wants to be in two places at once."

"I guess so."

"Maybe you ought to divorce yourself," Imam Ahmad cracked, making Roc laugh. "Just think about what I said, Rahman," Imam Ahmad urged and Rahman acknowledged his sincerity.

** ** ** ** **

"So, you want your divorce that bad, huh? You couldn't even wait until I was here?" Roc growled into the receiver of the pay phone. He was so upset that he was speaking more with his hands than his words, as if Ayesha was standing right in front of him.

"As Salaamm Alaiykum to you, too," Ayesha quipped. "And I ain't do *nothin'* behind your back, *Rahman*. You already knew my position."

"Yeah, and now, so does everybody else."

"So, what do you expect…me to sit here and suffer in silence? Is that it?"

"No, I expect you to get on wit' your life, like you said. Ain't that what you want?"

Silence

Ayesha took a deep breath to calm her escalating temper. "Sticks and stones, Rahman. I'm not gonna let you beat me with

201

your words. But, you're wrong. The Qur'an tells you not to abandon your wives, not to leave them hanging –"

Roc held up his hand, eyes shut tight against his own frustrations. "I know what the Qur'an say!"

"Well, I can't tell –"

"No, *I* can't tell. Maybe you got a point, you know…maybe I am wrong. Maybe I'm wrong as a father, wrong as a husband…hell, wrong as a Muslim. So, maybe all I can do right is wrong," he huffed with the tone of a man ready to embrace his faults because he was too weak and confused to correct them.

Silence

"So, what are you saying?" Ayesha questioned.

Rahman sighed hard, "Goodbye, Ayesha," and then slammed the phone even harder. A few people walking by looked at him curiously and he glared them down. No one wanted a part of the huge madman in the middle of downtown Newark.

He looked around, wondering to himself about where he would draw the line. There was no doubt that what he wanted to do was right, so *why was what he was doing so wrong?* Everywhere he looked, all he saw was pain and misery. Buildings of banks and corporations scraped the skylines of every major city, yet the homeless starved at the very base of its structure. Millions of dollars were spent to build more prisons, while urban school children had to share dated textbooks.

Where was the justice? No, where was the mercy that everyone desired, but refused to give? He understood the nature of choice and that if God stepped in every time we made a bad one, it would negate choice itself. Still, it seemed like the only choice for him was to fight fire with fire, and that's exactly what he intended to do.

** ** ** ** **

"Yo, Roc."

"Yeah."

"I just got on the New Jersey Turnpike. I'm on my way.'

"What, you run out of parties or somethin'?"

"I'll tell you about it. I would've been here sooner, but I got mixed up in the District of Columbia."

"D.C."

"Huh?"

"D.C...the District of Columbia is just called, D.C."

"Oh"

"Exit 13 A. Call me then."

"Cool."

A little while later, Roc drove his rented Chrysler 300 and met M'Baye on Frelinghuysen Avenue.

From there, M'Baye followed him to Harlem – Amsterdam Avenue – where Squeeze of LaFamilia had gotten them an apartment. M'Baye looked touristically out of place in the Autumn weather wearing shorts and a wife beater. But, the sleek yellow Ferrari made it hard to see his fashion faux paux.

Squeeze led them to the sparsely furnished apartment. The living room had the bare necessities of a T.V., a Dreamcast and a couch. Roc walked over and sat on the couch.

"First things first. You can't be drivin' around New Yitti in a yellow Ferrari. It'll attract too much attention," Squeeze explained to M'Baye.

"The Feds got more soldiers on the street than we do, and for what we here for, we don't need none of that," Roc added.

M'Baye shrugged it off. "No problem."

"Now, tell me what happened?" Roc asked.

M'Baye explained his meeting with C. Miller and then meeting the two chicks. "Truly, Roc, it would've been hard for even you to say no," M'Baye emphasized. He told them about their proposal and how he followed them back to their hotel.

"Hol' up," Squeeze chuckled, "you tellin' me you fell for that shit? The oldest trick in the book?"

Roc shook his head. Not only was M'Baye a trick, but he was a naïve one at that. He expected the next thing he said to be that he had been robbed at gunpoint, stripped naked and humiliated. He would find that he only had the naked part right. He didn't expect for M'Baye to tell him what he did. And, it wasn't just what he said, but how he said it. The way he described the whole ordeal, the murders – without malice, almost jokingly.

Roc saw M'Baye in a whole new light. He knew then, that he was a cold blooded killer. Under all his French finesse, M'Baye possessed the savageness of the beast Roc shared, and therefore, he recognized and respected it in the young cat.

"And these bastards didn't even have the decency to at least let me get a nut!" M'Baye chuckled, relaxing back on the couch.

Roc fully agreed with Dutch's assessment. He had a lot to learn on this side of the world, but if he caught on as quickly as he did with that situation, he had a lot of potential. He even reminded him of Dutch when he was on the come up. And, in the following days, he had ample opportunity to prove it.

Like the Month of Murder, Dutch's plan for the streets was a restructuring of the way things were. Dutch wasn't of the mentality that you work from within a system to change it. Dutch would dominate the street sweeps – as they would be called by the media – which were in effect, street cleanings, top to bottom, coast to coast.

The first to go were the snitches – the known informants in every city that were allowed to operate with federal blessings, in exchange for the freedom of others. Snitches in Cali were found hung from street lamps, in New York, floating in the Hudson or slumped in car seats, next to equally lifeless girlfriends and baby mamas. In Chicago and St. Louis, they were massacred like it was

St. Valentines Day all over again. And, in the Dirty South, New Orleans and Mississippi, they simply were never found, except on the bottom of swamps by hungry alligators.

The string of murders resembled a serial pattern to the Feds, because they were the only ones that knew what each victim had in common. Once the chief got wind of it, he worried even more about the absence of Goldilocks.

Even the dry snitching in the music industry was dealt with, with the same swiftness. M'Baye, after securing the key from the head of security of a plush hotel in Los Angeles, himself a member of the Bloods, entered the room of the number one rapper in the country and gunned him down along with his hype man, body guards and three groupies. The media ate it up, sensationalizing the violence in rap and its gory consequences. But, on the streets, no one so much as painted a mural or wore a t-shirt for the bastard.

The message was loud and clear, the street revolution would not be televised on B.E.T. Violate and the penalty was death. The point was made – Crip walking and set throwing were no longer fads.

The next phase was consolidation. Sets that were established illegitimately were legitimized by the national affiliation they claimed – by having their leaders executed and official gang leaders installed in their places. Local and regional gangs with no national membership were ordered to pay tribute to Dutch's commission or be disbanded.

With the distribution networks now organized, Dutch's coke, via the cartels, hit the streets and, within weeks, caused epidemics not seen since crack's first introduction in the early 80's. Fiends unknowingly sniffed or smoked their way into heroin level addiction, dealers stepped on the product repeatedly, increasing profit, but decreasing quality, causing fiends to get more desperate and more violent. The streets were filled with the walking dead and even the social sniffers in Hollywood, Wall Street and Capitol Hill manifested the zombie-like effects. Dutch had turned cocaine from an epidemic to an all out disease.

The only social upside to the street sweep was, after the elimination of many known snitches, pirated sets and studio gangstas, violence between gangs became almost non-existent. The truce was real because there was more to lose than community peace – millions were at stake and no one wanted to jeopardize that over any petty squabbles. The sets also spent paper on programs for the youth, seed money for new businesses and real estate in the neighborhood, so even though they feasted on the flesh of the rotting fiends and were turning new ones out daily, the commission enriched themselves, while advancing community development as a whole. The strong survived by the laws of Ghetto Darwinism. The process wouldn't be overnight, but as the success of the operation began to take shape, Roc executed it with deadly accuracy and a smile. In every hood, he had a Muslim controlled area where no drugs were allowed. Strip clubs were forced to relocate, the willing strippers given jobs like he had done in Newark. Liquor store owners were paid up front and willingly or unwillingly watched their stores torched, and then collected insurance on the back end. The Muslim enclave stood securely in the middle of all the madness.

Roc and M'Baye relaxed at the 40/40 Club in Midtown Manhattan, taking in the sights and sounds and enjoying their success. Around them, were members of several of the gangs on the council, all of them basking in the glow of knowing they were virtually untouchable. Roc looked around the room and knew that they were truly making history, and not only was he a part of it, he was the general.

A surge of power filled his arrogance to the point of spiritual intoxication, which is to say, he was truly feeling himself.

M'Baye drunk straight from the bottle of Petrone, feeling tipsy. "You know," he slurred, slouching up against Roc, "after all this shit, I might as well run for president." He and Roc laughed, and then he added, "Imagine a French nigguh in the White House. I'd have *two* first ladies! Bill Clinton wouldn't have nothing on me!" M'Baye threw back his head, turning up the bottle and emptying it, and then cracked another one.

"Well, I don't know about you, but I'm not sitting here all night wit' all these chicks wit' my name on 'em," he held up his bottle. "To myself. I'm young, rich and hung like a horse! Ha! Ha! The world is mine!" he exclaimed, drunkenly, threw back the bottle and then handed it to Roc as he staggered from the booth and dove into the sea of women on the dance floor.

Roc chuckled because he agreed. The world, *their world*, was indeed theirs. He couldn't argue with success, and all the smiles and flirtatious eye contact he was receiving confirmed it. His hand still gripped the bottle, as he nodded to the beat of Keisha Cole's new joint. Roc tilted the bottle to his mouth without fully realizing what he was doing, until he tasted the alcohol on his tongue. He caught himself before swallowing, swished the liquid around in his mouth and then, the *might as well's* kicked in. *Since you already sipped, you might as well drink it. Since you drank it once, you might as well drink it twice. Since you're drinking, you might as well get drunk*. And so…he did.

The more he drank, the fuzzier the bright lights of the club, and so did the line between who he was and who he was becoming. His soul screamed the warning that his arrogance laughed at brazenly.

The world was theirs…why not indulge it?

The night took on new meaning in Roc's eyes. With the Petrone bottle in one hand, and his nuts in the other, he made his way into the crowd, returning the flirtatious glances and exchanging respects with the other members of the commission.

Squeeze looked surprised, but let it go, knowing that the spirit is always willing, but the flesh is sometimes weak and handed a cigar to Roc.

Roc inspected the craftsmanship and asked, "What's this...a Cuban?"

"Naw," Squeeze winked, "it's a Dutch," he joked, lighting the tip for him. You just in time, too. I was just about to escort these lovely ladies to a private party, but I ain't greedy. It's enough to go around."

Roc eyed the three chicks around Squeeze – two were Latinas and one was Black with acute Asian features. A Kimora Lee-like attraction held Roc's attention. He held out his hand, introducing himself. "How you doin' tonight? I'm Rah -...Roc. Just call me Roc."

"Roc?" she grinned suggestively, taking in his height and line backer physique. "Are you a pirate, Roc, or is that just a fashion statement?" she asked, referring to his eye patch.

"Naw, Ma," he chuckled. "Unless you gonna lead me to the buried treasure."

She giggled, but didn't blush because she was a grown woman with no pretensions. Roc scoped her from her long mocha toned legs and the way her Baby Phat dress clung to her shapely petiteness.

Shortie had style about herself, and the kind of eyes that could become more expressive behind closed doors, and Roc's voice of warning became less audible as he stared into them.

"So, what's up...we out or what?" Squeeze interjected, arms around both of the Latinas.

"That's up to Miss..." Roc let his voice trail off so she could fill in the blank.

"Angela. Angela Crowder," she smiled invitingly.

"Well, Miss Angela Crowder...are we or aren't we?"

"Oh, we definitely are," she replied with sass over her shoulder, giving Roc a view of her sway as she walked away, towards the exit. The way her ass jiggled under her dress, there was no way she was wearing panties underneath and Roc hated to admit it, but he couldn't wait to find out.

** ** ** ** **

The look that Goldilocks was giving Angel could've shot daggers in her back, and the grayish color of her eyes looked like cold steel. She watched Angel on her knees, gripping both sides of the toilet, throwing up. This hadn't been the first morning, but the last few mornings, and Goldilocks had taken all that she could take. They both knew what the problem was – Angel was pregnant.

Angel's emotions were a mixture of surprise and confusion. She knew that she wasn't the motherly type, but she could never hurt anything that Dutch loved. She only debated when she would tell him. She and Dutch's relationship hadn't changed into some lovey-dovey affair. They were both already married to the game. Besides, it would've been hard to get any closer than they already were, therefore their physical relationship only consummated their bond.

But, every night, Goldilocks lay cold and alone while Angel warmed Dutch's bed...and the floor...and the balcony...and the shower.

Everything was so new to Angel and her curiosity was insatiable. She finally had the only man that could tame her.

Goldilocks was through playing games though. The only reason Angel was still alive was because of Odouwo's orders.

"Spare Angel...for now," he'd said, "after I meet with Ceylon, then we'll decide her fate."

Still, Goldilocks wanted to see her suffer. Instead, she settled for, "Bitch, you ain't shit."

Angel looked over at Goldilocks, her hair hanging loosely over her face. "Goldi," Angel replied calmly, "get dressed. We got business to take care of."

They were in Paris, staying at the Hotel de Lute'ce until they met with Quintero. Then, they were headed to Vegas for the 2007 All-Star weekend to begin putting the gold diggers on the team and rebuild Angel's Charlies.

Goldilocks stood in the bathroom door in her bra and panties. "It's always business. Is it business when you fuckin' him, too?" Goldilocks huffed.

Angel brushed her teeth and then washed her face, making Goldilocks wait for a reply. She grabbed a towel to dry her face off with, walking towards Goldilocks. When she was right up on her, close enough that Goldilocks could smell the Crest on her breath, Angel replied "Was it business, you fuckin' Craze? Huh?" Angel quipped with a smirk, and then kissed Goldilocks on the nose and walked around her.

Goldilocks spun around, scared at what else Angel might have known. "Fuckin' Craze?" she echoed, her voice cracking slightly.

Angel stood in the mirror, brushing her hair. She thought about putting it in a ponytail, but decided against it because she had to look like a woman today. She eyed Goldilocks through the mirror.

"Don't look so surprised," Angel chuckled, "you thought I didn't know?"

Goldilocks regained her composure and shot right back, "And? Yeah, I fucked 'em, so what? Maybe if you had been payin' more attention to me, it —"

Angel shook her head, smiling. "It wouldn't have mattered, Goldi, and believe me, I'm not upset 'cause I know…you gotta let a ho' be a ho'."

"So, now I'm a ho'?" she exclaimed, the truth hurting, but her rage greater.

Angel approached her, wrapping her arms around Goldilocks' bare waist and running her tongue along her neck, sending shivers up Goldilocks' spine. Angel's touch always had that effect on her, which is why she craved it, why she loved her and why she hated her too.

"You know you a ho'…a sexy ass ho', but a ho' just the same," Angel told her, pushing her bra off of her shoulders, then down around her waist. Angel tweaked her nipples until they stood taut on her heaving chest. "Maybe you could fuck Quintero, make him see our point."

"May…." her voice broke off in a grunt as Angel ran her tongue over her nipples and then sucked the slope into her mouth. "Maybe I…ummm…could fuck Dutch."

Angel lowered to her knees, tonguing her belly button. "And I'll kill you myself," she replied calmly, never breaking her caresses, but there was no mistaking her seriousness. Angel turned Goldilocks around, bent her over the bed and pulled her panties down to her ankles. She ran her nose along the crack of her ass, and then used her fingers to spread Goldilocks' throbbing pussy. As soon as Angel's tongue entered her pinkness, she jumped like something had shocked her. Angel darted her tongue in circles while fingering her hole with two fingers.

"Ohhh…why are you doing this to me," Goldilocks moaned, her anger melting away while her lust heated up.

Business, Angel thought, because it was no longer personal. The feelings she had for Goldilocks were still there, still a factor, but her relationship with Dutch added another dimension to her life, and took priority over all other considerations. But Angel knew Goldilocks would be an asset in reestablishing Angel's Charlies, so she was securing the locks on Goldilocks' commitment…and her pussy still tasted sweet.

** ** ** ** **

211

They met Quintero at the Café de Flore, an open air café that sat on the corner of the Boulevard Saint-German. The dining inside was more private, but outside, the street corner patio was abuzz with excited tourists speaking a cacophony of languages, and the natives laughing in French. It was perfect for the type of dialogue they needed to have.

Quintero was already there when Angel and Goldilocks hopped out of their taxi. His three bodyguards were at three separate tables in strategic positions, while he sat alone, awaiting their arrival.

Dutch had told him to expect Angel, but he didn't expect such beauty.

Angel made eye contact as she approached and then said, "Hola, Jorge. Desculpa por aserte esprerar," she apologized for making him wait.

Jorge stood up to kiss her hand and then Goldilocks', smiling slyly. Angel definitely looked all woman. She was wearing a body hugging Lauren dress and Goldilocks was just as gorgeous in her Chanel, two-piece dress, her dreads in a bun atop her head with a few locks left out to frame her face.

"They say good things come to those who wait. Now, I'm a believer," he replied, then added, "Please, sit. What are you drinking?"

"Remy," Goldilocks answered.

"Make it two?" Angel seconded.

Quintero got the waiter's attention and ordered the two drinks. After the waiter walked away, he said, "Dutch told me to expect Angel, but I didn't know he was sending a real one," he complimented her, holding up his glass.

When the waiter returned with their drinks, Angel got hers and had sipped it before catching herself, remembering her condition. She was starting to hate motherhood already. "Looks can be deceiving, Papi," she warned him with a smirk.

"Si', which is why, regardless of beauty, I never believe in illusions, 'eh," he told her as he sipped his drink. "It's a shame Dutch couldn't join us."

— "And, he sends his apologies, but it was unavoidable."

"You are far from an apology, but I understand unavoidable matters, especially with another cartel," Quintero signified.

"He sends his apologies, but it was unavoidable," Angel repeated for emphasis, poker expression revealing nothing. Still she had to hand it to Quintero, he was sharp. Either that, or he had ears within the other families. The cartels were conniving. Dutch actually was heading for another meeting with the Arellano cartel as they had discussed.

Quintero leaned forward onto the table, adjusting his cuffs, and then folding his hands. "Dutch is a smart man and I love to do business with smart men. Less mistakes, less chances for…misunderstandings. So, I said to myself, 'Jorge, what would a smart man do in a position such as Dutch's?'"

Angel asked: "And, what did Jorge say?"

"Jorge said, a smart man in such a position, would not hoard, because then, he would create enemies…too many enemies…hidden enemies. So he would do business, but he would also make friends. And these friends should be, if he is a smart man, enemies of the enemies…this would create…how you say, equilibrium, no?"

Angel shrugged. "There's already equilibrium, dealing with everyone equally."

"Ah, that, La Bonita, is business. Friendship must be given…sparingly, to a chosen few…or exclusively," Quintero replied.

"Exclusive, meaning you?"

"Si'…I am willing to pay double for what I am getting now."

"Then, you'd have a monopoly."

"No, an advantage...one that would benefit Dutch as well."

Angel's expression said that she was listening.

Quintero continued, "Because the Arellano, Cali and Camorra are all old, they prefer twelve year old girls to war. They don't want to make waves, so they bow to the Italians, the Russians, they politically compromise their countries, they are under their thumb. But, if they starve, then the Italians and the Russians must come to Dutch, they must compromise because they prefer money to war."

"So, maybe we take 'em to war. Chase 'em the fuck outta our hoods."

"You could...and you'll probably win, but it would be foolish. The mob is no longer strong in the streets, but they don't have to be. They have done what all successful criminals have done...merged into legitimate society. They have the judges, the police...the politicians. Fight them, and the system fights you."

Angel nodded. She remembered what Frank Bonno had done to Dutch, and it confirmed the accuracy of Quintero's assessment.

"But, for me to have a monopoly," Quintero shook his head, "it would cost me too much in production. The others would continue...but they will be under *my* thumb instead of the Europeans,"

Quintero smiled, sitting back and finishing his drink.

"Double for double?" Angel asked, Quintero confirming her question with a nod. "We'll be in touch."

Chapter Twelve

There are men in this world with the power to control the masses with the simplicity of a chess move; men who control the value of world currency, therefore the artificiality of economic booms and recessions; men who control Democratic and puppet presidents and dictators, men, that the masses are foolish enough to believe, control the destiny of their souls – therefore they pay in blood. They are the power elite and the underworld is no different.

Omar Ceylon and Joseph Odouwo were two such men. They were meeting in Monaco, the true playground of the rich and powerful, located in France on the Italian border, with all the attraction of Vegas, but without all the gaudiness of false glitter. Compared to Monaco, Vegas was a Mini-Me.

They met in an exclusive suite atop the Hotel Monaco. They met alone in the spacious suite, because these were the type of men that needed no bodyguards – who they were and the connections they held were more than enough protection. Many things were at stake, but at the center of it all was a pawn that had become a knight and was aspiring to be king...Dutch.

"Omar," Odouwo smiled, shaking Ceylon's hand, "You are looking well," he complimented as he reclined in a plush armchair. To Odouwo, Ceylon always struck him as having more Israeli features than Turkish. He had long suspected him to be of a faction of Mossad, the Jewish Intelligence Agency, but had never voiced it to anyone.

Ceylon sat across from him. "Tank you, Joseph. I believe it is the wine, good for the heart, the French believe. And you? You are looking well."

"It's the women," Odouwo chuckled, who, despite his age, still had the virility of a bull, "and I was just blessed with my twenty-third. A boy, you know though, that most of my offspring are males," he boasted.

"Congratulations," Ceylon remarked. "Although, some believe that when a man dies, a child is born."

"That is the circle of life."

"As we have come full circle."

Odouwo smiled at the smooth segue Omar used to turn the conversation. "Yes, it is true that we have not always seen eye to eye, but the world has changed, and former...adversaries...must become allies to protect common interests," Odouwo stated diplomatically.

"Such as?"

"The sea gates," Odouwo replied, "I know you are familiar with military strategy, and that anytime any maritime nation must maintain a strong Navy to protect its ports and harbors. America is such a nation and does possess the strongest Navy in the world. But, they have come to rely on that strength, but without intelligence. Cowboys have been elected to the White House, with little manhood between their legs, and sought to compensate with bigger guns, bigger armies – more strength. But they have been outmaneuvered politically and strategically by the Chinese."

"You are referring to the sale of the Panama Canal and the Bering Strait Sea Gates, no?"

"Primarily, but there are several others. As you know, these sea gates are of primary importance to our drug smugglers as well. Ninety percent of international trafficking comes through these ports. The other ten percent are in bits and pieces and of no real consequence, so, in fact, that ninety percent is effectively one hundred percent, all owned by the Chinese."

Ceylon was well aware of the emerging world dominance of the Chinese and the threat to his interests. The Golden Triangle, the biggest producer of heroin in the world, was Turkey's biggest rival.

But, Turkey - aligned with France and Italy – was able to maintain the advantage over the Far East. But times were indeed changing, and now, the Nigerians – who were aligned with the Far East – could pose a more direct threat to Ceylon.

"A very strategic advantage."

"But you, Omar, possess the technological advantage," Odouwo conceded, "with this new strain of coco you are backing. You have effectively cornered the market. Now, I am aware that you are the Pope," he smirked, "and that it will take more time to see how adverse the climates will become for you, but I advise that you do not wait. Let us agree, as men, to prosper together and share in the collective feast."

Ceylon understood totally. Presently, Odouwo posed him no threat, but the time would come when he could, and if that potential could be offset with minimal loss, then so much the better. "I knew that you would call on me soon...especially since you've unleashed an assassin into my home," Ceylon told him, looking directly into his eyes.

Odouwo wasn't surprised that Ceylon knew, but he waited to hear what he felt about it.

"Miss Reese is subtle, I must say, but one must know what to look for. Espionage is my expertise.

I simply had her fingerprints on a drinking glass processed. Kimberly Reese, a federal agent. But the F.B.I. to *me* has no more power than a county sheriff, and, in France, a security guard. I would've told my young friend, but then, Chris was killed and also his wife. I don't believe in coincidence, Joseph, therefore, I waited for this mystery to solve itself...and it has."

Odouwo's eyes narrowed. "His head, Omar, I require his head. My vengeance for my slain countryman...my slain blood cannot be quenched by anything less. Reese is expendable, of no consequence, but I needed her federal connections to get inside of

217

his confidence and take away all that he loved. Now, the time has come to avenge Kazami," Odouwo swore.

"And you are asking me to deliver him to you?"

"Or, merely concede. Either way, I'll have my revenge."

"Then, so you shall, Joseph, so you shall."

The two shook hands over another man's blood and departed company.

** ** ** ** **

What happened to you? Roc couldn't get those words out of his mind, and, as he stared at himself in the bathroom mirror, he wondered the same. The last few days had engulfed him in a whirlwind of liquor, women and gambling. If Ceylon was the Pope and Dutch a King, then he was the Don of street generals and he moved as such. He copped a metallic green BMW 650 to reflect his status and dove head first into the life he had sworn off. *Or had he?*

Sometimes, causes are followed because people want to feel more a part of a cosmic whole, and sometimes they want to feel less of themselves. These are the robots, the cattle, the goyim. Yet, others led causes to change the world and deliver it from temptation, only because they are too weak to fight those same temptations within themselves. As with the writers of the Bible, unable to control their own lust for women, they blamed that lust on the women themselves. These are the lawmakers, and the category of men in which Roc admitted to himself that he fell.

He had gone to prison a gangsta, sincerely embraced Islam and sincerely realized the gangsta life was wrong, but instead of fighting it from within, he projected it out on the world, grabbed his gun and went to war. *What happened to you?*

That had been the question of Sonia, a.k.a. Miss Grown, a.k.a. Jamilah. He had been in Newark with a chick named Kim he had recently met. He double parked the BMW on Bergen, near Lehigh, only to run into a store for a quick snack. On the way out, Jamilah, walking with another Muslim sister, spotted him.

As she approached she said, "Rahman! As Salaam Alaykum!"

He turned his head and saw the two beautiful sisters approaching. They both wore full length jalibbiyya dresses and the khimar head coverings. Jamilah's was a royal blue and her friend's was burgundy.

"Wa Alaykum As Salaam, Khayfa halli??" he asked how she was doing in Arabic.

"Tayyib. Wa anta?" – Good and you?

Roc was pleasantly surprised to find that she responded fluently.

"This is my friend, Tamika. She just became Muslim."

"As Salaam Alaykum," Roc greeted. He was good with faces, so he knew that he had seen Tamika before. What he didn't know was that it had been with Nina and Dutch.

"Wa Alaykum As Salaam," Tamika responded, stressing to pronounce the greeting correctly.

"I've heard a lot about you, Rahman. You've done a lot for the community. That is a blessing."

Roc didn't know how to respond. He felt all he had done of good, would cost him his soul.

"I just got married, Rahman," Jamilah glowed. "His name is Basim, and he works for you and Hanif. You know him, right?"

Roc shook his head. It was then, that Jamilah really focused on him, furled her brow and said, "Rahman, are you okay? What happened to you?"

It wasn't an accusation, but deep down inside, it felt like one. Roc stared in the mirror and knew that it had nothing to do with his appearance. He had the same beard, same eye patch, same nononsense disposition. What Jamilah had seen was far deeper. He remembered the Prophet, peace be unto him, as saying, *Beware of the believer, for he sees with the light of Allah.* That realization scared him, slapped him out of his stupor and made him confront himself honestly and unflinchingly.

He hadn't offered salat in days, he mixed the scent of one woman on top of another's and his breath carried a hint of Hennessy. But, it wasn't too late…he wasn't too far gone not to recognize his mistakes, and now that he knew his weakness, he could rely on his strength to change it.

Without hesitation, he walked out of his room in his and M'Baye's apartment, and into the living room. M'Baye slouched deep in the couch, scratching his nuts and flicking the remote like he was bustin' shots at the screen with it. He heard Roc come in and looked up.

Killer to killer, M'Baye recognized the death stare in Roc's eyes. He didn't flinch, because he knew it wasn't for him. But, he knew that someone was about to die. He didn't know it would be Roc.

Not in the physical sense, but in the sense of what he had allowed himself to become.

Rahman would kill Roc.

"What's up, mon'frere?" M'Baye asked lazily.

Roc tossed him the keys to the BMW, and then pulled his gun from his waist and tossed it on the couch.

"What's –" M'Baye started to say, but then, he understood. He knew Roc had been torn, and the last few days weren't like him. Still, M'Baye didn't expect him to leave and he stood up. "Ock…you okay?"

"I will be."

"What about Angel? We're supposed to pick her up at the airport."

"Go pick her up, then call me. I'll be to see her. But, I'm through, M, period. The car is yours, the position is yours. I don't expect you to honor my position with the Muslim spots, but that, I can't help. Allah is the best of planners."

M'Baye looked at the keys in his hand, and then back at Rahman. "I admire you, brother. I wish I had something to believe in sometimes myself," he admitted.

Roc nodded, and then extended his hands. "You a good cat, M'Baye. Hold it down."

Roc was headed for the door when he heard M'Baye say, "I will honor your position, Roc. My word!"

Roc smiled slightly. "Call me when you pick up Angel," and then he walked out.

Once he hit the streets of Harlem, he felt like, after all this time, it was only now that he was getting out of prison. The steel bars and gun towers are often no more real than the prisons we sometimes construct for ourselves. Destroying those prison walls is when we are truly free.

Rahman admired Harlem in it's Autumn attire - the brown, orange and maple reds of the trees.

As he walked, he pulled out his cell phone and dialed that all too familiar phone number. He didn't know what to say, what he *could* say, and he still hadn't figured it out by the time the line was answered.

"As Salaam Alaykum," Ayesha answered.

Silence

"As Salaam Alaykum?" she repeated, and then, "Hello?" She listened for a second and then added, "Rahman?"

"Save me."

"Rahman, are you okay? What did you say?" her voice quivered slightly, a sense of urgency in her tone.

"I'm drownin', Ma...save me."

Silence...but, this time...it was hers.

"Where are you?" she finally asked.

"Harlem...Amsterdam and 101st.

More silence...then... "I'm on my way."

She met him on the uptown side of the street. When she pulled up in the Escalade, Rahman was sitting on the back of a bench and he looked at her in the driver's seat.

Marriage is half your faith, so it was no wonder he had been so weak after neglecting his marriage. Ayesha was not only a blessing, she was also a beautiful woman, inside and out. She had held him down through thick and thin, but he had taken that for granted.

He got up from the bench and walked over to the passenger's door, but found it locked.

Ayesha hadn't taken her eyes off of him since she'd pulled up, her gaze, one of a Black woman willing to forgive and unwilling to compromise.

He lifted the door handle and uselessly, so she would get the message and unlock it, but, she didn't, so he tapped on the glass. "You gonna open the door or what?"

"Why should I?" she asked, cracking the passenger's side window two inches.

"Because you came," he countered.

Ayesha got out of the SUV and walked around the hood to the other side of the car. She looked gorgeous in her multi-colored jalibiyya and matching Khimar. "Yeah, I *came.* I came so that you could tell me *one* reason to save you, as you put it, that you haven't used before. You can't use, *It's gonna be different this time,* because you used that up," she huffed, counting off on her fingers all of the lame excuses he had given her in the past. "You can't use, *It's about you and the kids,* either, because you used that up several times over...and you can't use, *It's over,* because you used that up, too. They all used up, Rahman, and now I feel used up!" her bottom lip quivered, but she was past the point of tears.

Rahman didn't know how to respond. *What could he say to the woman he had neglected and taken for granted for so long? The woman that had borne his children and made his house into a home, but he was never really around to appreciate?* She had come and answered his call, but her presence alone, reinforced the guilt he felt, not only for the years, but especially for the last few days.

"Ayesha, I can't give you no reason because they'll all seem to be excuses. Whenever I needed you, you was there. You know, you —"

Ayesha folded her arms. "Maybe that was the problem, you know, maybe I was *too* good to you. Maybe if I gave you all types of drama, kept you jumpin' through hoops, kept something stirred up to keep you close...but I was secure in what we had, in what I *thought* we had, and I didn't. I always gave you the benefit of the doubt. I was always giving more, so tell me, Rahman, *please*, how much did I have to *give* to *get*?"

Rahman heard every word she said, but what struck him the most was the way she spoke of their marriage in the past tense. "But, you still came. That's gotta mean something."

"I...I just don't think its enough."

"So...you still want a ...a divorce?"

Ayesha dropped her head, looked away, and when she looked back at him, she could no longer hold back the tears. "What do you think?" She held his gaze a few more seconds, and then went back around to the driver's side, got in and unlocked the passenger's door.

Rahman stood, looking at Ayesha, who wouldn't return his gaze Instead, she looked straight ahead, hands on the steering wheel. He wondered if this was the price he had to pay. Would letting her go be the only way to repay her for the neglect while he had her? He couldn't accept that, but it seemed that she had her mind made up.

The traffic on the West Side Highway was bumper to bumper along the Hudson River, leading them to the Holland Tunnel. A talk radio station babbled on and on as the Escalade crept closer and closer toward Newark and reconciliation.

"Ayesha, I know how much I hurt you when I walked out on you and the kids over those nine little girls, but what else could I do? I couldn't just let 'em die when it was my actions that put 'em in that position in the first place," he explained, but Ayesha ignored him, blowing the horn impatiently at the driver in front of them.

"Yo, its crazy, Ma, I came home from prison ready to change the world, or at least try, but I didn't know how to change myself. I thought that just changing my allegiance, changing what I stood for was enough, but it wasn't. And, it took these last few months to understand that...I'm fucked up inside. I wanna do right, live right...and I can, but I need you to help me," Rahman admitted.

Ayesha looked at him as if she was about to say something, but then shook her head and turned the radio dial to Hot 97 to drown out her thoughts with music. Rahman got the point and looked out of the window at the piers. She was trying to shut him out, but he refused to let her. He grabbed the CD changer remote and clicked through the CD's until he found what he was looking for.

The familiar rhythm of Lolita Holloway filled the car as he turned it up a notch. Ayesha just looked over at him. He read her expression and shrugged, "You wanna listen to music, then let's listen to *music*."

Its not ovaaa ovaaa

Its not ovaaa ovaaa

The melody forced a smile from his lips, taking his mind back to happier times, and he hoped Ayesha's, too.

"Now, that's music. Remember that? Huh? Remember how you used to wear the big bamboo earrings wit' your name in 'em and every time we had an argument, you'd play this song over and over," he reminded her, grinning.

"It won't work, Rahman, I was a little girl then, but I'm a grown woman now," she affirmed, but the song still held a special place in her heart as well.

I'm surprised to see your suitcase at the door
Remember the good times...don't you want some more
Its not a perfect love, but I'll defend it
Because I believe in what God intended...

Everyone has a time in their life where, when things get rough, they look back to a happier time for comfort, and associated with that time, there's always a song, a melody, a rhythm so sweet, so much a part of their happiness, that that song can even make death easier to accept. Like that first real kiss, it never fails to cause a tingle inside, and make you cry out, *That's my song!*

"Shoot, you was grown then, least you thought you was," he snickered and Ayesha hid her smirk behind her lips, but it escaped through her eyes. "What was your friend's name...Sheila? Sheila Evans and...Hasanah."

"I ain't surprised you remember Hasanah, the way you used to sweat her."

"Hasanah? Please! She was cool as a fan, and yeah, she was cute...but it was always you, Ma. Word up. You was the only chick that could keep me in check I look in them eyes, and I could never lie to them. Ain't nothing changed either, I still can't."

Ayesha gazed at him evenly.

Its not over between you and me
Its not over, I don't want to be free...

"Rahman, why are you doing this? You know –"

"Look, you asked me for a reason, and this is it. That feeling that we still share, deep down, past all the drama and all the madness our lives have become. And I'm through with all that

225

madness...through. I just want to be Muslim, be your husband, raise our babies, you know? I mean, yo, if I gotta wash the dishes or clean the clothes, I'm willing to do whatever...whatever it takes. I know you done heard it a hundred times or more, but I swear, I done changed, I swear I done changed."

I can still hear the words spoken as we stood
Making vows to love through times bad or good
I'm convinced that what is meant to be will be
Even the stars declare that you belong to me-ee-ee...

Ayesha didn't believe in the stars, but she *did* believe in the power of love and she wanted to believe in Rahman as well. She leaned her forehead against the steering wheel, shaking her head, and then rolled it around to look at him.

"Nigguh, I swear, if I didn't love you so much –"

"Then, I'd find a way to make you, so what up? Yes?"

Ayesha sat up straight. "Rahman, I'm gonna believe you, but I want you to believe me, too. If you so much as try and organize a cookout, I'ma put a bullet in yo Black ass myself, and oh, you gonna jump through some hoops this time, too," she smirked, eyes narrowed with Newark attitude sassing up her tone.

"Yo, back flips, semis, tap dancin' naked on the bathroom tile, just say you still my heart," he asked.

"I'm your heart," she said, allowing him to lean over and kiss her.

His cell phone rang and Ayesha pulled back, eyeing him hard.

Rahman held the cell phone up in the air, "Whoa...its only a call, its only a call" he laughed, seeing that it was M'Baye. Opening the phone and placing it to his ear he said, "Speak."

"Roc."

"Yeah."

"I'm at the airport and I don't know, but...Angel never got off the plane..."

226

Chapter Thirteen

The reason Angel never got off the plane, was because she was never allowed to get on it.

Goldilocks had seen to that. After Odouwo called her and confirmed the success of the meeting with Ceylon, he gave the instruction.

"Spare her…she's worth more to us alive."

Goldilocks understood why, but she didn't like it. She wanted to watch her die with her own eyes. She sat in the suite, in the corner of the room, while Angel showered in preparation of the trip to Vegas she would never take. Goldilocks was already dressed in a pair of black Dolce jeans and a gold Trina Turk lace blouse, held closed by three tiny gold buttons. There was no way that she was going to give up the opportunity to get Angel back in some way, so, she retrieved her F.B.I. badge, gun and handcuffs from the secret compartment of her bag, and then sat back in the chair, waiting for Angel to come out of the shower.

She sat and listened to the spray of the shower and the sound reminded her of sizzling bacon. She smiled, imagining Angel's skin sizzling with the same intensity. Goldilocks got up, laid her badge open
on the middle of the bed and returned to her chair.

A few moments later, the water was turned off and Angel emerged from the bathroom with a large white towel wrapped around herself, hair pinned up on top of her head. When she saw Goldilocks smirking at her, she asked, "What's so funny?"

"Inside joke."

Angel shrugged it off, thinking, *Whatever, this bitch is still trippin'*. Her mind was on other things, like the child growing in her womb. The feeling of pregnancy warmed her and worried her at the same time. *How would Dutch react? Would he be happy? Would he be upset?* Angel knew his thought pattern, shared in it,

227

but his emotions had always been a mystery to all who knew him, even her. So, she wondered – the seed in her belly suddenly feeling like a load – *would he even care?* She would tell him as soon as she returned to the states. No matter what she...her eyes moved across the bed...

The leather wallet lay open. The face on the picture, she knew, but...not the words underneath...and not what it had to do with the shiny bronze shield that bore the unmistakable acronym – F.B.I.

"Even smooth criminals one day must get caught," she vaguely heard Goldilocks taunt.

Angel blinked, and then blinked again, not wanting to really see what she was seeing. "A fed?" she said aloud, more to herself, her voice in a semi-whisper. Pictures went through her mind rapidly from their meeting in prison, the way she asked questions, what she asked, her expert marksmanship in the mall shoot-out, to her disappearance right before they left for France, and then, finally, the smirk she wore a moment ago – *Inside joke.*

Angel turned to face Goldilocks and found herself staring at the barrel of a .45 caliber handgun, Goldilocks still seated calmly in her chair. "You a *fuckin'* fed?" Angel spat in disbelief, with emphasis on the word fuckin', like she was spitting mucus in her grinning face.

"Sometimes," Goldilocks shrugged, "but, not right now. Right now, I'm that bitch you shoulda' never crossed."

"Cross you?" Angel raged, "you fuckin' slimy bitch! You was crossin' me the whole fuckin' time!"

Angel started to rush forward, but Goldilocks stood up, quickly, gun poised, handcuffs tucked in the waist of her jeans. "Please," she trembled intensely, "please try it, so I'll have a reason to spill that bastard in your belly all over this motherfuckin' floor! Please do!"

"I'm not goin' back in no cage, yo, so you might as well kill me now."

"Then make it happen," Goldilocks replied, eager to pull the trigger. "You chose him, Angel! Over *me*! *Me*! The only one that really loved you. Dutch don't! Where was he while you was rottin' in prison, huh? Who was wit' you then, huh? Me! Regardless of *why*, what I felt for you was *real*. Dutch was the target, not *you*! I was there, I woulda' died for you, Angel! There wasn't nothing I wouldn't have done for you! Now...I can't do *shit* for you!"

Angel realized that Goldilocks was a woman scorned, so she knew that any emotional plays would be useless. But, she felt everyone had a price. "Goldi, okay, I fucked up. I see that, but, yo, look at all the shit we did, *you and me*. We killed together, fucked, got high, I mean, damn, you already broke the law and you a agent! What good is taking me to prison when we about to touch *millions*, me and you, whatever the price, I'll pay it," Angel proposed.

Goldilocks laughed in her face. "You don't get it. You think this is about the feds? Naw, baby, its much, much deeper."

"Everybody has a price, Goldi."

"The price is Dutch's life. You willin' to pay me that?" Goldilocks quipped.

Angel was confused. Dutch's life? But, she had no time to figure it out because Goldilocks was moving towards her, drawing her cuffs.

"Turn around...slow...and put your hands behind your back," she ordered her.

Angel complied with the first demand, but, in a flash, defied the second. She shot her right elbow up and around, trying to smash it into Goldilocks' nose, but she missed because Goldilocks was too agile. She ducked the elbow, tackled Angel from under her raised arm and dumped her on the bed.

Angel, from her side, tried helplessly to kick Goldilocks like a mule, but Goldilocks wrapped her leg around Angel's with expert wrestling technique and flipped her over on her stomach, placed the gun to her head and twisted her arms behind her back.

"Bitch, I coulda' *been* smashed yo', ass," Goldilocks bragged, barely out of breath. "Street tough Boricua, 'eh? You a weak ass *bitch!*"

Angel lay with her face to the side, seething. "Maybe, but you loved me, 'eh? Deep down, you still do...but me? I never gave a fuck about you," she lied, "you was my peon, my piss and...rotten pussy bitch," Angel spat. She knew that if she couldn't get Goldilocks to love her, she could make her hate her.

Either way, all Angel wanted was time. Time to work the hair pin she held in the palm of her hand.

While they were struggling, and Angel saw that she was outmatched, she had snatched the pin from her hair...right before Goldilocks flipped her over. Now, as Goldilocks locked the cuffs, she could tell that her play was working.

"You chose him...you chose him," Angel mocked Goldilocks' cry. "You may've played me for my trust, but bitch I played you for your heart. *Now* who's the weak bitch!"

"Shut up!" Goldilocks bellowed, smacking Angel with the pistol and drawing blood. "Shut the fuck up!"

All the memories of being just a play thing for men, Black and White, growing up - being nothing but a booty call, fucked and forgotten – came flooding back to her. It was hard enough to know that her love had been betrayed for Dutch, but to hear that that love meant nothing... If she couldn't kill Angel, she would degrade her in the worst way she could think of.

"I never loved you, bitch," Angel said, still unable to use the pin because Goldilocks was still in a position to be able to see her hands.

"Naw, but you love Dutch's dick don't you? That's all you ever wanted, some dick. All you had to do was ask," Goldilocks hissed, grabbing her strap on from under a pillow. She didn't bother to take off her clothes because, what she was about to do, wasn't about sensuality – just raw, sexual violence.

She strapped it on over her clothes and snatched the towel from Angel's body. The blood streaming from Angel's temple excited her blood lust because, to her, it wasn't pain, and she wanted Angel to feel nothing but pain.

Goldilocks spread Angel's legs with her own, and then rammed all twelve inches up inside of her as if she were trying to ram it into her guts. Angel stifled her shout, not wanting to give Goldilocks the pleasure of hearing her, but the pain caused her temples to begin throbbing almost instantly.

"You like that? Yeah, you love it, don't you?" she gritted, pounding her harder with every thrust of her pelvis.

Still though, Angel refused to scream, concentrating on getting the pin into the cuff keyhole while her body movements continued to jolt her out of aim.

"Oh, you won't scream, huh? Well let me see how you like *this*!" Goldilocks pulled the dildo out of Angel's pussy and shoved it straight up her ass.

The dildo might as well have been a hot poker the way the pain seared through Angel's rectum, directly up her spine and exploded in her brain. She cried out in an effort to release the pain and avoid a potential black out. She almost dropped the pin, fumbling it between her fingers.

"Ut-unh...don't holler now, bitch! See how it feels to be used?! You see how it feels to be used?!" Goldilocks barked, trying to rip Angel's rectum apart.

With Goldilocks' body positioned on top of her, she didn't jolt as much, finally giving Angel the chance to key the hole with the pin. She tried not to focus on the excruciating pain until she was finally able to free her wrists.

Goldilocks felt Angel's hands under her stomach, but mistook them for clawing and scratching.

The gun was at the base of Angel's skull and gripped tightly in Goldilocks' hand.

Angel knew she'd never be able to get her hand free and grab the gun without catching a headshot, so she would have to get better leverage. Despite the pain, she forced herself to throw her ass back at Goldi, fronting as if she liked it. "Mmmmm…harder, Goldi, do it harder," she moaned, pushing back and raising up on her knees slightly.

Goldilocks didn't expect Angel to like it and her words infuriated her, but she allowed Angel to raise her body, giving Angel just enough room to duck her head to the side and swing her arm up and around. Goldilocks fired without hesitation, but Angel was already out of the way and throwing her weight into Goldilocks' awkward position.

Angel grabbed her wrist as Goldilocks tumbled from the bed, firing another shot straight into the ceiling.

"I'ma kill you," Goldilocks screamed, completely disregarding Odouwo's orders, but Angel had other plans.

Angel held on to her wrist for dear life, and with Goldilocks falling off of the bed and onto the floor, she finally had the advantage. She bent Goldilocks' wrist in the opposite direction of her falling body and pried the gun from her hand.

With it now firmly in her own hand, Angel wasted no time firing directly into Goldilocks' face, the Hydroshock bullets bursting and butterflying in her brain, completely blowing out the back of her head and leaving less than half of her head still attached to her body.

"Arrggghhhh!!" Angel screamed, firing again and again until the gun sat back on its cylinder, empty and smoking. "You shoulda' killed me when you had the chance, bitch!" Angel cursed her, then spat on her dead body.

She tried to stand, but her legs were too weak, so she collapsed to the floor, blood spilling from her rectum. But, she had to get up and warn Dutch. She knew Goldilocks was a fed, but she also knew that shit was much deeper; she just didn't know how deep. But, as fate would have it, she didn't have long to wait.

The door was suddenly kicked opened, damned near off its hinges, and in rushed three Black men, brandishing pistols. They spotted Angel on the floor and each of them turned their guns on her.

"Don't move!"

She couldn't have, even if she wanted to...

** ** ** ** **

As soon as Dutch hung up with M'Baye, he called Angel's cell. He got no answer, so he called again. There was still no answer, so he deaded the line and focused his attention on the streets of Paris.

"Is everything okay?" Ceylon asked.

Ceylon and Dutch were riding in the back of Ceylon's Phantom, heading for a meeting, which Dutch thought was with the Camorra cartel, when in fact, Ceylon was delivering him to the Nigerians.

"Yeah...it's cool," Dutch lied, because it wasn't cool. M'Baye had told him that Roc had walked away from the commission. It was something Dutch expected, but had hoped wouldn't happen. He needed Roc to hold the newly established commission together, and on top of that, he wanted his man to be with him. He knew Roc was Muslim, but he thought it was just his profession, like so many other Muslim brothers in the game. Now he knew better, and the realization angered him because it seemed like Roc was abandoning him.

After this, I'ma talk to Roc. He owe me that, Dutch thought. And now, Angel was missing. He tried her cell once more with the same results. *Where the fuck she at?* In his finest hour, it seemed like everyone had disappeared for one reason or another, and he wondered if something was trying to tell him that this was the price for true success.

Ceylon watched Dutch from the corner of his eye. A tinge of regret touched his conscience because he truly liked the young man. But, he had no regret for what he was doing – that was truly business. The Nigerians could, quite simply, offer more than Dutch. So, not only was it business, but it was smart business – Dutch's death being merely an inconvenience.

They arrived at a small cabaret in the Latin Quarter of the city.

"Ceylon, get your people to check and see if Angel made that flight. If not, then why not, okay?"

"Don't worry my young friend, we will locate her," Ceylon assured him, while patting him on the forearm.

The chauffer opened the suicide styled rear door and Ceylon stepped out, followed by Dutch and they proceeded to enter the cabaret. Inside, all the chairs were atop the tables and the room was dark and quiet. They passed through to the back hallway, over which a bright red sign that read Sortie – Exit in French – hung, marking the rear door.

To the left was the entrance to the kitchen and to the right, a large entrance to yet another room which served as a private dining area for large parties. The pair turned the corner, and inside, were several Black men, including Joseph Odouwo. Dutch didn't recognize Odouwo or any of the other men, but he *did* recognize the setup.

He had expected to meet Columbians, so seeing all the Black faces, left him to conclude the obvious. Knowing what must be done and – fraught with the knowledge that time was of the essence – Dutch swiftly pulled his gun before anyone could react, yoked Ceylon up and put the gun to his head, using his body as a shield.

Two of the Black men pulled their own weapons and began to speak to each other in a language that Dutch didn't understand, but knew was the dialect of the Nigerians.

"Ceylon...what the fuck is this?" Dutch growled, watching everyone intently. "You set me up!"

Dutch's arm across Ceylon's throat was tight enough to choke off his already nasal tone, but he remained calm, confident that Dutch wouldn't kill him...yet.

"Dutch...the apparent is obvious, but I implore you to listen... for more than *your* life is at stake."

Joseph Odouwo stood in the middle of his entourage, smiling triumphantly Dutch noticed the chain around his neck as being a replica of Kazami's - the twin jeweled dragons intertwined, the Ekwensu's symbol, representing the constant force of duality. Odouwo's was only slightly smaller than Kazami's had been and Dutch found himself wondering if he cut Odouwo's head off, *would it fall to the ground as quickly as his nephew Kazami's had done?*

Joseph eyed the man whom he had hunted for so long. He admired how quickly Dutch had responded to the situation – the look in his eyes devoid of any fear of death – and he reminded him of Kazami, the man whose life he would finally avenge.

"No!" Dutch barked. "You gonna listen to me! Tell them muhfuckas to drop their guns, now! Any hesitation, and its *your* fuckin' life at stake!" Dutch's voice boomed with authority.

Ceylon nodded to Odouwo, who commanded the men to lower their weapons. "I think you should speak to someone before you make any hasty decisions, Dutch," Ceylon suggested.

"Speak to who?"

One of Odouwo's men brought a cell phone over to Ceylon and Dutch. "Your mother."

Upon hearing Ceylon's mentioning of his mother, Dutch tightened his vice grip even further, pulling the shorter man almost completely off of his feet.

"Ch...choking me...will not save your mother," Ceylon gasped.

Slowly, Dutch loosened his grip to allow Ceylon to breathe normally.

"Now, Ceylon began after catching his breath, "She is expecting your call. We have two men there who told her that you'd sent them, so she doesn't know that she is any mortal danger."

The Nigerian held the phone to Dutch's ear. He listened to it ring and his heart dropped when he heard, "Hello?...Bernard, is that you?" Her voice carried a hint of worry because her motherly instincts said that something was amiss.

"Yeah, Ma'...its me."

"Is everything okay? I have visitors here...you did send them, didn't you?"

"Yeah, Ma'," he lied, "I sent 'em. I...I just wanted to check to make sure you were...okay."

"I'm fine, baby...are you sure you're okay?"

"Listen, Ma'...let me call you back."

"O...Okay. I love you."

Dutch closed his eyes tight, wishing that she hadn't said that – hadn't reminded him of her love right at that moment. "I know you do, Ma'," Dutch responded, refusing to allow Odouwo the pleasure of hearing him openly admitting his love in return.

The Nigerian closed the cell phone with leer on his face as he stepped away.

"What the fuck is this all about?" Dutch questioned.

"After you speak to one more individual, then I'll explain," Ceylon replied.

Ceylon nodded to the Nigerian with the cell phone and he keyed a second number, then placed the phone to Dutch's ear once more.

Dutch knew instinctively who it was before he heard the voice...*Angel!*

"Dutch! Goldie was a fed! I don't know what the fuck is goin' on, but those bastards bagged me up!"

The Nigerian didn't give Dutch a chance to respond. He just hung up.

"Now that you are able to understand things better, I'm sure you realize that holding me hostage in such a way is...useless," Ceylon said.

Odouwo stepped into the middle of the floor, his hands clasped behind his back. "Drop your weapon, Dutch. It is over. You will die tonight, this is certain. But, I will permit you to die with your honor," Odouwo told him.

"If I do, so will Ceylon," Dutch reiterated, grasping to hold on to his last card.

"And you will be doing me an inevitable service," Odouwo said, only half jokingly. "But, you would be doing *yourself* a disservice, because your mother and Angel will both suffer the same fate."

Dutch shrugged, "then kill 'em...then I'll really have nothing left to lose, and my last breath will be spent puttin' a bullet in your ass, too," Dutch warned.

The Nigerians, on hearing Odouwo threatened, leveled their guns at Dutch.

"What ya'll waitin' for? Pop off!" Dutch dared them, prepared to meet his maker, while taking a lot of mothafuckas with him in the process.

Odouwo respected the young man's heartless philosophy. But, he was ready to call his bluff.

"Bring her in," he told one of the Nigerians, who immediately got on the phone to relay the order. "It is one thing to know someone you love is dying...but watching them die is quite another."

The standoff remained tense – one squeeze away from a bloody mess, and if it went down, anybody could catch one. They may have had Dutch cornered, but a cornered man is potentially the most lethal to face.

A few moments later, two more Nigerians escorted Angel into the room, wrapped only in a sheet from the hotel. As soon as she came in and saw Dutch holding Ceylon, she screamed, "You fuckin' shit! I knew we shouldn't have trusted you! You betrayed us!"

Ceylon, his suaveness tempered with anxiety, replied, "No, my dear. Betrayal is something much deeper and can only occur between friends."

Dutch knew that this had nothing to do with betrayal; he had simply been out maneuvered.

"Dutch, your death is inevitable. If you choose to kill Ceylon, then...as I stated, you'll only be doing me a favor," Odouwo reminded him with less humor than before. "But, then Angel and your mother will die...just like Craze and Nina."

Dutch tensed up and shot Odouwo a menacing stare that was returned with a smug grin.

"That's right...I have been the answer to your question of...*why?* When Craze was killed and you asked in your mind *why*...it was Odouwo. When Nina was killed and your heart cried *why*...it was Odouwo," his voice grew in intensity. "Goldilocks took them from you because of *Odouwo*. Pain for my pain...lives for the life of Kazami."

Dutch kept his composure, but inside, he was boiling. Odouwo stood only a few feet away...nothing to prevent Dutch from avenging Nina and Craze...nothing but the blood of Angel and his mother. Odouwo's protection was Dutch's own heart.

Odouwo walked over, closer to Angel, and then turned back to Dutch. "Do you want to see her die right before your eyes? Do you want to see her blood shed for your stubbornness, and…the fetus of your child crushed under the very heel of my shoe?" Odouwo threatened, assuming that Dutch had already known of Angel's pregnancy.

But, he hadn't known, and he instantly looked to Angel.

"You fuckin' liar…you *lie!* I ain't pregnant…Dutch, I ain't!" she lied, knowing what Odouwo was doing to Dutch. She wanted to protect Dutch from giving Odouwo any more leverage.

Angel couldn't meet Dutch's gaze as she said it, so he knew she was lying. He closed his eyes, just long enough to steady his head.

"Oh, you didn't know?" Odouwo chuckled. "Then… congratulations, I too just had a child – a son, and a son carries the legacy of men, a legacy I will gladly destroy unless you accept Ceylon's demands."

A child? Dutch thought. There is no greater feeling to a man, a real man, than to know his loins have borne fruit, and Dutch was no exception. But, to find out like this, was like finding out you were a father after the abortion. The emptiness engulfs you and Dutch was engulfed because, in an instant, Odouwo had given him fatherhood, only in exchange for freely giving it up.

He loosened his grip on Ceylon, who stepped away, straightened his tie and cleared his throat.

"Dutch, it is quite simple. An unlikely alliance between Joseph and myself has been forged by geopolitical factors, outside of our control. We are, after all, businessmen and not politicians. For this alliance to be completed, Joseph requires your life, while I require the synthetic formula for the hybrid."

Angel growled, "Don't tell 'em shit, Dutch…don't tell 'em shit! He's gonna kill us anyway, he already betrayed us once."

Ceylon turned his attention to Angel.

239

"You are a woman, still, try to think rationally. If I wanted to betray you, as you say, I could've easily obtained that information from the scientists themselves. But, I was quite content with Dutch controlling production because it allowed me to remain...a silent partner," he explained, and then turned back to Dutch. "I truly commend you, my young friend...you have done what few could achieve merely with intellect and courage. But, the irony of it all is that the best move you ever made was also your worst mistake."

Dutch sat down in a chair and tented his hands in front of his mouth, gun hand on top. "What about the money?" he questioned, thinking of his legacy.

Ceylon smiled. "I may be a liar...but I am not a thief. Your share of the cartels will not be touched. I assume that Angel is familiar with the accounts? Of course, after that, no more will be forthcoming. Consider it a buyout."

Dutch thought about offering Odouwo the synthetic, but then knew it would be futile. Only with Ceylon, was this business. With Odouwo, it was personal. Ceylon extended a pen and paper to Dutch and he just looked at it.

"So, Dutch, as you see what is at stake...do we have a deal?"

Dutch slowly rose from the chair and took the pen and paper from Ceylon. Then, in a flash, he brought the gun up and smacked the shit out of Ceylon with it, knocking him to the floor, dazed. He then scribbled off the synthetic formula and tossed the paper and pen on Ceylon's chest.

Looking up, while holding his freshly bruised cheek, Ceylon nodded in acceptance of his punishment, "I'll take that as a yes."

Dutch walked over to Angel, who, sensing his decision, began to jerk wildly against the two Nigerians holding her arms. She started shaking her head, mumbling, "No...no...no..."

Dutch calmly shushed her. "Callete, Dada. Listen to me –"

"No!" she retorted angrily.

"Listen –"

"No!" she shouted. "Don't try and save me, 'cause I hate you! You do this and I'll kill your baby...I will!" she tried to threaten, not wanting it to end like this, not without her, regardless of the cost.

Dutch smiled, the trademark still intact, and kissed her gently. "This is my debt. Neither you, nor Mama can pay it for me."

The tears started to pour from Angel's eyes, it was only the second time he had seen her cry, and it would be the last time she would ever shed a tear.

"Look around this room, because now, they owe *you* a debt," Dutch told her, keeping steady eye contact, and then turning away from the pain in her eyes to face Odouwo.

He walked right up to Odouwo, eye to eye and told him, "Do what you gotta do."

Odouwo looked into Dutch's eyes and saw no fear of what was to come. He admired his courage.

Men like Dutch were few and far between. It was just a shame that he had been one of the few to oppose him. It reminded Joseph of the symbol of the twin dragons locked in battle - neither right nor wrong, merely determined to be the victor.

"The revenge is mine, but your blood is not...Ousmane," Joseph called, one of the Nigerians immediately stepping forward. He was younger than the rest, and in his hands, he carried a sword.

Dutch looked him in the eyes, saw the look of resolve on his face and knew exactly who he was...Kazami's son.

He was the same child Dutch had held in his arms, the same tool he had used to break Kazami...and in his hand, the same weapon of destruction. Dutch remembered the look in Kazami's eyes when he saw him holding his child. Dutch had thought of Kazami as a weak man, and not a caring father. Kazami hadn't feared, he had loved...and now Dutch stood in those same shoes. Love is the most formidable weapon in the world – stronger than hate, fear, and even stronger than death. This was truly his debt.

Joseph Odouwo stepped away as Ousmane stepped up. His English was broken, but he managed to say, "On knees...theah," he ordered Dutch, pointing the sword at the floor.

"Fuck you," Dutch spat. "I'll die for my family, but I'll die on my feet."

Odouwo wouldn't allow it and nodded to one of the Nigerians, who fired a single shot into Dutch's knee, causing him to fall face first onto the floor.

"Dutch!" Angel screamed, seeing him go down.

Dutch grimaced from the pain, trying to prop himself up with his hands as Ousmane stood over him.

"Dis...is for my fadda," he vowed, and then raised the razor sharp sword.

Angel fought desperately, but felt the energy draining from her body. She couldn't look.

The sword glinted under the lighting, the perfect arc, aimed for the back of Dutch's neck. The last thing Dutch thought of, was his mother's words, *"Is it worth it?"*

In his mind, there were no regrets. If everything in his life had come down to this moment, then this moment was worth his life. He was a man that accepted his consequences. If you live for it, then you must be ready to die for it.

"It's worth it."

Ousmane stepped back. The blade was so sharp, that there was hardly any blood on it. He bent to retrieve his prize, depositing it into a bag.

The Nigerians who had been holding her, released Angel, but she no longer had the energy to stand and she sunk to her knees. Odouwo walked over to her, and when she looked up, there were no more tears. "Now, you better kill me."

Odouwo smiled at what he saw as an empty threat. "You're free to take...what's left of the body."

"Burn it," she hissed.

Odouwo walked away, laughing, and Ceylon and the other Nigerians followed him out, leaving Angel alone with Dutch's corpse. They saw it as his remains, but she didn't.

Angel still had Dutch's army, she had his share of the money – which was close to three billion dollars – and she knew the synthetic formula as well. But, she also had what no one else in the world had.

She had his son growing inside of her. She would birth that son...and she would name him...Angelo James.

Dopeboy Folklore
By Monte Smith

Another night
High on cocaine

It wasn't cheap
Nor is the pain

Been down for weeks
So the days look the same

Can't sleep
Too wired for bed

Barely alive
Better off dead

Can you believe
That's what the police said
As they tried to off me

But what do they know besides
Guns
Cuffs
And coffee

Kill you
Too tight
Hot or cold

They don't give a fuck

Do the math

They ride
We stuck
They jive
We shuck

It's time poor people chose
The gun over the buck

Truth over the lie

But who am I to talk
I can't even draw a straight line

[For more info on this poem's author:
myspace/montesmith]